KU-175-314

ANIMALS

Also by Emma Jane Unsworth

Hungry, the Stars and Everything

ANIMALS

EMMA JANE UNSWORTH

CANONGATE
Edinburgh · London

Published in Great Britain in 2014 by Canongate Books Ltd, 14 High Street,
Edinburgh EH1 1TE

www.canongate.tv

1

Copyright © Emma Jane Unsworth, 2014

The moral right of the author has been asserted

Every effort has been made to trace copyright holders and obtain their permission
for the use of copyright material. The publisher apologises for any errors or
omissions and would be grateful to be notified of any corrections that should be
incorporated in future reprints or editions of this book.

Extract from 'Fair Weather' by Dorothy Parker reprinted by permission of
Gerald Duckworth & Co Ltd.

Lyric from 'Evidently Chickentown' words and music by
John Cooper Clarke, Martin Hannet, Stephen Hopkins
© 1980, reproduced by permission of
EMI Songs Ltd., London W1F 9LD and BMG Dinsong Ltd.

British Library Cataloguing-in-Publication Data
A catalogue record for this book is available on request from the British Library

ISBN 978 1 78211 212 9

Typeset in Minion by Palimpsest Book Production Ltd,
Falkirk, Stirlingshire

Printed and bound in Great Britain by
Clays Ltd, St Ives plc

For Alison

WHITE PISS GOOD; AMBER PISS BAD

You know how it is. Saturday afternoon. You wake up and you can't move.

I blinked and the floaters on my eyeballs shifted to reveal Tyler in her ratty old kimono over in the doorway. 'Way I see it,' she said, glass in one hand, lit cigarette in the other, 'girls are tied to beds for two reasons: sex and exorcisms. So, which was it with you?'

I squinted up at my right arm, which felt like it was levitating – but no, nothing so glamorous. The plastic bangle on my right wrist had hoopla'd over a bar on the bedhead during the night, manacling my hand and suspending my arm over the pillow. I wriggled upwards to release it but only managed to travel an inch or so before a strange, elasticky feeling pulled me back. I looked down. My tights – or rather the left leg (I was still sluttishly sporting the right, mid-thigh) – had wrapped itself around a bed knob. I tugged. No good. The knot held fast.

'Get that for me, would you?' I croaked.

She'd moved across the room and was leaning against the wardrobe. *Her* wardrobe. Her room.

We'd been out. Holy fuck, had we been out. A montage of images spooled through the brainfug. Fizzy wine, flat wine, city streets, cubicles, highly experimental burlesque moves on bar stools . . .

Tyler took her time looking for somewhere to put her cigarette. I knew that she was really savouring the scene. This was one for the ever-burgeoning anecdote store; to be wheeled out,

1

exaggerated and relished on future nights that would doubtlessly end in similar indignities. *Hey, remember the time you tied yourself to the bed?* Killer.

'Where did you sleep, anyway?' I said.

'I didn't sleep. I Fonz'd it on the back lawn with a spritzer and my shades on.'

'Fonzing it' was making yourself feel better about things (aka the inevitable existentials) by telling yourself that you were cool and everything was fine. We also referred to it as 'self-charming'. It had a 55% success rate, depending on location and weather.

'What time is it now?' I asked.

Tyler tugged at the knot, raised an eyebrow and unthreaded the tight-leg into a straight black line, which she held taut to show me. 'Half past five.'

'And what time did we get in?'

She pinged the tight-leg at me and held up her hand. I thought she was saying five – but no, she was saying no. *No forensic autopsies.*

I nodded. The effects of the day's self-charming were stable but critical. Don't think about endings. Don't look down. There were rules that had to be obeyed in order to guarantee a horror-free hangover: no news, no parental phone calls, some fresh air if you could tolerate the vertical plane. Sitcoms. Carbohydrates.

I ran my swollen tongue over my unbrushed teeth. A farm-ish smell. Furriness.

'How do you feel?' she asked.

'Like an entire family of raccoons is nesting in my head.'

'Nesting raccoons? How nice for you. I've got two bull-seals fucking a bag of steak.'

I sat up. Woof. Liquefying headrush. I looked down and caught sight of the prolapsed duvet on the floor by the side of the bed, its insides lolling between the missing buttons of the striped cotton cover. I squinted at Tyler. Five-two with cropped black hair sprung into curls. Face like a fallen putto. Deadly. She gripped her fag between her teeth as she opened her kimono and re-tied it tighter. She was wearing knickers but no bra: a bold move for the garden in March. She pulled the fag from her teeth and exhaled. 'I know this will only concuss you further,' she said, 'but I'm getting excited about the Olympics.'

I held my head with one hand, squeezed my fingers into my temples. 'The Olympics? Fuck! What month are we in?'

'March.'

'Thank Christ.'

My paranoia wasn't so paranoid when you took into account the time we'd gone to bed on Saturday only to wake up on Monday morning. On that occasion I'd raised my head to see Tyler frantically shrugging off her kimono in front of the dresser.

What are you doing, you maniac? It's Sunday!

It's fucking Monday and I'm fucking late, she said, batting a dimp out of her regulation baseball cap.

What's that on your eye?

She turned to the mirror. Gasped and sighed. *It's a low-budget high-definition eyebrow.*

It's permanent marker.

It's A ClockworkmotherfuckingOrange. Oh Lo Lo Lo, what am I going to do?

There were still red wine stains on her kimono from that night some months ago. She took another drag on her fag. 'And then the rover is almost at Mars, just a few months now until it performs its neurotically precise landing. There's too much happening this summer. My hope can't take the strain. There was this Olympics ad just on with a cartoon man diving off a cartoon cliff. It had me in *bits*.'

'Cartoons can be very moving.'

'Why do I feel more for cartoons than the news?'

'Because you're perverse. And American.'

'Barely, any more. American, I mean.'

'Say "vitamin". Aluminium. *Herbs*.'

She'd lived in England for ten years and hadn't lost her accent – I especially liked hearing her say the words 'mirror' (*mere*) and 'moon' (*murn*). Tyler had moved over from Nebraska when her mum, an English lecturer, decided she wanted a divorce and applied for a teaching job at Manchester Met. The Johnsons were well off, the profits of her dad's family's cattle-farming mostly. They had a ranch in Crawford with stables and turkeys and a porch with a chair-swing. But for all the perks Tyler said that living there had been like standing on a mathematical plane drawing: eerily flat and evenly portioned into squares of sallow crops. Just you and the horizon, waiting. More specifically: filling the hours. You had to tell yourself you were waiting or really there was no point in eating your breakfast, changing your shirt.

'I was thinking of boiling up some pasta bows,' Tyler said. 'Reckon you could eat?'

'Possibly.'

She looked at her watch.

'By my estimation this culinary extravaganza should be ready in about fifteen. Now, do you need some help getting up?'

'No. And don't be nice to me, or I'll cry.'

'Roger that.'

She retrieved her cigarette from the side of the dresser and left the room, fagsmoke trailing. On the back of her kimono was the logo of a Thai boxing club in Salford – the Pendlebury Pythons – along with their motto, in looping gold font: DEATH BEFORE DEFEAT.

I lay still for a moment, planning. An order of ceremony was needed. Become upright. Brush teeth. Find phone.

Phone.

Jim.

My fiancé (although we both hated the word) was in New

4

York performing a piano recital on a barge in Brooklyn. We'd spoken the previous night before he sound-checked. *You be careful*, he'd said. He knew me, knew the way the night rose in me, knew the way Tyler and I egged each other on. *Course*, I said. At the time I was *carefully* smoking outside a bar on Oxford Road, while Tyler was inside *carefully* transferring the number of a dealer from her dying phone onto her forearm in lip-liner. The rest was – well, not quite history; more a chain of events that amounted to the same headache, the same ransacked purse, same wasted day-after. But at least we'd made it home (you congratulate yourself with the *avoided* crimes when you're clutching at the grubby straws of self-charming) – why, I'd been positively restrained, getting home and sort-of into bed. The previous week we'd ended up at a house in Stretford with a fifty-year-old air traffic controller called Pickles who'd invited us for a (purely friendly) nightcap to discover he only had an eighteenth of a bottle of gin in the cupboard. *How he could have over-estimated that situation quite so much is beyond me*, Tyler had said. *It's enough to make you never get on a plane again.*

I looked to my side and saw a glass I'd somehow had the sense to fill and place there before I collapsed. I reached for it, gulped one twice three times. My gunky mouth made the liquid milky. Swallowing was an effort. I drank water like it was a job to do, an unpaid internship at my own inner (highly corrupt) Ministry of Health. Getting the whole pint down was hard work. As soon as the water was in me it wanted to come out. I ran along the thin hall to the bathroom, left tight-leg trailing. Slammed the door.

The tiles were blissfully cool under my feet. Bathrooms were the best kind of room. You knew that whatever happened in there, you were going to be all right. You had a sink, a toilet, no soft furnishings, usually no audience. I pulled down my knickers and sat. A thunderbolt of piss plummeted and the rest trickled through.

The wall next to me was full of holes – a succession of injuries from various toilet-roll holders, towel rails, shelves and, I could only imagine, fists and fingers – that had been botchily plastered and painted over in sickly pale yellow by the tenants before us. On the other side, my knee rested against the flimsy fibreglass bath-side. The slightest pressure could dint the bath-side in and out. Sometimes I did it for fun – just pressed in and out with my knee. (Sometimes I did it for hours.) A cityscape of curdling beauty products sprawled along the bathside and then, at the foot of the bath, the winking sink with its hot tap head missing. A red metal heart, dusty and hollow and punctured with crescent shapes, hung on a long chain from a nail above the sink, next to an extending shaving mirror that Tyler used to do her eyeliner. Next to the sink, two folded banknotes balanced on a rung of the towel rail, drying. I stood and looked in the bowl before I flushed, recalling the adage of a girl I'd once worked with: *White piss good; amber piss bad.* Orwellian in its visceral simplicity. Meanwhile the liquid I had dispatched into the toilet bowl was almost ochre. Not good, not good at all. More water was in order.

I walked down the hallway to the kitchen, past the coats, hats and bags dangling from hooks like the vaporised hanged. Tyler owned the flat – her dad had stumped up the cash (not just the deposit, but The Cash) not long after she moved over – and I was meant to give her a hundred a month for my bare little box-room, but I never had it and she never asked. The flat was part of a wood-and-chrome cooperative that had been built in Hulme, south of the centre, in the late 1990s. The block shared a central courtyard with a patch of grass and a few raised beds where people with the time and organisational skills grew their own vegetables. Someone had tried to keep chickens in there once (*Stuck in Fucking Chickentown*, said Tyler, quoting John Cooper Clarke), in a little sustainable-wood hutch they'd whittled themselves or something, but they hadn't lasted long with all the foxes. Zuzu alone had dragged in four hens, limp-necked and lovingly punctured, through the cat-flap, leaving each splayed in the centre of the kitchen floor and she'd looked up at us as if to say: *I caught it, bitches – the least you can do is pluck it and cook it.* It was mostly hippy types who lived in the surrounding flats; 'hippysters' as Tyler called them (*eco-friendly toilet cleaner and fifty designer jumpers . . .*). In the shop space on the ground floor of the block there was a vegan café that Tyler and I ate in when we forgot to buy food (often), taking in our own ham and honey, applied under the table to liven things up – the latter because a) Tyler liked sweet toppings on toast and b) they'd reprimanded her once when she asked them whether they had any, thinking it would be a safe bet. *They looked at me like I'd just slaughtered an orang-utan in front of them*, she said. *And this was HONEY. It's a natural product. Bees LIKE MAKING IT. No one forces them to. Where will the madness end???*

She was in the kitchen merrily slicing up a bumper jar of German Bratwursts. Zuzu wound expectantly around her ankles. Zuzu was muscular; more military hardware than cat. She barrelled up and down the hallway. When she trod on my foot it hurt. Tyler walked over to the sink and drained the pan, tipped the pasta into a bowl. A few greasy bows spilled over the sides and slid steaming across the draining board.

'We're gonna need a bigger boat.'

Spinning around looking for a larger bowl, she eventually shrugged and tipped the pasta back into the pan. 'Fuckit. Those are for you, by the way.'

I looked over to the opposite counter and saw a pint of iced water and two ibuprofens. I necked them and edged around her to refill the glass with water at the sink.

Tyler scraped the slices of sausage into the pan, squirted ketchup over the top and stirred it all together with the handle of a rusty fish slice. 'So Tom texted.'

I put the glass of water down, goggled her on.

'Jean's gone into labour.'

Jean was Tyler's sister. Lived in London. Did something to do with funding for museums. Or at least used to, before.

'Shit.'

'Yeah. She's *dil-ating*. Saying it's all his fault. You know the drill.'

A grimace with this. Tyler and Jean were close – so close that it had been a composite betrayal when Jean got pregnant, considering the fact that at twenty-eight Jean was a whole year younger. *Another one lost for a decade!* was Tyler's initial reaction, delivered with a sweep of her kimono sleeve, like a Roman emperor declaring the closing of the games.

'Is she all right?' I said. 'What – ' It was hard to know what to ask about someone who was in labour. How's her perineum holding out? Has she shat herself yet?

Jeannie Johnson. Who'd once accidentally set her own pubes ablaze standing naked on a candlelit dinner table. She'd out-spectacled us all. Now where was she? Spouting clichés, in stirrups.

'Yeah,' Tyler said. 'Tom's going to call when there's news.'

She handed me the bowl and a mug, a fork and a teaspoon, and walked ahead carrying the pan with two hands. She paused at the kitchen door and turned. Nocturnal woodland eyes, black and glistening. 'Do you want some wine?'

We looked at each other for a few moments, assessing the weights of our various desires and reservations as they rolled and pitched inside. After all: the first rule of intoxication was

8

company. Do it together and you have a party; do it alone and you have a problem. I felt the dryness of my insides, tubes crackling and gasping.

'I don't know, are you having wine?'

'I do not know.'

'Well, we might as well, if it's there.'

'Yes!' Tyler said, dancing with the pan. 'Make like mountaineers!'

She jogged through to the lounge, deposited the pan on the plate-glass coffee table and jogged back to the kitchen. She returned a few minutes later with two grubby tumblers of white wine. Drops of water clung to the top of the glasses where she'd rinsed them. She put one on the table and drank heartily from the other.

Somewhere, my phone started to ring. I ran around, uprooting cushions and rifling through papers. There were books all over the flat, poetry mostly. The previous Christmas we'd made a Christmas tree out of them: hardbacks at the bottom, working up through paperbacks, finally to slim modern collections (Spenser's *The Faerie Queen* propped up on top). We'd wrapped the whole thing round with fairylights that turned off looked like barbed wire. Now, only the bottom three branches remained. I pulled them apart and threw them across the room.

'It's in your jacket in the hall,' said Tyler, sitting. 'It's rung twice already.'

Out in the hall I located my jacket on the coat-stand and patted the pockets until I felt the hard boxy telltale form of Phone. It was Jim, of course it was Jim – only two people ever called me and one of them was in the next room. I picked up. 'Hello.'

'Hi.'

It struck me as it always did: the contradiction. The beauty of phones! But also the inadequacy. Jim's voice was a tonic: a

Midlands accent softened by natural sibilance and university down south. Henry Higgins might have clocked him but everyone else found him hard to place. Me, I was instantly Mancunian: too clipped for Lancashire; too glottal for Cheshire.

'How was your night?' he said.

I clutched at the phone, hunched in the hallway, feeling suddenly goblin-like. The long-distance line buzzed. I thought of Jim's sharp agile lips, the colours of the political world map, slowly looping satellites. In the lounge, the TV came on.

'Fun,' I said.

'Great!' Jim said. 'How fun?'

'Home-and-sleep-but-a-bit-hungover fun. How was the recital?'

'Not fun, but nice people.'

Jim had been teetotal for two months – a decision made when his workload increased to such an extent that he rarely got a day off with travelling and rehearsals. As a concert pianist he couldn't take any chances. Classical music fans were ferociously attentive.

'How's Tyler?' he asked. He always asked. I had to give him credit for that.

She snorted a tequila slammer through a straw. She stole a Magic Tree air freshener from a taxi. She –

'She broke a shoe. Otherwise she's intact.'

We'd been running across a road when the plastic heel of her ankle boot – which had been threatening to go since December – had snapped clean off. She'd sworn a long, lusty *Fuuuuck* and then started singing, cornily: *You picked a fine time to leave me, loose heel . . .*

A fraction-second of silence. A conversation drawing to a close. I tried to picture New York in my mind, seeing Earth from low orbit, then falling through the sky, zooming down and down through map scales, to the hotel room where Jim was sitting, holding the phone. The image disintegrated as it smashed into memory: Jim, the way he'd looked leaving for the airport with his Bart-Simpson-church-hair, side-parted and slick from the shower, in his white shirt and diamond-pattern tank top. The memory put more miles between us rather than fewer.

'Get back to your girlfriend,' he said. 'I'll see you Friday.'

'See you Friday.'

Exhalation.

Love: funny how you knew you'd found it, when you found it. I didn't like believing in fate, it struck me as a concept for happy people to cling to. Majestically unfair when you thought about it. Someone gets a shit lot – that's their *fate*, is it? Oh, bad luck – sorry about that Alzheimer's, that dead kid, that bombed-out family home. *Sor-ry*. It's just . . . well, it's destiny, you know? At the same time I knew I felt lucky, having found someone to make some promises to; to be in turns fascinated and reassured by. Jim was solid and separate: hooded eyes, pointed chin, black widow's peak – not dissimilar to young Spock and just as logical, just as smart and self-contained. Knew exactly who he was. And there's *nothing* more attractive than someone who knows who they are, especially when you're – well, a fucking shambles. Lately, our love, too, had been assuming more of a definite shape – a *marriage* shape. I'd never really known whether marriage was for me; I'd just said it as a word, an abstract – *When I'm married* – without thinking about what it meant. But the abstract was manifesting. It was white and huge and heavy and expensive, like a Fifties American fridge appearing at the foot of the bed, and I didn't know what the fuck I was going to do with it.

'How's loverboy?' Tyler said as I walked back in the lounge.

I looked at her and I could see she was reading me, seeing how the conversation with Jim had gone, getting everything she needed to know – the words were just her playing for time.

Since meeting Tyler I'd believed that a psychic connection between human beings was possible. 'Kinship' is the best word in English for it. The French call it *une affinité profonde*, which I also like it but it still doesn't quite get there. It's that doppelgänger effect that can go either way: to mutual understanding or mutual destruction. Someone sees right to your backbone and simultaneously feels their backbone acknowledged.

'Fine, thanks.'

'Does he think we're savages?' (This with her mouth full, spraying pasta bits down her front.)

'Of course he does. We *are* savages. How's the pasta?'

'Functional.'

Tyler was a dreadful cook, not that she gave a shit. She liked food but she wasn't fetishistic about it – quantity not quality gave her her kicks. 'Yeah, it's definitely done the job,' she said, getting up and patting her stomach. 'I could dump a corpse right now.'

We'd met nine years ago. I was ordering a coffee in a shop halfway along Deansgate. The shop's leather sofas and hat-sized sponge cakes had looked inviting as I passed on my way to the library after work, which at the time involved standing on Market Street with a clipboard selling £9.99 baby photos to people with babies. (Of all the jobs I'd had it had been the simplest – new parents were the most vulnerable demographic, the most desperate to preserve and present their legacy; the easiest to sell shit to. *And yet you're still going to die – that's the punchline!* I thought as they proffered their tenners, bloodshot, sleep-starved, unsexed, their offspring indifferent.) The coffee shop was part of an Italian chain and hadn't been open long. She was at the coffee machine grappling with a metal jug – the milk wouldn't froth properly by the looks of it – and she was shaking the jug and frowning and pouting. Her pinny was skewiff, her baseball cap was backwards like Paperboy's, her name badge said DENISE. She looked up and I saw a look pass through her eye that I'd caught in my own, in bathroom mirrors – it was a look that said she was outside somewhere, and running. She made the coffee with the milk as it was and came to take my order. I ordered a frappé and as I ordered it I said, *I never believed the day would come when I'd order a frappé* and she nodded at the books I was pressing to my chest and said, *That's a Moleskine, isn't it, like Hemingway used?* and I said: *Touché.*

I picked up my bowl of pasta and stabbed it with my fork, failing to spear a single piece. Zuzu glanced at me. The cat only trusted Tyler, an exclusivity Tyler had ensured by getting her when I was away on a random week's holiday with Jim. When I came back the cat was already indoctrinated to Tyler's ways, brain-washed in some kind of one-cat cult. 'I've trained her to recog-nise only my face,' Tyler said. 'The rest of humanity are inferior mutants in her eyes.' Zuzu tolerated the odd pat or stroke but always with hackles-ready suspicion. She never came on my lap, never took food from my fingers. Tyler was unhealthily proud of her hairy little devotee.

The pasta was rotten – overcooked and laced with the poison-tang of too much basil. I ate it anyway. The small flatscreen TV in the corner was tuned in to a tacky Saturday night dating show I liked. Tyler was objecting. The elitist in her often stropped centre-stage, raised as she had been amongst poetry and horses. Conversely, light entertainment was mother's milk to me. It relaxed me, rendered me junk-drunk at the teat of British terres-trial telly. That was how my four-strong, two-up two-down family had rolled: takeaways in front of game shows and horror films. (I'm not trying to *out-working-class* you, by the way; I went to grammar school and university, but my first touchstones were forged in the garish gore of Granada TV.)

The dating show was a bit like *Blind Date* except instead of a screen and the old 'love is blind' philosophy there were thirty girls behind a bank of white-lit pillars and one man standing in front of them for their perusal. The poor bastard descended onstage in a lift, the 'Love Lift', and thrashed about like a landed fish under the studio lights to whatever godawful tune he'd chosen to come onto (in this case, bludgeoning irony to within an inch of its life with Sister Sledge's 'The Greatest Dancer'). He proceeded to further fuck up his chances by doing a 'party piece' (juggling bananas) and allowing his friends and family to defame him via an impishly edited video of them all discussing his personality down the pub (*Steve's VERY close to all his exes and his mum, such a nice guy . . .*).

I was on the floor, practically laughing out toxins. Tyler – fork poised chin height, split pasta dangling – was aghast.

'Someone get him the fuck out of there,' she said. 'Preferably *not* someone he knows.'

It got worse. The second part of the show began with Steve in an energetic headlock courtesy of the comedian host, and the line of girls manically dancing behind their booths to the theme tune.

'Christ on a cracker,' said Tyler. 'Did they crop-dust them with poppers during the commercials?'

The camera homed in on one girl in a partially see-through dress, her nipples almost visible beyond the corners of a diamond of fine black net. 'This is Our Lou,' said the host, 'and she has a very special talent: she can pick men up!'

'Presumably in the literal sense,' Tyler said. 'Or she wouldn't be involved in this fiasco.'

Tyler had been single as long as I'd known her. I'd once overheard her saying to a boy at a party: *Sharing your life with someone is like Marmite. It's FUCKING SHIT.* She took him home after.

On the TV Lou came out from behind her pillar, grasped the host round the thighs (face practically in fellatio-proximity) and lifted him a good two inches off the ground to deafening applause. 'I bet you can do it with Steve, too, can't you?' said the host. Steve gulped but looked game. *Pick him up! Pick him up!* chanted the audience. Steve came forward and Lou lifted him, nose-to-crotch. After she'd returned him to his feet she did strongman arms to the roaring crowd.

'You utter cunts!' said Tyler. 'What are they doing? Do they think stupid is sexy?'

'They probably make a lobotomy mandatory in the early stages of the selection process.'

When the women had been whittled down to the final two it was time for Steve's decider question. 'I like to buy myself fresh flowers every week,' he said. 'How would you guarantee romance blossomed on our date?'

'Sunsets and sunrises,' said Lou, who had unsurprisingly made it down to the final cut. 'They make romance blossom.'

'Get me a gun,' said Tyler. 'I'm going to shoot the TV, then myself. No wonder people go postal in shopping malls. The populace deserve it.'

'You'd have to get me there and then you'd find out,' said the other girl coquettishly.

Tyler mock-vommed. 'This piece of shit is an *assault on my soul*. Every second of it that I endure robs me of MILLENNIA. Just so you know.'

'Oh shush,' I said. 'Just go with it.'

'I can't believe *you* enjoy this,' she said. 'You, with all your high-falutin' ideals of "romance" . . .'

I stopped laughing. 'This is not Romance,' I said, pointing at the TV. 'This is the other end of the spectrum. It's the dregs of reality.'

Her hand shot to her eye.

'What now?'

'I've lost a contact. No, seriously.' She blinked and rubbed at her eye.

I looked at her. 'Well, fancy putting your lenses in today when you've got no moisture in you.'

'It was more a case of not taking them out.'

'Not to mention how old they must be.'

'Best-before dates are for pussies.'

A few days after I'd met Tyler I was walking across town, heading home to my parents' house, where I was living at the time. I stopped at the tram tracks at the top of Market Street when a tram tooted to indicate that it was pulling away from the stop. As I stood waiting by the track I looked up to the front of the tram and saw inside the driver's cabin. And there, in the driving seat, *driving the tram*, was Tyler. I blinked. It was still Tyler. Driving a tram. The driver was standing behind her, grinning and waving. I waved back. It must be her dad, I thought, he must be a tram driver. But when I questioned her the next day she said: *No, I was just on the tram and I thought,* I don't want to die not knowing what it's like to drive a tram – *so I asked the driver and he said I could have a quick go. That's what I call Society.*

I lay in her bed later, Tyler snoring next to me, Zuzu curled between her legs. When Tyler's phone rang I nudged her and she moaned and reached over to the bedside table.

'Hello?' Louder: 'Jean? JEANNIE?'

She sat up, flicked the light on. I sat up, too. Zuzu opened one thin green eye.

'Oh fuck! Oh fuck!'

It was a good *Oh fuck*. She was grinning. I grinned back.

'What is it?'

Tyler looked at me. 'A girl! Shirley.' I held onto her arm. 'More wine,' she said to me and then, down the phone: 'We're toasting you, Jeannie, we're toasting you all right now, you beautiful bovine bitch.'

I ran to the kitchen and swooshed a couple of glasses clean. We had a fine collection of branded beer pots and family-sized ashtrays we'd pillaged over the years. (One time Tyler had tried to steal a chair from a bar – and not a small chair either but an *armchair*. She'd got stuck in the doorway, like a dog with a bone.)

I came back with a Kronenburg half-pint and a Duval goblet, both filled with wine. Tyler was off the phone, sitting with her back against the bars of the bed's headboard, one hand holding the bed knob, resplendent. The swirls of teenage tattoos on her upper arms were slowly greening, like algae on a shipwreck.

'Congratulations!'

Tyler sniffed like a football rattle. 'Jean sounded rinsed,' she said. 'And it's only just begun. Give it a week and it'll be like when she used to take meth except she won't be able to hide away because she'll have this *thing* to feed.'

'*Shirley.*'

'Imagine suddenly losing all your privacy, all your hope of self-development. You put everything on hold. Oh, the feelings, Lo!'

It was something we said often: *What to do with all the feelings.* They ambushed you sometimes. They rioted. They were legion.

'Yes yes, just drink.' I cheers'd her glass.

After she'd fallen asleep I took the glasses through to the kitchen, placing them quietly in the sink. The sky was dark beyond the window, starless and moonless, the city muddled with reflections in the glass. I lit up a cigarette.

Babies. I didn't know how to feel about them. I had a recurring dream where I was walking through a room with babies sitting on the floor, regularly spaced, and I bent down to each one, took its chin in my hand and looked at its face. They stretched away in every direction, like a prism of mirrors.

I stood staring out the window and sensed a huge thing turning in the supposedly great beyond. The pull of it made me grip the sink.

GIRL VERSUS NIGHT

Five days later I was in my room replying to emails about the wedding. As always when otherwise occupied, I wanted to be writing – a desire that rarely withstood the presence of actual writing time. *Bacon*, my novel-in-progress, was the story of a priest who fell in love with a talking pig (I could already see the movie trailer: Gene Hackman in a dog collar, the back of a pig's head in the foreground as they desperately embraced: 'God help me, I love you!'). I'd been halfway through the thing for a few years now and needed to crack on if I was ever going to escape the call centre. I'd reduced my hours there to the minimum but I still spent every second pondering quiet desktop suicide. The previous week I'd been losing the will to live ten minutes into my shift when my boss came over and asked whether I had flu.

'It's just a cold,' I said, stoically.

He looked at the pile of congealed tissues on my desk.

'You know, Laura, it's best if you don't come in when you're infectious.'

'I'm not infectious.'

He leaned in. 'I'm trying to give you *a reason*.'

I looked at the whiteboard on the wall. My rating was second from the bottom in an office of sixty-three. I looked back at my boss. He was a man who enjoyed golf.

'Noted,' I said.

'It's a tough climate,' he said. 'We need to pull together. You should really flush those.'

I took my pile of tissues to the Ladies and threw them down

the toilet, then took a piss on top of them. I stared at the fish-head hinges and drunk-fighty-octopus hook on the door. Beneath the hook, a graffiti conversation was scrawled in three different-coloured pens.

Gas gas gas the middle class!
To which someone had replied:
I put my semi in West Didsbury on this cunt being middle-class.
To which someone else had replied:
I put my semi in your fat mam.

The sooner I finished my novel, the better.

I stubbed out my cigarette and pressed send. Ping! Off the last email went, specifying breaded ham instead of honey-roast for the buffet. I felt free and proud. I located my phone and called Jim. He was in Vancouver. A long flat ring tone, then a pause, then another, then –

'Well done!' he said.

'I'm wondering how I should celebrate.'

'I land around lunchtime tomorrow, shall I see you at mine?'

In the background someone was hacking at a cello, the *Jaws* theme but faster.

'What?' His voice was quieter, as though he'd moved the phone away from his mouth. 'Yes, okay.' Then he came back at full volume. 'Look, Laur, I've got to – '

'Course. Hey, why don't I cook for us tomorrow?'

What can I say? I was delirious with success.

'Oh, you don't have to. We could – '

'No, I want to.'

Just before he went I heard the whole orchestra strike up. I tossed my phone onto the unmade bed. It stopped solid on the sheet, like a brick. I turned the router box off at the wall. I didn't like it just being on, it made me feel located, matrixed. I had a strange relationship with the internet, avoided it most of the time. I didn't do social networking because I didn't trust myself, I got too *involved*. Plus, drunk and home alone it could too easily go tits-up, as Tyler had proved. She'd sunk two bottles of wine (they were half-price so buying two was right and just) and signed up to a dating website under the pseudonym 'Vivian Fontaine'. She then proceeded to maraud round the site, sending obscene messages to random men. *I was looking for connections* – that was how she'd defended it – *you know, like normal people do on the internet*. She'd even sent one man – who, to be fair, encouraged her – a photo of herself prancing in a half-mast leotard and a werewolf mask. She eventually got into bed with her laptop, where only the irresistible coma of max-capacity drinking saved her from further disgrace. The next morning, snouting out from under her duvet at 6 a.m., she'd seen the open laptop and shrivelled. Called me.

'LO, I'VE DONE SOMETHING BAD LIKE REALLY BAD.'

'Calm down.' I was at Jim's. I got out of bed and walked into the hallway so I didn't wake him. 'It won't be – '

'It's the worst yet. I'm in TEFL City.'

'TEFL City' because we called those times 'TEFL-pondering mornings', when your only option felt like emigration, and teaching.

'Did you hit anyone?'

'No.'

'Vomit on anyone?'

'No.'

'You didn't kill someone, did you?'

'Does cyber-suicide count?'

I sighed. 'Sit tight, I'll be round in ten.'

With no hope of self-charming her way out of it, between the phone call and my arrival Tyler had gone back online and messaged each of the men under the guise of Vivian's sister saying that Vivian would sadly be unable to attend any of the arranged three-ways since she'd been admitted to hospital with a nasty case of gout. The most annoying thing was she'd used *my* laptop and, thanks to the guile of direct marketing, ads for dating sites were still popping up in the sidebar of my email inbox three months later. She was holding her right hand to her nose and smelling her first two fingers the way she always did when she was scared ('oysters and bonfires' was how she described the smell). 'I panicked!' she cried. 'Anyway, *you* had gout when you were twenty-five.'

This was true. When I'd hobbled my cartoonishly swollen left big toe into A&E the doctors had been taken aback. Super-strong anti-inflammatories were all they could give me – those and the official literature on recommended weekly units of alcohol for women. Fourteen. Seven glasses of wine. Per week. Barely enough for a vole to have a good time. But you know, they had to try. We all have to fucking *try*, don't we.

Now whenever a dating site ad appeared by my inbox, I informed Tyler and she displayed suitable mortification. And this was *Tyler*, who was generally unshockable and certainly un-embarrassable when it came to sex. Aged ten she'd been caught masturbating in the school sickbay and the school nurse had hauled her into the headmaster's office. 'I apologised,' Tyler said wearily in the re-telling, 'but the headmaster was a joyless soul, a non-carrier of the *fuckit* gene. And it's not as though I lied. I DID have a headache – I had a headache because I *needed to jerk off.*' Tyler's parents had been called into the school and her mum had defended her. You know people are really rich, like *generations*-rich, when they're not embarrassed discussing sex in public. One of the things I admired most about Tyler's family was their openness. They told it to each other straight. This ranged from *That dress doesn't suit you* to *That thing you said to me yesterday made me very upset.* My family pussyfooted around, especially when it came to illness. Last autumn, my mum had answered the phone with a cheery *Hello!* and when I asked her where she was she replied *Oh, just in A&E!* in the tone you might expect someone to say *Oh, just in B&Q!* She said she'd burned her hand on the oven (even went so far as to wear a bandage when I saw her next) but it eventually transpired that my dad had been going back and forth with a bad cough they nailed down as stage-two lung cancer. You know the Black Knight in Monty Python's *Holy Grail,* when he's getting his arms lopped off and saying it's just a flesh wound? That's my family. If we end up having a family mausoleum our epitaph should be *Don't worry about me, I'm just having a little lie-down.*

So apart from checking email, odd facts (I listed them and did them in bulk at 5 p.m.) and sometimes – when I was feeling particularly brave – my overdraft balance, I kept the wi-fi off. The book was proving hard enough without the added worry of where it might or might not fit in the world, especially when I was yanked every day into a heinous, staticky place, a grey carpeted box of lies concerning credit cards. All that got me through was telling myself I was buying as well as biding my time, a dangling carrot for most people who worked in the call centre. There were musicians, playwrights, poets, novelists – all of us detesting every second in our headsets; all of us dreading the time someone would turn round and say: *I'VE GOT MY BREAK! I'M OUT! SEE YOU LATER, LOSERS!*

GCSE English class. Tuesday afternoon. Me – thirteen, ginger, unstylishly myopic – navigating my way through Yeats' 'When You Are Old' with rabid intent. I loved it, loved it without knowing exactly why. Loved the words, the rhythm, the idea of someone having a 'pilgrim soul'. Didn't think it could be anything to do with a bitter albeit complicated man putting a hex on a girl who'd said no. (For the record I still loved it at thirty-two, experience notwithstanding.)

The teacher waited until we'd all finished reading and asked a question. 'What do you think he means when he says "hid his face amid a crowd of stars"?'

Mrs Coan had seen countless kids like me wriggle their way up through the grammar school: first-generation middle-class with an unstable core of entitlement and parents poised at home for results; for *a better way for you, easier than I had, one with options.* I didn't know much but I knew I had to impress. And as Pope said (Pope! Listen to me! I told you . . .): 'a little learning is a dangerous thing . . .'.

Mrs Coan didn't smile as she acknowledged my raised hand. A slightly exasperated tone in her voice. 'Yes, Laura.'

'Did he die?'

'No, but I can see where you're coming from.'

I got the next one in fast. 'Did he get famous?'

Mrs Coan ignored me and looked expectantly at the rest of the class. I kept my hand up, Rolodexing options and collating them into a list of descending likelihood. Meanwhile Rachel Atherton lifted a slender, tanned arm. She was the girl I always vied with for top of English. We wound up sharing the sixth-form English prize – the first time in the school's history there had been joint winners. A photo from the ceremony, in a silver frame on my parents' dining-room radiator shelf, showed us gripping the small plaque on either side in an almost invisible tug-of-war. Rachel was smiling in the photo. I was not. We might have locked horns intellectually but she surpassed me when it came to dignity.

'Yes, Rachel?' said Mrs Coan.

Rachel cleared her throat. Took her time. Knew she had a winner. 'Did he retreat into his art?'

Mrs Coan clasped her hands and smiled as though all her years of pedagogic graft had finally been validated. Here it was! Lo and, while you're at it, behold: a shining pearl in a sea of gritty little oysters. 'What a beautiful answer,' said Mrs Coan. 'Yes, Rachel. He did.'

My inner swot hawked and spat and I spoke again without being asked to. 'I disagree,' I said. 'It's not just that.'

Mrs Coan rolled her eyes. *This girl. This girl who chews her fingers and won't sit still, who whispers in assembly and reddens when she's looked at.* She levelled me with an assassin's grim, unimpeachable gaze. 'Your problem, Laura Joyce, is that you *try too hard.*'

And yes, that's my name. Laura Joyce. Quite a blinder from the great beyond, I think you'll agree. A fine example of blistering cosmic humour – and one I didn't truly appreciate until I first started sending out submissions and received several rejections referring to the discrepancy between my own writing and that of my streamy namesake. Want to know what the mysterious 'dark matter' they're searching for actually is? It's Irony – billions of tons of the stuff, lurking, ready to go. The Universe is not indifferent; the Universe is *amused.*

To get out of my bedroom I had to slide a clothes rail out of the way of the door. It was tricky getting back in again. In addition to the clothes rail and a small desk I had a single bed, which was why I often ended up in bed with Tyler.

I went to the fridge and found a beer – the last. The kitchen was in its usual state of neglect – the fridge full of things mouldering or threatening to moulder. Philadelphia Light with a green, hairy thing in it that had almost as much character as a muppet. Curling dried bacon, half the pack used and left ripped open as though it had been attacked by a badger. An array of slowly rotting condiments, pickled this and that, bought on drunken whims in express supermarkets. A bowl of withering fruit on the top of the defunct microwave. Bananas that had furiously ripened after being placed beneath apples and grapes (how many times had I warned Tyler that the banana was not a sociable fruit?) that had themselves softened in more sanguine defeat. We didn't really keep on top of things (Tyler: *I'm thrilled when I put the right fucking bin out on the right fucking day*).

I drank my beer looking out of the window. The pub over the road had been boarded up for months. It was long and thin like a pale yellow torpedo, built to suit the shape of an old junction that had since been altered, so the pub wasn't on a junction at all any more and looked lost even before it was put up for sale. Further down the road was the community garden centre, its chicken-wire fence crocheted with wet spider-webs. When I'd finished my beer I went to the 'cocktail cabinet', a kitchen cupboard where we kept the random glasses and anything that had survived the previous weekend. A quarter bottle of whisky glinted from the cupboard's shadowy depths. I pulled it out. Maybe it would help. Whisky was a lucid kind of drunk. You kept your faculties, mostly. Wine and whisky were my favourites because they felt – and I'm aware of the tragic-sounding nature of this – like *company*. The easy kind. Maybe it was the names. Merlot – that rambunctious exchange student who talks all night. Chardonnay – the girl with the steam-hammer laugh who's crashed her sports car on the way over. Pinot Grigio – the quiet one who stuns the room with a braining bombshell. Chianti – total psychopath but charming with it. Chablis – point-blank refuses to go in a tumbler, gets acidic when talked down to. Laphroaig – earthy; always up for intensity without getting po-faced. Lagavulin. Oh, Lagavulin. But for all my appreciation of booze's plethora of personalities, I didn't subscribe to the old Romantic lie: if you were sozzled you'd produce works of genius.

Hey, lose your mind! Get the opium in. Get tanked. Go fucking bonkers. You'll produce masterpieces . . . No no no no no. The point of intoxication for me was not to create but to destroy the part of myself that cared whether or not I created. I drank for self-solidarity; to settle the battles within, or at least freeze-frame them. Because the truth was: I *had* tried too hard at school. I'd done everything too hard. I sketched too hard (even kind Miss Spooner, the wispy-voiced art teacher, threatened to resort to violence: *What am I going to have to do to get you to sketch lightly, Laura, WHIP YOU?*); I brushed my teeth too hard (the dentist: *Really, Mrs Joyce, if you don't get her to calm down on this then we're going to have to worry about receding gums . . .*); I played netball too hard – overshooting, overshooting, terminally overshooting.

I filled a Fosters glass a quarter of the way and carried it back to my desk. Sat staring. Drinking. Staring. It was no good. I picked up a book of poetry and took it with the whisky down to the grass. It was sunny for March – not warm but the light was cold and yellow and cheap, like margarine. I sat in the shade by the wall and bent my legs, making a lectern of my knees. Strained to read as the sun shifted meanly over the Manchester skyline. A blackbird clucked in a nearby hedge. A thousand tiny flies went about their business. Early spring. Things awakening. I kicked off my shoes and socks and surveyed my feet. Oh, they were ugly, my feet. Monkeyish. Almost clawed. They hadn't yet invented the kind of therapy required to console me about them. When I was younger I'd tried to make myself feel better about them by telling myself that Lolita had monkeyish feet and *she* was desirable. Granted, in a sick, twisted way, but beggars couldn't be choosers – or rather, mill-workers couldn't be choosers, because that's where my long-toed feet had originated from. The girls who worked in the mills of Lancashire (my maternal grand-mother being one of them) had to limbo under the moving threads to clear detritus as it fell from the looms. They couldn't bend for fear of cotton-cuts (think *machine-driven* paper cuts) so they developed a way of picking things up with their feet, snatching and gripping with their toes then kicking their legs back against their bum to grab the bits between their fingers. Toes stretched and became more dexterous as a result. Darwin got involved (I *know*, impossible, but throw me a toe-bone here). Jim said I might be able to play the piano with my feet, that he'd teach me.

Jim. I missed him in a physical way, like a thirst. Missed his mouth and his composure and his steady loving eyes. I didn't buy the whole 'absence makes the heart grow fonder' spiel. I was with Rochester on the matter: a cord was tied to my ribcage at one end and tied at the other end to Jim's, and the further away he got, the thinner the cord stretched. Memories helped and didn't help. What had he said to me the other day? *We are not defined by how we are but by how we try to be.*

What if you try too hard to be everything? I countered.

Lie down, he said. *Lie still.*

I finished my whisky, picked up the glass and got to my feet. I walked to the stairwell and up the stairs. As I walked past my desk I checked my phone. Two missed calls. Tyler. I called her back. She answered on the first ring.

'I'm outside a city-centre drinking establishment and there's a chair opposite baying for your ass.'

'I'm writing, remember.'

I heard her suck on a cigarette.

'Fine. I'll still be here when you change your mind.'

The bloodrush of temptation. An alfresco drink (and a cigarette at the same time, a rare luxury) with my best friend on a sunny eve. In March, too. How many evenings like this did we get in March? If that wasn't an oasis in the wilderness then –

'Are you on your own?' (As if I could somehow make this about compassion . . .)

'Only until you get here.'

Ohhhhhhhhh. She cajoled me like an over-confident boy at the bus interchange. She was persistent. She was cocky. She was *good*.

'Jim's back in the morning.'

'So just come for a couple.'

'Ha! That's a good one.' I inspected my fingernails. 'Anyway, I've already had a whisky and a beer.'

'You do know that beer *isn't even alcohol.*'

Another drag on her fag. She was enjoying this. The practice scales of her siren call. I said: 'Don't you have work at seven tomorrow anyway?'

'Baby,' ('Baby', was it? Three drinks at least, likely on her fourth) 'I've got work at seven tomorrow every day for the rest of my life, serving mochafuckingchickenlattes to people counting off the days in little coffee stamps. What gives? *Only* the fact that there are nights in between.'

And there it was, as always, swinging my way: The Night. With its deals, promises and gauntlets, by turns many things: nemesis, ally, co-conspirator, master of persuasion. It tosses its promises before you like scraps on the road, crumbs leading into the forest: pubs, parties, booze, drugs, dancing, karaoke . . .

Here, kitty.
Here, kitty kitty.

Whatever your peccadilloes, The Night knows.

I looked at my laptop, at my desk with its dirty mugs and fag-ash archipelago. The grubby keyboard from eating on the job. The dimp-filled saucer (had I smoked that much today? Holy fuck). The hob lighter I used as a lighter. The Marlboro packet with the take-heed photo of the bloke with the big neck tumour and bigger moustache (Tyler: *Difficult to say which of those disturbs me more . . .*).

I said: 'I have £1.72 to last me until payday.'

'Are there no notes on the towel rail?'

'No.'

'Check underneath.'

'I did, yesterday.'

'Well, I'm buying. Correction: I have bought.'

She hung up. My laptop screen flicked to sleep mode, displaying a bashful black-and-white photo of Jim sitting outside a pub the previous year, a half-drunk pint of Guinness in front of him. It was a confusing sign: half-warning; half-endorsement. I chewed my thumb. I'd need a shower and something quick to eat although I could always get something when I got there, yes that made more sense. I could throw my jeans on, a t-shirt, cardigan, trainers – no need to dress up. No need for much make-up. But then . . . Didn't I want to be full of the joys of productivity and rejuvenating sleep tomorrow? I could make it quick. I could. 'A couple' might be optimistic but five drinks was a good number to have in mind. Yes, five drinks was jolly but not silly. Five drinks was just *normal*. I could use the last of my money to hop on a bus the few stops into town, Tyler could pay for a cab home, saving more time, getting into bed Even Earlier – because I hadn't been out all week. That was right, I hadn't been out all week. I deserved a break. Also it made sense to get some input, some fresh inspiration, no one ever wrote anything good in a vacuum . . .

My phone beeped in my hand. A text.

THIS WINE IS SO COLD AND IMPOSSIBLY REFRESHING THE GLASS IS STICKING TO MY HAND AND I'VE GOT YOU A PRESENT

Here, kitty.

THE RETURN OF JIM

Thirst woke me. Thirst and Fear.

Oh fuck. Oh holy *fuck*. What time was it? My head pounded with its own globe-splitting seismic beat. I scrabbled for consolations. I was in bed. I had made it there. But I was meant to be going over to Jim's and cooking a meal and giving him a hero's welcome and on top of all that I was going to have to make myself stop smelling like a six-week-old bar towel that had been twice through the digestive system of a yak. My armpits were cadaverous. I liked smelling of myself but *this* – I took another sniff and boaked: sour booze and raving and not nearly, as always, enough water – this was pushing even my own tolerance. My hand found my phone, finger pressed it awake, eyes and brain interpreted numbers. 10 a.m. Jim was home at lunchtime, which meant twelve at the earliest, to be safe. Two hours. Doable. Just about. I could have a bath at his place once I'd put the food on. Yes yes, this was shaping up fine. Now all I had to do was work out how to move my limbs.

I'd arrived at the pub to find Tyler resplendent on a picnic bench with a bottle of wine in an ice bucket on the table in front of her.

'GREETINGS!' she shouted across the beer garden.

Oh god, I thought. She's doing Christian Slater in *Heathers*. We're there already, are we? I did a little wave and weaved between the benches. She poured me a glass of wine. I took a swig, felt the wine do its thing – the smacky whack hitting my stomach and brain simultaneously. Bliss. The promise of more bliss to come. Tyler was on the more already. Her wormhole pupils and tangible gravitas gave it away. Coke. Nothing else provided quite the same inflation; quite the same *Fuck all y'all*. I took another swig of wine and she grabbed my hand, pulled it under the table and shoved the wrap into my palm. My fingers obediently curled around it. No point asking how she afforded it. No point asking where she got it. Probably from 'The Queech' – a man with Dennis the Menace hair who'd locked us in his flat the previous month to wait for him (or rather the deal, drug-lust nullifying social niceties) while he went to buy milk to make us a cup of tea. *That* was an hour of my innocence I was never going to get back.

The Queech had two dice tattooed on his wrist and waved a fist-sized iron padlock at us as he left. *I'll just be putting this on the outside of the door, won't be two mins.* (He was thirty-two mins.) I'd looked at Tyler as the lock clunked into place and his footsteps receded down the hall.

I don't even want a fucking cup of tea!

I don't want a cup of tea either!

What are we going to do Tyler what are we going to do?

I don't fucking know. How high are we?

I'm not high at all – what have you had? Is that why you went to the bathroom?

No, dick-head, I meant LITERALLY off the ground. Is it jump-able?

We got out of the lift at the NINTH floor, remember?

Fuck. I need more wine. I'm getting my sense of reason back. Any minute now I'm going to sober up and wonder WHAT THE FUCK I'M DOING LOCKED INSIDE A DRUG DEALER'S FLAT.

Oh god oh god shall we check the fridge?

Well if he hasn't got any fucking milk he's unlikely to have any fucking wine, is he?

I guess not.

Hey.

What?

I'm just thinking.

What?

Well unless he's got it on him which is unlikely it must be in here somewhere.

Do not even think about it. Do NOT even think about it. Tyler. Tyler. Look at me. No. Listen THAT is how people get shot and die. Sit your ass back down I mean it.

Ohhh he doesn't seem the type to have a gun . . . What?

From her seat across the table in the beer garden, Tyler eyed me like the superior being I knew she knew she was. She was up in the stratosphere, one arm around Space and the other around Time, looking down on the world and saying *You haven't got a clue, not a fucking clue*. It was a cosmic can-can I wanted in on. *Wanted.* Therein lies the crux. The knowledge of non-addiction was, ironically, grist to the mill. That was how it went: down, down and down, deeper and deeper, until I reached, as I always reached, the final pre-*fuckit* outpost. The saloon on the edge of the desert. The 40,000-league crab shack. The brothel on Pluto.

This is my will.

Tyler leaned in saucily, breasts first. 'You know it's really good when it scares the shit out of you,' she said. 'I had to stop myself from roaring in the bathroom earlier. Like this,' she tipped her head back and waggled it from side to side, 'RAAARRRRRRR.'

I rolled out of bed and leapfrogged around the square metre of rough carpet, lifting balled papers and carrier bags, looking for clothes. Eventually I found some: a clean t-shirt and – gusset sniffed – some just-about-acceptable jeans. I stuffed random toiletries and – even more randomly, a bag of decomposing grapes (For Health) into a bag and called a cab. I usually walked to Jim's, it took twenty minutes or so, but time pressures plus Bambi-legs made walking as unlikely as successful social inter-action.

The cab company sent a minibus. Oh great, typical, I thought when I saw its hollow bulk chugging away by the kerb. *Te-rrific.* If there's one thing sure to amplify the existentials it's a minibus ride across town on your own. I nodded at the driver as I heaved the sliding door open. Threw my bag across the seats and climbed inside. Didn't put my seatbelt on. The cab smelled of hot fabric and pine. Four empty seats stared back at me. Another four empty seats behind. I found my phone in my bag and called my sister.

'Minibus, is it?' Mel said when she answered.

'Eh?'

'You only ever call me when you're in a minibus after a big one.'

'Do I?'

'Yep.'

'Sorry.'

'It's okay.'

'Where are you?'

'At the folks'. Dad had chemo again this morning.'

'Oh god. Is he – '

'It went fine. He's resting.'

'They didn't hear you say that, did they? About the *minibus after a big one.*'

'No, but even if they did I doubt they'd give much of a shit right now.'

'Course. Sorry.'

'Look, drink some water. Get some sleep.'

'I'll try.'

I hung up feeling wretched, and then wretched for feeling wretched, and then proud for feeling wretched for feeling wretched. I asked the cabbie to stop at the Co-Op opposite Victoria (the tenner rolled itself up in the plastic money-tray, I unrolled it, it rolled itself up again – I got out without waiting for change). In the supermarket I scuttled to the meat section, past the cold huddles of vegetables and uniformly stacked pasta and rice. Nothing smelled of anything. In the meat fridge there was a pack of mutton that had been discounted and I picked it up without thinking. What else should I get? A bottle of wine. A Shloer or something for Jim (fuck's sake). Bread. Milk. Fags. Loo roll. Cooked chicken. Crisps. Credit card the lot and worry about it next month, if I was still alive. I bought too much and when I pulled the bags off the counter I swayed with the weight and thought I might vomit. Oh god, no. I looked around. There were never any bathrooms in these little supermarkets. Could I feasibly get outside and find somewhere discreet? The last time I'd vomited was before Jim had left. He had a late flight so I'd stayed at his, drinking wine on my own and playing *Portal 2* on his PS3. At 2 a.m. I was starving and there was nothing in so I staggered to McDonald's in St Ann's Square in his canvas espadrilles (did they ever record for Google Earth at night, or was that just during the day? Mortification). I bought too much food and ate it walking back, and then – schoolgirl error – got in bed too soon. The internal tide turned and I knew there was only one way it was going to go. Just thinking about that night made vomiting inevitable so I paid quickly and left the shop. Around the corner I leaned against a wall and dropped my bags. The glass bottles rang against each other. The sound, and the lurch of worrying about them breaking, made me even sicker. Jim's street was about five minutes away, towards the arena. Did this require another taxi? Yes, my stomach said, yes it did. I reached for the wall and pressed my palm flat. I retched. Nothing. Sometimes a retch was worse than a gip. I tried not to think about food or fun of any kind and definitely not Jim. My nerves surged. You know that feeling. You feel pins and needles rushing and wonder if it means you're healing.

When I felt like I could move I walked to the rank outside the station and got in the front cab. The driver was nice enough about the shortness of the journey. I think he saw the panic in my eyes. When I got to Jim's I walked up the steps at the front of his building (he lived on the ground floor, mercifully) and let myself in.

He'd had a key cut for me in January and the plan was for me to move in when we were married but I couldn't see it yet. Cohabitation. Would I have to contribute to the décor, posters in clip frames, that kind of thing? Was Athena still open? I loved Jim's place but it didn't feel like home. Still, where did? Not Tyler's. Tyler's was Tyler's. Maybe when I made some money I could rent my own flat opposite Jim's and we could wave to each other over the road, like Woody Allen and Mia Farrow across Central Park. That would be romantic. Or lonely – would it just be lonely?

My phone started to ring. Expecting it to be Jim, I hunted through my bag and cleared my throat. The screen said ICE. In Case of Emergency. My parents' house. Dad, probably. I watched the letters flashing. His body. My body. What I'd done. What he hadn't. Oh, the shame of raiding my body's chemical joy-stores! I was no better than a looter. When it stopped ringing I noticed the time on the screen. I had just over an hour.

I put a pan on the hob, heated oil. Sliced onions. Fried spices. Tipped the mutton in. I'd never cooked with it before but I knew that it was basically the same thing as lamb, the archaic name reassuring. Dickens probably did a lot with mutton. The steam from the searing meat made me feel like I might vomit. I stepped back and flicked on the extractor fan in the hood over the hob. I added ginger, garlic, curry powder. I turned down the heat and went for a little lie-down on the settee. When I felt up to it I went back to add water and tomatoes to the pan. There.

That could sit awhile. Next: washing. But first . . . Jim had some rehydration salts in his medicine cabinet. I took a glass from the cupboard and tipped a packet of rehydration salts into it. The salt sat at the bottom of the glass in a little pile. It looked like cocaine. I took the glass to the sink and turned on the cold tap. Water twisted out in a clean, violet-edged ribbon.

Tyler and I had stayed a few hours in the pub, growing raucous with much table-pounding and face-gripping. We'd sorted plenty out, over tables, over the years. It was dark when we decided to head across town. We walked along the canal towpath, up, over bridges, under arches. Above Deansgate Locks there was a row of chain bars. Outside each bar was a small, roped-off section, guarded by doormen, where clubbers stood smoking. Tyler unhooked each rope as she passed, as though she was opening the pens in a zoo, saying: *RUN, BE FREE, NOW'S YOUR CHANCE*. Canal Street was manic with revelry. Boys in fairy-wings. Gazelles in hotpants. The homeless and their hounds. Dishevelled after-work drinkers for whom one drink had turned into one too many. Teenagers cramming burgers in their mouths outside neon-lit takeaways. We went into a club because someone told us it had a balcony, reserved for VIPs – not that it stopped Tyler. In the unisex toilets I got talking to a man who said his name was 'Chicken Sandwich'. He slipped me a green pill. I split it with Tyler and she said she'd got two Valiums for us for later from the doorman. We danced like wardrobes.

I went into Jim's bathroom and ran myself a bath. Looking around, I knew that if I was going to have an input on any room, then really it should be this one. Some new tiling. Maybe I could do it myself. How hard could tiling be? I could get into DIY as a hobby. Keep me busy. I liked the idea of a wedding list at Wickes; *that* would be funny. Screw John Lewis! Our guests

– all forty-eight of them – could race to snap up the under-£20 items: the bog brush holder and impractical wicker bin. I lit the half-collapsed candle by the side of the bath and stripped. Looking in the mirror I saw a thread vein had burst on my cheek, just beneath the bag of my bloodshot left eye. *You are a total dickhead*, I said. I felt the whole bathroom swell and nod in agreement. Yes, you are. A total dickhead. What the fuck was I going to do about this fucking veiny thing? Would Jim notice? I stepped back from the mirror. Squinted. Stepped forward. It was noticeable. I could wash my face and then attempt to cover it with concealer. These things happened anyway, with age. It could just be an age thing. It all started to change in your thirties. Things popped up all over the place. I had a ganglion at the base of my right middle finger that had sprung out of nowhere the previous month. I had a fallen arch in my foot that hadn't been there when I was twenty. Now I had a thread vein. Furthermore, I deserved it. It was as though the huge, punishing hand of God had reached down during the night and flicked me really hard in the face for being such a total fucking dickhead. I walked into the bedroom and checked the time on the radio. I'd wasted a good fifteen minutes inspecting my face and it was now quarter past eleven. T-minus forty-five minutes until Jim landed. Fine, fine. Cool, fine. Finecoolfine. A bath was all about the first thirty seconds anyway, that almost unbearable immersion when the water feels so hot it's cold, your skin's receptors in blind panic mode. Washing, like imbibing water, felt like a chore. I did it as little as I could get away with. I cringed in the shower, like a cat. Besides, I liked the various smells of myself; I often sat with my head to one side, nose close to my armpit. I liked the raw smells of other people, too; in particular scalps, ears, and the insides of wristwatches – these smells were more comforting than perfume or aftershave, which set me on edge with their keen social purpose. I went back into the bathroom,

38

turned off the taps and stepped into the bath. Sweet holy JehooHEEsus! It was a hot one. I gripped the bath handles and lowered myself, teeth gritted, legs reddening, pausing as the tide of firewater lapped at my navel.

The last thing I could remember from the club was the lights going up and seeing Tyler's hair flattened to her cheeks and forehead, glued in place with her own sweat and also communal condensed sweat, dripping luminously from the ceiling. Over on the bar a man was on all fours as a second man held his arse-crack open and a third poured a bottle of beer into it. The man on all fours was Chicken Sandwich. Tyler said: 'I think if I tried right now I could probably do the Caterpillar.' Time to go.

I dipped myself fully into the bath and dunked my head, came up gasping. I washed the holy trinity. I shaved my armpits. The hair on my legs was downy, mostly invisible; worse when meddled with. I shaved it occasionally in summer when my own treacherous aesthetics meant I couldn't go tightless otherwise. Tyler – coarser, darker – kept hers in honour of feminist historian Janet Fraser: *All that time I save in body hair removal I devote to revolution.* I teased her about it whenever I caught her coming out of the bathroom.
How much revolution this time?
Oh, heaps. There's a LOT of blood . . .
I got out of the bath, pink and quivering, and hobbled to the clothes I'd taken off, lying in the middle of the floor. I didn't keep clothes at Jim's as such, just the odd thing. A black vest, greying with age. A pair of thermal leggings. A silver lamé thong Tyler had bought me as a joke (*That, my friend, is just a yeast infection waiting to happen . . .*).
My mobile rang. Where was it, where was it? I ran into the

39

hall and tipped the contents of my bag onto the floor – running out of time now, that ten-ring emotional crescendo before the maddening voicemail tag-team that would ensue – saw the phone, grabbed it, and answered.

'I can't feel my legs, Keyser.'

'I'm not quite dead. I'm just very badly burned.'

Film quotes. Self-charming standards. The dream-house was our helpless Hotel California.

'I thought you were going to be Jim.'

'Sorry to disappoint you.' She sounded like she was lying down, her voice flat and gargly.

'Actually, it's a relief to hear you,' I said. 'Mastering meaningful speech is next up on my list of Things to Achieve Today. I'm not quite ready for Jim but I can just blart vowel-sounds at you and it's okay.'

'It's more than okay. I understand your blarting perfectly.'

'You're the world's leading expert in the field of my blarting.'

She inhaled and sighed. 'You staying there today, then?'

'Jim's back shortly – you know that.'

'Ah.' She sniffed. 'Pulling rank, is he?'

'It's not like that, I just need to get things straight. Myself, mainly. I'm practically brain-dead. Jim might as well be coming home to someone on life support – hey, at least he might have some sympathy for me that way . . .'

'Listen, just don't apologise, whatever you do. That only feeds the fire. I made the mistake of reading the news earlier. You know what the biggest problem is right now with Western society?'

'Our lack of real commitment to addressing climate change?'

'Our pornographic appetite for contrition. You have to be sorry for everything, all the time. Are you *sorry* you ate all those burgers? Are you *sorry* you smoked all those cigarettes? Are you *sorry* you said that dumb thing online? It's not morality, it's just another fix, another kind of greed: give me all your sorry, I'm

40

so hungry for sorry. But sorry changes nothing. There are more progressive motivations. When you go out and tear the night a new hole you do it for a reason, even if that reason is taking a vacation from Reason.'

'Yeesh, Tyler, I really hate that expression.'

'Sorry – I forgot, you have previous.'

'Hey, they were only internal and very small. I was eating too much bread.'

The curry was a predictable disaster. I ruined everything I cooked because of my inherent lack of cruise control. I had to remind myself to stand by pans. *You are cooking. Concentrate. Stir.* When I heard the key in the lock I ran to the door, hurling myself into his arms before he'd put his bags down.

'Whoa,' he said. His eyes were tight and sunken with travel: the red-eye flight from JFK and a connection at Heathrow. I held his face, kissed him hard. He tasted of mint and coffee. He smelled of plastic and his own delicious sweat. I drew back and we stood there for a minute taking each other in, the fear-excitement that there might have been a change in the space of a week; the slow-swell satisfaction-disappointment in knowing there wasn't. I did *Brief Encounter* like always – tight lips, Old English posh: 'You've been a long way away. Thenk you for kemming beck to me . . .'

I dished out the food. We sat at the table. The curry was too hot, the spices raw, the sauce floury, the meat fibrous. The last time I'd cooked for Jim I'd made a tortilla without pre-cooking the potatoes. It was almost as though I enjoyed failing. Was I, as I had long suspected, one part optimism two parts masochism, like all the best cocktails?

'You shouldn't have,' Jim said, squinting.

'I know.' I dropped my spoon into the still-full bowl. 'Tell me about New York.'

'Oh, you'd love it, Laur. It's all your favourite things.'

I picked up my spoon again, made a fist round it. 'Like what?'

'Lively, contradictory, seemingly organised on the surface but beautifully chaotic underneath.'

'Does it have a dark, complex soul?'

'I think it wishes it had.'

'Very good, Mr Partington. Now, take all your clothes off.'

Sex with Jim was, amongst other things, a way of reminding myself I had a body. I'd had sex in my teens to get out of my body; in my twenties and thirties, so far it was about making me remember again. Jim's body was springy and curved in a woodish way – he'd lost weight since he'd stopped drinking and his work kept his arms high-toned. He pulled me on top of him and I tried to encourage him to do the things I liked, be rougher and smack my ass so I pushed harder onto him. *You are here, here and here. Close your eyes. You're still here, aren't you?* But Jim had gone shyer since he'd stopped drinking, like he'd lost his bottle in more ways than one. It was sort of okay and sort of . . . frustrating. I didn't know whether bringing it up would make him more self-conscious (was there anything *less* sexy than a conversation about sex?) and we had so much on, so I enjoyed the feeling of his spread hands, holding me (convincing me), and his chest hair that smelled of salty-smokiness.

We lay in bed afterwards discussing the wedding. 'We're pretty much on track,' I said. 'Listen to me! No, Jim, seriously, we're *moving forward* on this . . . You can shoot me, you know. Any time you like. So tomorrow I've got a few more emails to reply to, which I'd have done today if I hadn't been so head-rottingly hungover. The caterers have more questions about the ham and we've had a few more RSVPs, also people are still asking about presents and if I have to use the *Your presence is our present* line one more time then I'm going to have to wire my nipples to the mains and beat myself to death with a knotted rope just to feel original again.'

He kissed my eyelids. I told him about the club. He laughed. I showed him my thread vein. He said it was cute. I felt invincible. Such is the inner sanctum of bed: when you're in there with the person you love the rest of the world can go to hell. At least that's the way it feels when you're not discussing logistics. The wedding chat invited quite literally the rest of the world in. I decided to only ever bring it up again in the kitchen; that was where it belonged.

The Northern Quarter, Friday, October. Tyler and I had gone drinking after our shifts. By 8 p.m. we were ten drinks in, wedding-drunk and almost dancing. Over by the bar I saw him stirring his drink. It wasn't the kind of place you stirred your drink (no ice, no fruit, straws of dubious cleanliness) so I knew something was up. After I'd been watching him a few seconds he looked at me and back to his drink. Another two seconds, me, his drink.

Game on.

Tyler was sitting next to me, her head drooping as she looked at her phone. A few feet away, the sound periodically blunted by gyrating bodies, 'She's A Rainbow' by World of Twist belted out from a bass speaker.

'Tyler,' I shouted over the music, 'do you fancy a shot?'

'Tequila,' she said without looking up. 'I had too much sambuca on Tuesday, I can still feel it coating my tonsils. And he's gay but go for your life.'

I bounced up to the bar. His mouth twitched but otherwise his expression didn't change. The marine wash of bar lights gave him an elvish opalescence, his skin a pale contrast to black hair and brows. So hard to say how you sense that peculiar attraction, the kind that shakes you to the root of your own mythologies (there was the bad child on the settee, the fourteen-year-old running from the parked car, the twenty-year-old shyly saying actually she'd like that more maybe, the thirty-year-old bored and guilty in her boredom, each former self acknowledged as he passed, yes hello hello, present, present if not quite correct. He had all of me in all of five seconds). He looked like he was drinking something with tonic, which boded well: something with tonic was my drink of choice for going the distance. I've always believed you can tell a lot by someone's drink. He delicately – nimble fingers, I noticed those straight off – took the straw he'd been stirring with out of his drink and set it down on the bar, where a little pool of shiny liquid seeped around it. I looked to the barmaid and ordered two shots. As she turned to the optics I turned towards him and offered to buy him a shot. He shook his head. Smiled. Still not a word. I wondered whether he was mute. Could I love a mute? We could write each other notes, that would be romantic. He took his drink up to his lips and sipped. Swallowed. Put the glass back on the bar. The moonish meniscus swayed to a standstill. Was he ever going to speak? He smiled again. He was like the Mona Lisa. I almost said, *You're like the Mona Lisa* but stopped myself. I was aware I looked odd enough as it was, sweaty and stone-eyed with ranting and wine. My shots arrived. I handed over the cash. Waited for my change. When I'd put my change in my purse I tucked my purse under my arm and took a shot in each hand. Turned to him. 'Well,' I said. 'Have an intense one.' Wankerish of me, I know. But I mean, really, it's one thing being all intriguing and beckoning but when –

'Hang on.'

I stopped. Turned. The shots quivered in my grip. This could go one of several ways but it definitely wasn't done.

I said: 'I come here every week and it's a lot nicer than me and my dad isn't a thief but he probably knows a few although

44

as far as I know he's never been anywhere near the stars and I don't even like *raisins*.'

He grinned. Actual teeth. I stood there, poised with two tequilas, wondering whether to put them back down on the bar, take them over to Tyler, or neck them right there just for the fuck of it. I looked over to where Tyler was sitting. She nodded and mouthed GAY. I turned around and placed the shots back on the bar.

'You sure you don't want one of these?'

He looked over to Tyler. 'Is one of them not for your friend?'

'Oh, she's fine.'

'Okay then.' I handed him a tequila and cheers'd his shot with mine – momentary awkwardness, first proximity, dangerous angles, then clear all clear. My fingers wide on the glass I tipped it back with a seasoned pelican swallow. He did his in two and ran his tongue over his top teeth, throat twitching.

'So,' I said, 'what do you do with yourself when you're not standing in bars being enigmatic?'

He smiled. 'You really want to talk about *that*?'

'No,' I said, burning for my crassness. I skittered, recovering. (This is the way it is with me, I don't know whether I want to be the life and soul or the mystery.) 'Not at all,' I said, 'I don't want to talk about anything. I just feel like I should because I'm a product of my generation and we abhor a lull in communication. Sometimes I envy Neanderthal times. A caveman moment, where you could just stand there throwing meat at each other. None of the inane chitter-chat.'

A single nod. The firmest eyes. A chin not unlike the horn of a saddle.

'I'm a pianist,' he said.

No penis jokes.

'Classical or jazz or . . .? I can't think of any more.'

'Both, but mostly classical. I mean, that's where the big bucks

45

are.' A twinkle at this. Was he? Yes – yes, he was. Ripping the piss. Oho, this boded well.

'Go You.'

'Go me,' he said, squinting. That squint. He had me at *that squint*. 'I played the RNCM earlier. That's why I'm here.' He looked around, raised his eyebrows and sipped his long drink. '*Some*one recommended it.'

'Was it your girlfriend?'

'No, it wasn't my girlfriend.'

'Is she quite boring, then?'

'You could say that.'

'Boring in a kind of non-existent way?'

'There's no "kind of" about it.'

(HOORAY.)

'So,' he said. 'What do you drive?'

'A hard bargain.'

'Let me guess: you're a comedian.'

'Way off. Freezing, in fact.'

'Let's have it then.'

'I'm a writer.'

'A writer of what?'

Words. Laura, I scolded myself, YOU ARE NOT BOB DYLAN.

'Short stories mostly. But I'm working on a novel. I know everyone says that but it's nearly finished and I'm quite determined.'

Quite determined? Jesus. I sounded like Elizabeth fucking Bennett.

'Great,' he said. 'Anything published?'

I did a sour little tequila burp and hoped he hadn't noticed. 'A few things, in a small way.'

He stuck out his hand then. 'Jim.'

'Laura.'

His was a good hand. Clam-shaped nails, raised veins,

46

knuckles just worn enough. I had a fleeting erotic vision; a rush that spilled from jaw to ribs to pelvic floor – lowering myself, holding his hips, not losing eye contact, seeing what his face did. I hoped the vision hadn't passed through my hand as I took his, and then I hoped it had. I sensed a gentleness emanating from him, a soft lamp on somewhere inside. I wanted to collapse like a blooming flower in reverse stop-frame animation, rush to the point of his hand, and go in there. I wanted to be inside him. I felt – as I did again and again whenever I had hold of Jim – Yeats' *loveliness that has long faded from the world.*

I woke up naked in a bed that wasn't mine. Someone next to me who wasn't Tyler. A not-unpleasant achiness. Memories of deep kissing, his hands on my shoulder blades, the nape of my neck attended to. Closeness. Intimacy. I remembered undressing, the condom, the carpet. A rented room. Magnolia paint, sloe gin his niece had made, no cigarettes. I rolled over, and *there*: the back of him pale and straight like a candle. I reached out – atoms displacing atoms, that's all it was, funny, just before the moment of contact – then my hand was on him. Warm, downy skin prickled. He murmured and turned to face me.

We'd stayed in the bar until two then we got a taxi back to his place. Tyler ended up at a party in Salford, bum-grinding with a *Coronation Street* star who wouldn't admit he was in *Coronation Street* – not surprising under the circumstances; the circumstances being nitrous balloons and Arrested Development on Spotify. *Actors*, her morning voicemail said. *Actors.*

I called her back at the end of Jim's street. *So how about you and your fancy friend?*

So how about that?

Well, I'd only gone and fallen in love.

Beyond all fantasies, this one, right from the start. It's a beautiful thing when you know you have a bolder look in your eye and can bolt one back. That sudden ownership of someone's body, the requited favouritism when it comes to yours. That sense of communion. I can touch you here, here and here – look at me just touching you all over. I made love to Jim religiously; it felt like prayer or what I knew of prayer. The ritual. The bending. I felt a new point to things, a new purpose, an endlessness in that. I'd been so disappointed to discover at the age of sixteen, after losing my virginity to a gentle, shy schoolmate and dating him for a year or so, that an orgasm was merely what I had been giving myself all those years (Is that *it*? Oh, it is. Oh, well). Jim and I explored each another, turning stones, dropping depth gauges. It was about what I could do to him, and it was about seeing what what I was doing was doing to him; the tease and retreat, the whispered exchange of devils. And beyond all that, the purity of possibility. You haven't had the chance to fuck up. You could be anything. You could be *perfect* (unlikely, but the freedom of having the whole rainbow of potential flaws in the running is not to be under-estimated). He doesn't know yet about your limited geographical knowledge; that you don't read the papers every day; that you sometimes hide instead of answering the door (and the phone). You are yet to drink white wine and turn into a complete fucking lunatic over absolutely nothing. You are yet to, yet to, yet to.

We got engaged just over a year later on New Year's Eve, after a party at Tyler's that we left early (she was in the process of kicking up a fuss but then someone had put 'Buffalo Stance' on and our departure had gone unnoticed). We sat on the rug in his lounge drinking a bottle of port that his parents had left and we were so drunk that we couldn't remember who had asked who in the end, but it didn't matter; it was a minor detail. We'd been talking about the future and what we both wanted, and agreed that being together for ever was The Thing. The idea of marriage suddenly felt – well, a bit crazy and dramatic, over the top really (SOLD!). We woke up on New Year's Day and turned to each other with that heart-filleting, hungover *something-big-happened-and-is-it-okay* wariness.

Did you mean that?

Yes. Did you?

Yes.

(Phew.)

Since then things had got busy. In January we took a trip to Scarborough before his spring touring picked up. We stayed two nights in a wind-blasted B&B and spent the Saturday afternoon skimming stones down at the beach in our scarves and hats. From a distance we could have been any age. I turned from throwing a particularly good skimmer – four bounces, my dad had taught me well: keep the stone flat, like that, direct it with your first finger like you're trying to hit the horizon and not the surface – and said to Jim, who was looking out to sea: 'Can we always live in the city?' The sun was low, like a bubble on a spirit level, and Jim didn't turn round so I carried on talking to his back. 'When we're married, I mean. Let's not put ourselves out to pasture. Let's keep having adventures.' I didn't know where it had come from, that panic, the feeling that we were somehow closing down, reducing possibilities.

When Jim turned he was looking at me in an odd, epic way; as though he'd been looking at the sea too long and his irises had absorbed an extra element. *Infinity* is a grand word, but you know what, fuckit, sometimes only the grand ones will do. I knew that whatever was coming, it was big. If we hadn't already been engaged, I'd have thought that he was about to propose. If Jim had been a woman, I'd have thought he was about to tell me he was pregnant. Behind him, waves broke regularly in fat little flops.

'Laura,' he said. 'I've made a decision.'

I tensed, prepared myself. Did he not want to marry me any more? Ah, it was silly idea anyway, marriage. I'd been having my doubts, hadn't I? We didn't need it to prove our commitment. Tyler was right –

'I'm giving up drinking.'

I shook my head to shake the words he'd said into place. 'WHAT?'

'I can't do it any more, with work. With what I want for our future. It doesn't . . . agree.'

I was so flabbergasted I couldn't say anything else. Jim and I had had so much fun together when we were drinking. Drinking, unlike smoking (he bought a ten-pack sometimes drunk or stole mine, yep, one of *those*), was something we shared. And then, the beginning of a strange feeling, deep down inside. Hard to put your finger on. Inner space stretching, and despite the unease, my heart perversely rejoicing. *A new feeling! A new feeling at thirty-two! This is something!* I looked back to the town. Was there a pub nearby? We should really get a – Oh.

Jim took my hand. 'Is that okay?'

I shrugged, the polite words coming on instinct. 'Well, of course it's okay. It's your choice, you know.'

It was a steely sky, a steely sea, and I had that hollow feeling I always got in my gut whenever I saw the horizon or the night sky.

'I've never been as good at it as you, Laur,' he went on. 'So I might not be your man for adventures. But I can be your rugged base.'

I kissed his hand hard and fast, it was cold as a stone and my lips burned on it. 'You're not rugged, I'm rugged. I'm rugged

50

enough for two! Anyway, what makes you think that I think that all adventures have to involve drinking? Do you think I'm that shallow, that ridiculous?'

We bought bags of chips on the way back to the B&B. I've never been able to finish a full bag of chips so I gave most of mine to the gulls.

HOME NOT HOME

Psssshhhhhht.

I ducked as a jet of fine mist shot towards my face from the automatic air freshener on the medicine cabinet. I shook the remaining water off my hands and stepped to the other side of the bathroom. *Pssssssshhhhhht!* Another shot fired from a second air freshener on top of the toilet cistern.

'Fuck!'

I crouched and shielded my eyes, peered up through the gaps between my fingers. Above me a nimbostratus of 'Cashmere Woods' began to precipitate.

'All right in there?' My dad's voice on the landing beyond the door.

I unlocked the door, opened it. There he was in his green plaid shirt, grinning, hunched, visibly thrilled he'd heard me swear.

'Sorry, Dad. It's like an FBI training zone in here.'

He backed up against the wall and made his hands into a gun shape. 'Come on, Clarice. I've got your back.' The effects of the chemo were showing. His hair was thinner and ashier, the skin mottled on his cheeks, dark umbra eclipsing his eye sockets. He darted his eyes back and forth and jerked his head.

I walked ahead of him down the stairs. His downward pace was fast for a man of his age in his condition, and I wondered whether he was trying too hard, which made me think of something my mum said sometimes – partly to embarrass him and partly to endear him to us. *He follows you and Melanie round the house, you know, whenever you come home.*

Home. It was and it wasn't, any more. (Hovis Presley helped: *Wherever I Lay My Hat, That's My Hat.*) My old bedroom had been redecorated and besides I'd only spent a few years in Middleton before moving away to Edinburgh and university. Most of my childhood memories were from the house before, where I'd lived from the age of eight to sixteen – in fact, my child-self was attached to the terrace in Crumpsall so tenaciously that a few times on my way home from the doctor's in my mid-twenties, fever-dazed and comfort-hungry, I'd given the taxi driver directions to Crumpsall only to get halfway there and realise that I lived in the other direction entirely, as a grown-up.

Down in the hall, which reeked faintly, perennially, of mice, Jim was helping my mum put on her coat. I rotated Jim and Tyler as my date for family meals – it seemed only fair. I'd taken Tyler before I met Jim and it felt wrong for him to suddenly usurp her, and besides her mum had moved to London to help Jean so Tyler didn't get many dinners out. I didn't like to admit it but the meals with Jim were easier. He was golden amongst the Joyces; they hung on his every word, saw him as a bona fide exotic mystery. It was a different relationship to the one I had with his family, which had been sullied from the start. That memory! How it burrrrrrrned.

We were on the M6 on the way to his folks' place in Birmingham when I'd felt a sudden painful and irrepressible need.

Darling, I said, *I need you to pull into the next Services.*

But we're nearly there.

No – I mean I REALLY need you to pull in. This isn't desire. It is necessity.

Fifteen minutes and we'll be there, Laur. Can you not wait?

Nnnnnnngggggggggggggg.

I hung on against my better instincts, hunching and groaning and cursing and feeling magma shifting inside. I loosened my seatbelt and hooked it around my knees but it didn't help. As we got close to his parents' cul-de-sac Jim handed me his keys and I held them in my sweating hand, ready to run. When we pulled up outside the house I threw the door open and toppled out before the car had come to a halt.

Top of the stairs and first left! Jim shouted. *They won't be back from church yet.*

I ran to the front door and fumbled the Yale key in the lock, swearing. I ran up the stairs, pulling down my pants, swearing and shaking. I dived into the bathroom and sat on the toilet, releasing a Niagara of scalding diarrhoea. When it was purged I exhaled with relief and wiped the sweat from my brow. I turned to unspool some toilet paper, only to see Jim's dad sitting in the bath next to me, a white-knuckled flannel obscuring his nethers, the newspaper limp in his hand.

They hadn't gone to church that day. They'd prepared an extravagant Sunday roast instead. And what an awkward occasion that was. *No gravy for me, Mrs Partington . . .*

'Thanks, love,' my mum said to Jim when her arms were in her coat. She touched her hair and I saw the mauve veins of her inner wrists bulge and flatten between her bracelets. Quiet and proud (my mum hardly ever drank but when she did it was as though every thought she'd had for the past forty years spilled out), it was only her love of outlandish costume jewellery that might direct a stranger to the Sixties fairground of her heart – the heart that had fallen for and stuck with my dad.

A copy of the *Daily Mail* sat folded on the sideboard, its masthead scowling out in Satan's own handwriting. Mel and I – liberal upstarts that we were, politics worn as flashily as our Levi 501s and Doc Martens – had been so pleased with ourselves when we'd convinced our parents to stop buying the *Sun*. And what had they started buying instead? Oh, Universe. You and your jokes.

My mum batted non-existent dust from her shoulders and set about buttoning her coat. 'Jim, be a love and close the Very Front Room door, would you? Give it a good slam. It's started to stick and Bill – well, there, yes, that's it. You are a marvel.'

The 'Very Front Room' was the result of nobody knowing what to do when we moved into a house with two front rooms (although crucially did this mean two TVs?), but one was at the front of the house and one was at the back, so we christened them accordingly. At the time it seemed like logic but now, like so many things that had once seemed logical, all that was left was a needling sense of the surreal. The Very Front Room was kept for special occasions like when Dad got three balls on the lottery and threw a bit of a party. There was an uncomfortable antique sofa in there, thick-veined with loosened springs, and a throttle of disintegrating bulrushes in a pure 1970s vase.

I got in the back of the car and put my seatbelt on. Jim drove us to the restaurant – a Tex-Mex place a few miles away. As we passed the Baptist church on the main road I read out the billboard, which was always comical.

'WHAT IS MISSING FROM CH CH?

U R'

'Puh,' said my dad. As a child I'd questioned him – repeatedly – on his upbringing and all he'd said was: *Religion trains you to take things personally.*

Before I started at the grammar school I was buddied up with a Jewish girl called Dina to ease me into the new regime. I went round to her house with my mum in early September before term started. Our mums talked at the breakfast bar while Dina and her younger sister Danielle took me upstairs to a bright pink bedroom full of Barbie vehicles and voile fabrics. I was wearing a Garfield digital watch at the time – a cumbersome thing I adored, with a plastic Garfield-in-relief face that flipped open to reveal a liquid crystal display. Dina and her sister were admiring it when I heard myself say: *Oh, this thing . . . they were giving them away at our local kosher butchers . . .* I trailed off, let the suggestion hang there. Dina and Danielle looked at me. *You're Jewish?!* they exclaimed. I pouted, looked around the room. After an hour or so they dropped it.

When I actually got to prep school it wasn't by accident that I made best friends with Jessie Roberts – a tall, Poochie-fringed Catholic girl. I bought garage freesias for her mum and complimented her dad on his cooking. Eventually she said I could accompany her family to church one Sunday. They expected me to just sit there and take it in, sing the songs, kneel during the prayers, but I got so involved (rituals had me rapt) that I followed them up to take communion. I saw Jessie's dad glance at me curiously from where he stood further up the queue. I finally gave the game away when I said *Thanks* to the priest instead of *Amen*, the host melting helplessly on my tongue like a very thin ice cream wafer soaked in Calpol. The priest looked to Jessie's dad, who shrugged and then glared at me. They didn't invite me round again. I seethed, silently, about it. I had a *right* to be there, didn't I? MY FATHER WAS AN ALTAR BOY. And so it was my dad I took it out on, making excuses to go up to my room straight after dinner. He won me round with fishing trips, Sunday drives, trips into town to see the retired satellite, a glinting blue drum of circuits, at the Science and Industry Museum. What else did I try? I had a friend who was a Methodist (the church hall was dull; the nativity was lively, but I abandoned my faith when I was told off by the minister for wearing earrings in the shape of a cross – a bizarre humiliation). Another friend was a nerdy Quaker, and made a convincing case for how to be religious and scientific at the same time, but her pervy uncle put me off the meetings. Another friend was Muslim (I over-appraised the self-discipline of fasting, I was dismissed as a creepy little voyeur). In GCSE Maths I sat opposite a big-eyed Sikh girl who I was obsessed with but never plucked up the courage to talk to. I realised what the awful feeling was when Rajveer asked everyone else in the maths group to go and watch *Batman Returns* for her birthday: God was just another party I hadn't been invited to.

At the restaurant, Mel and her boyfriend Julian were waiting for us in the foyer. Mel waved when she saw me. Julian stood with his hands in his trouser pockets. Melanie, two years older than me, was still in many ways my idol. I always thought I'd catch up height- and beauty-wise, but never did. That's not false modesty; it's irrefutable fact. I was always able to live with it because: a) I loved my sister; b) I wasn't that superficial most of the time, *most of the time*; and c) Julian was The Most Boring Man On Earth. He wasn't unkind (or we'd have had him killed), but I'd never felt so genetically alien to my sibling as when Julian had come round to the house for the first time and spent three hours telling my dad (who didn't have a pot to piss in after forty years' window-cleaning) about his new foray into property development and why now was the time to BTL. My dad and I had briefly rendezvous'd in the kitchen for a large whisky, and neither of us had felt the need to speak. But Melanie loved Julian and we had to give her credit for her choices – after all, she *was* thirty-four. So I stopped appealing to her with my eyes whenever he launched into a tirade about one of his many problematic tenants (they never sounded particularly unreasonable in their requests to me as a lifelong renter) but I couldn't help but wonder about her private happiness. I mean, what was he like in bed? If he wasn't forthcoming with boiler repairs then it didn't bode well for cunnilingus.

'Bill! Heather!' Julian stepped forward and shook hands with my dad then hugged my mum. He shook hands with Jim next, leaving me until last given that I was a deplorable little free-loading wastrel who was transferring her debts from her parents to her partner (or was I being paranoid?).

I shook his hand and hugged Melanie. She smelled of too much Chanel, like always. 'I saw about Jean on Facebook,' she said.

'Yeah,' I said. 'Tyler's thrilled.'

Mel smirked. 'I wouldn't have thought she'd be thrilled about any baby – what is it she calls them? *Human grubs*?'

Jim snickered.

'Don't start,' I said.

'Start what?' Mel's nails were a shiny maroon colour and she had one of those bras on where you weren't supposed to be able to see the clear plastic strap but you could.

'The Tyler-bashing.'

'You look great, Jim,' Mel said, hugging him. '*Great*.'

'Nearly three months now.'

'It's really agreeing with you.'

I looked at Jim. He did look good but then he always looked good. I wondered whether the vein on my face was visible. I looked around the restaurant and saw my dad looking around, too. He jerked his head towards the bar and I nodded and went over. We ordered a Guinness and a red wine, followed by the other drinks in order of interestingness: half a lager, an orange juice, a diet coke, a lime and soda. The Guinness swirled stormily on the drip-tray.

'Know what I've been thinking?' he said.

The barmaid put our drinks on the bar. My dad picked up his pint. His fingers flickered around the glass, tightened, loosened, flickered again. He spoke in little fanfares, swinging his head from side to side, posing and gazing for a moment before carrying on. Children and animals flocked to him. How many times had he caught something in the old pond behind our estate and held the net up to show us. *Look here, girls! Hard to believe that within this tiny space is a beating heart, a circulatory system, a rapidly sparking brain* . . . Me and Mel standing there, leering in our anoraks. He was why I picked stranded worms off the pavement and threw them into gardens even when I was on my way out. He was why I couldn't kill wasps even though I hated them. He was why I looked for, and loved, the creatures in people. They were always there. As family legend went, it was my dad who'd got the first proper grin out of me. I was six months old; he was thirty. We were sitting at the dining table. Way he told it, I was sliding soggy Wotsits around the plastic tray of my highchair, he was eating chops and gravy. He stopped eating for a minute and angled his head to one side to match the angle of mine. Stayed that way until I noticed. He said he saw it dawn on me that there was no sensible reason for him to be doing that – so what then? Something else . . . Something . . . Something . . . Searching . . . Then, CRACKLE. A spark by the black obelisk. Delight. So it was his fault, you see, when I was at the blaming stage of my existentials. He didn't fuck me up; he funned me up. Despite all the years my mum smashed loaded dinner plates onto the back patio; despite all the nights he didn't come home because he didn't want the men he owed money to following him; despite the countless bookies' I'd stood outside, kicking the toes of my trainers in the cracks in the pavement, desperate, *desperate* to see what was beyond the *No Under-18s* sign and the postered-out windows. Despite his selling atheism to me as a simple truth. He was forever the man who let me balance, buttocks tensing, on the back wheel-arch of his window-cleaning van as he drove down Jutland Street (the steepest street in Manchester) at a friction-hot forty-five. He'd taught me to read: a double-edged sword. I wanted to learn to read so badly. Learned quickly. But then came the frustration at not being able to look at words without understanding them.

I tried to glance at road signs and away, but it was always too late: to see words was to understand them. I sensed a loss there. (Later, Emily Dickinson would confirm it: *Hope is the thing with feathers that perches in the soul, and sings the tune without the words . . .*). Meaning was everywhere. And once you started with meaning, well, you got a taste for it.

In Los Nachos, Guinness in hand, my dad said: 'Lately I've had this feeling that as a species we're on the brink of something; something that redefines everything. Like when they discovered the world was round instead of flat.'

'They're closing in on the God particle . . .'

He grimaced. 'The *Higgs boson*, you mean. Maybe it's that at the back of my mind. Although it doesn't feel that specific, it's more a general feeling of . . .'

'Vertigo?'

He looked at me. Swigged his pint and grimaced again. Mel said he had mouth ulcers. 'Yes.'

We ferried the drinks to the rest of them and then went back over to the bar, just the two of us. I said: 'This brink, Dad. Don't you think every generation has thought the same thing?'

He cleared his throat. Sipped his drink and swallowed hard. 'Laura, I've been alive for the equivalent of two and half generations now and this is the first time I've felt it.'

I did think he was being sincere even though the harder part of me thought: *Dad, you're shit-scared, that's all this renaissance talk is. You need to feel something mind-blowing might happen before . . . Before the curtain's pulled back and you see the man with the megaphone. Or worse still: the great big Fuck All that's there, waiting, just behind the Irony.*

And of course I'd heard him, hadn't I. At his outer limits. Hedging his bets. It was six months since he'd found out (five months since he'd told me and Mel, on Mum's insistence, two days before his operation).

60

A grey day. The world in ugly molecular detail. Stones in the driveway. Dust in the air of the house. I went upstairs to use the bathroom while Mum and Mel sat downstairs not drinking tea out of matching floral mugs. Mel kept saying, *I can't believe we couldn't tell* – as though our ignorance was more horrifying for her than the fact of the cancer itself. I heard him as I got near to the bathroom, whispering at first and then a shout breaking through on certain syllables. At first I thought he was on the phone. I crept closer.

You cunt. You fucking cunt. You waited until I'd retired, didn't you?

I stood rigid on the landing, knowing how mortified he'd be to know I'd heard him.

Just give me ten more years. Ten more years and then you can do what the fuck you want with me.

We sat down to eat. I ordered a rare steak and a salad and another glass of wine. The waiter took my dad's order next.

'I'll have the beef fajitas.'

'No, he won't,' said my mum.

'Yes, I will.'

'Four more months and you can eat all the red meat you want, that's what Dr Grayling said. Now behave.'

The waiter looked to Mel. 'Salmon, please,' she said.

My dad leaned towards me. 'I had a bacon sandwich yesterday. Slipped through me like a greased otter.'

'Bill!'

He turned to my mum. 'I need iron, woman!'

'Have some greens!'

'I'm not a pet bleeding rabbit.'

'Oh, just let him have the fajitas, Mum,' I said.

She looked at me. 'You haven't been up with him all night when he can't sleep with cramps. You haven't washed your bedding five times in twenty-four hours. Mel saw what it was like when she stayed . . .'

My dad looked at me. The blotches on his cheeks had joined up with rage. 'Grayling said he'd never seen someone hold on to so much hair. I walked six miles on Sunday without stopping.' I nodded. 'All right, then. I'll have the grilled chicken and a side salad. With blue cheese dressing.'

My mum waited until the waitress had gone and turned to me. 'So where are you up to with everything?'

Jim produced a list and a pen from his pocket.

'What's that?' I said.

'My list.'

'You have a *list*?'

'I find lists very calming,' said Mel.

'I'll tell you one that isn't calming,' Jim said. 'The guest list. We've been trying to keep the numbers down but every person raises a few others. It's like that mythical beast where you chop a head off and two others sprout up in its place.'

'Just tell them all no,' said Julian. 'If we get married it'll be just the two of us on a beach. I'm not paying for every piss-taker I've ever met to come fill their boots.' He sat straight and breathed in bullishly through his nose, inflating his lungs to full capacity. It was a way of breathing that said *More Oxygen For Me*.

I looked at Mel. She didn't look at me. She didn't need to.

'I've nearly finished your invites,' my mum said. 'And I've bought the silk flowers for the table decorations.'

Jim crossed something out on his list.

'Least I can do,' my mum said.

Jim's parents were paying for the wedding.

My mum raised a finger, reached her other hand down under the table and brought out a magazine. 'And I got this for you, Laura.' I looked down. *Bride Be Lovely*. The actor-bride on the front, with her stony whited eyes and rictus grin, looked as though she had been saying BE LOVELY BE LOVELY to herself in the mirror through gritted teeth while getting ready.

'Thanks, Mum.'

Mel turned to me. 'Have you picked a dress yet?'

'I'm going shopping with Tyler at the weekend.'

Julian snorted. He'd first met Tyler at my dad's sixieth. I could still see his face as he watched her, off her tits on Prosecco, moonwalking across the dance floor to 'Moves Like Jagger', shrugging disingenuously. *You know what his problem is?* Tyler said whenever his name came up. *Too much fucking hair gel.*

'Where are you going to look?' asked my mum.

'Apparently there's some kind of bridal village in Cheshire,' I said. 'Tyler's driving me there.'

'Does Tyler *drive*?'

'You know she does.'

'Well, goodness knows what you'll end up with if you're going with that rum bugger,' said my dad. This was how my dad referred to Tyler – *that rum bugger* – with more than a hint of admiration. Unlike the rest of them, my dad liked Tyler because he knew a grifter when he met one and couldn't help but be enthralled when she wrinkled her nose and told him to *Get lost* and tell her another.

The last time I'd brought Tyler to a family meal she'd gone to the toilet and come back and sat on my dad's knee and started telling the whole table about how she'd stood on a chair in the coffee shop that day and recited *Beowulf* (Medieval Literature MA; she'd got a distinction). She said it had gone down well. I wanted her to shut up – or maybe it was because she was perched on my father's lap and it was making me queasy. I jerked my head, indicating she should get back in her own seat. She did. Only when the mains arrived and I saw her discreetly slide a cod fillet into her lap and wrap it in her napkin, unable to eat it – flinching as the hot fish burned her thin-trousered thighs – did I understand the real reason behind her sudden eruption of intimacy. Zero appetite. Conversation ramped up to eleven. Busted.

'So we need to plan a date for a rehearsal sometime in August,' said Jim, pen hovering.

'Second half of the month's best for us,' said my mum. 'Last chemo session's on the twelfth.'

My dad was supposed to be giving me away.

'Great. But see how you feel nearer the time, Bill,' said Jim.

'I'll be fine, pal, don't you worry. You just make sure *you're* around.'

When we got back to Jim's I went to the bathroom. As I sat on the toilet I heard him laugh. Rushed wiping, flushing, not wanting to miss out.

He was sitting on the sofa, the bridal magazine unfurled across his lap. He looked up. 'Blitz those bingo wings and be strapless without shame! What a bizarre choice of word that is. Shame.'

'Well, what could be more shameful than flabby upper arms? I know. These things offer no perspective. They should do a feature on what to do when you've fucked the best man or spunked the flower money on ketamine.'

Jim looked at me.

'I haven't done either of those things,' I said. 'I mean, you haven't even *got* a best man . . .'

He looked at the magazine. I sat down next him to hunt for more funnies. I thought, *How nice it would be to crack open a bottle of wine now and drink it together, getting merry and mocking the ridiculousness.* I felt a pang remembering how much we used to dick about together. The time we dressed up as Paula Yates and John Leslie for a Dead Celebrities party. The time we put on too much pink lipstick in Pere Lachaise cemetery and kissed the marble marker of Oscar Wilde's grave. The time we swam in a loch at lunchtime and had sex beneath a war memorial, causing a group of hikers to call the police. The time we did an impromptu 'My Baby Just Cares For Me' at a jazz bar and the manager asked if we'd consider being the house band. The time he held my knife. The time I wore his shoes. The time we danced – like, didn't stop, like constant, deadly dancing – for six hours at a trance festival in Germany; him mostly ballet, me mostly zumba. The times we talked all night, all night – grasping for those 'meaningful' conversations (I always meant Every Word). The time I christened him 'Poirot' after he drank so much brandy he pinballed along the walls of his flat towards the bathroom – me staggering behind and buffering him when I could – and bellowed several hearty blasts of puke into the sink, the shower cubicle, and finally, finally, the toilet. As I started to mop up with the bathmat he spun towards me, a thin vomit moustache on his top lip, and said: 'AND WHERE WERE YOO WHEN ALL THIS WES 'EPPENING?' As he said the word 'THIS' he twirled his finger round the outskirts of his face. I had to laugh because his vom-tash and accent (warped by booze-dulled enunciation) combined to give him the air of the Belgian detective. Also, a reckoning there: a responsibility to each other for the state we were in. For the states we got in. Together or apart. A vow of sorts.

Good times.

IT'S MY FUCKING WEDDING

A few days later I was sitting out in the garden ignoring my phone (my mum, ringing to ask about envelopes, the tentative voicemail revealed) when Tyler came tearing round the side of the block. She'd been out all night.

'GET INSIDE GET INSIDE!' she yelled. Her cardigan was hanging off, in one hand dangled a pair of ridiculously high wedges that her sister had given her, her other hand was pressed to her chest trapping a large glass jar that looked as though it was full of road grit. It wasn't winter. I jumped up and ran after her, kicking away the empty whisky bottle I was using as a doorstop. The door banged shut behind us. We pegged it up the stairs.

'What the fuck's going on?'

'JUST HURRRRY!'

She fumbled for her door key with the hand she was holding her wedges in; I shoved her out the way and used my key to open the door. She rammed it open and ran inside. I ran after her, slamming the door and double locking it. She went into the kitchen, opened the fridge and pulled down the plastic flap that sealed off the ice box. She started shoving the jar into the freezer, pulling out ice cube trays to accommodate it.

'What the fuck is that?' I said, moving closer. Then I recognised the sugary, beige crystals. I'd never seen them in such a large quantity before, but I knew them, and my stomach knew them, and my bowels. My lower insides contracted with hope and fear and all the big feelings. 'Jesus, Tyler, is that – ?'

She looked at me. Her eyes said it all. 'Mandy, yes. It's a fucking massive great big jar of mandy and we need to keep it in the freezer for freshness because that's where she kept it.'

I shook my head. 'That's where *who* kept it?'

Tyler turned away from the jar (which still wouldn't fit in the ice box, being one of those large jars with a clasp on the top, normally used for storing spaghetti or cereal) and looked at me. 'The drug dealer I stole it from.' She didn't need to add 'silly' to the end of the sentence.

I shook my head again, quicker this time, adrenaline and fear and panic all having their say in the choreography of my muscles. 'What. The. Fuck?'

Ice was melting on the floor. Tyler held the jar up aloft and shook it. 'This baby's gonna keep us rocking till Christmas.'

I pinched the bridge of my nose and closed my eyes. 'You stole drugs from a drug dealer.'

'Well, you know what she's like, what's her name. She's always dancing round to techno when you go in there. Stupid old dog slobbering in the corner and a few reprobates crashed out in the lounge.'

I said it again. 'You stole drugs from a drug dealer.'

'Oh, she won't miss it, believe me. She doesn't know what fucking day it is.'

'*What's her name*?' Tyler looked at me blankly. 'You know what she's *like*, do you? You know what she's like and YOU DON'T KNOW HER FUCKING NAME?'

Tyler did a slow, elaborate blink. It was the blink of someone whose eyes hadn't closed properly for a while. 'Marie,' she said.

'You just made that up.'

'I didn't. She's called Marie.'

I collapsed on the floor. The realisation of it all hit me. There would be a violent raid. We would be tortured by vengeful gangsters and then, at the end of it all, after much begging and agony and suffering, there would be death.

'Well, you've finally gone and done it, Tyler,' I said. 'I always knew you would.'

'You're worrying too much as per.' She turned back to the jar and continued trying to ram it into the ice box.

'So why were you running?' She ignored me. 'Tyler.'

'Just let me get this stored, then we can relax.'

'Tyler!'

She stopped ramming the jar but she didn't look at me. 'The dog followed me a bit of the way.'

I sat up straight. 'How much of the way?'

'I don't know, I was running!'

With one final thrusting push, like a wired, diminutive Elvis impersonator, she succeeded in securing the jar fully in the ice-box. Shavings of frost flew out and fell to the lino. She slammed the plastic flap shut, then the fridge door, and turned to me victorious. 'Look, Marie can't operate a door handle. She's officially tweaked out.'

I pulled a burn-marked tea towel down from the work surface and laid it over the ice and frost on the floor. Water bled into the cotton, darkening it.

'The worst thing we can do is panic,' Tyler said. 'You know how these things go. When you panic you invite the existentials in . . .'

I lay awake most of the night, clutching the top of my thin single duvet with rigor mortis hands, listening for the sound of a dog outside in the street. The next morning I found Tyler sprawled across her bed hugging the radio, tuned to some dance station on low volume, Zuzu stretched out alongside her, exposing her leopard-like belly. A floorboard clicked beneath me as I stood in the doorway and Tyler woke, sat bolt upright and raised the radio above her head. 'Wha – ?'

'It's me, Tyler. Put the radio down. Shall we get some breakfast before we hit the shops?'

She made a confused pig-face. 'Shops what shops?'

'You're coming with me to buy a wedding dress, remember?'

'A wedding dress?'

'Yes, I thought I should probably get one at some point. Either that or walk down the aisle naked.'

She groaned. 'Great. Now I've got an *erection* . . .'

'Variable-rate mortgages. David Cameron. The phrase "up the trumper".'

'It's okay, it's okay. I'm putting Radio 4 on . . .'

I sat waiting with a coffee and my laptop in the café beneath the block. I'd inched my way downstairs and outside, expecting to find the dog waiting, or a group of heavies sent round by Marie or whatever her name was. But no. Dear god, I thought. Has Tyler got away with this, again?

She appeared ten minutes later wearing a yellow hoodie and Aztec-print leggings.

'Inconspicuous,' I said. 'Excellent work, Tyler.'

'Dogs work by scent.'

She had her hand in her hoodie pocket, clutching something in there. If she's brought some out with her I'll end her, I thought. That had better just be her usual honey and ham heresy. She went up to the counter, where the café owner regarded her with the usual disdain. After she'd ordered she walked back to the table. 'I think twottyballs has had extensions on his dreadlocks, don't you? They're longer than they were last week.'

It was then I noticed her nose.

'Jesus, Tyler . . .'

There was no denying it: her nose looked like a

long-unemployed clown's. Rough, split and a sort of dirty crimson. She touched it with her fingers and winced.

'You snorted it, didn't you?'

She glared at me. 'Only once or twice. I couldn't feel it at the time. I got to the point where I needed *variety*.'

The café owner came over and threw a plate down onto the table in front of Tyler.

'Oh thank you that's so good of you this looks absolutely delicious,' Tyler said. The café owner moved away. As soon as his back was turned Tyler whipped the plate under the table and for the next few minutes looked as though she could have been having an angry toilet experience – I concluded that the runny honey must have solidified in the coldness of the flat, making it hard to squeeze into action. She persevered. When the plate remerged the slice of toast was dripping with honey and capped clumsily with a slice of wafer-thin ham. She cut it in half and picked up one of the triangles with both hands, balancing the ham carefully on top. Her red nail varnish was chipped on each nail. She nodded at the café owner and took a bite. As she chewed she murmured the word *Motherfucker*.

'Who were you out with last night, anyway?' I said. 'You know you're not allowed Other Friends.'

This was one of hers but she didn't acknowledge it. 'Oh, just some arty types, you know what it's like: I'm a magnet for creatives. I made the mistake of reciting some Chaucer to them while they were waiting for their panini and now they think I'm the Dalai Lama. Don't worry, it won't last, not when I run out of quotes.' She pulled my laptop round to face her and began tapping the keyboard. Honey-encrusted crumbs fell from her fingertips onto the keys. 'Can't we do this online? Surely there are wedding stores on here . . .' Then her face changed and she pushed her chair back and made a cross with her fingers. 'GET BACK! GET BACK!'

I swung the screen round to see a pop-up heart-shaped ad for HitMeCupid.com pulsing over the search engine homepage – *How great would it be if you knew everyone in the room with you right now was single?* I looked at the man behind the counter. Not so great. I clicked on the cross in the corner and the heart shrank to a pinprick and disappeared.

'Come on, you're taking me to the wedding village.'

'I'm just not sure I'm capable.'

'Tough. You're my matron of honour.'

'I'd rather be your matron of *dis*honour.'

'You're that, too. Now, as I love you and you love me you will bind my breasts and buy me a boy's wig . . .'

'*Shakespeare in Love.*'

'Help me, Tyler.'

The car shuddered as we pulled away from the kerb. Tyler banged the steering wheel. 'If this shitmobile starts stalling I'm going to kill myself on the hard shoulder.'

'Righto,' I said. 'What with?'

'A Spar carrier bag. For Maximum Tragedy.' There was a Spar carrier bag down by my feet, amongst empty crisp bags and dinted cans. She saw me see it. 'Don't doubt it, Lo-Lo-Pops, I've thought this fucking thing through.'

I lit two cigarettes, passed her one, and wound down the sticky window. Apart from her nose she was deathly pale.

'When did you last eat before that toast?' I said.

She cocked her head, thought about it. 'I had a peach on Thursday.'

'You shouldn't be driving,' I said. 'You should be in bed. With a mask on.'

'Oh, make me feel better, why don't you? I tried to cover it up with concealer but I looked like Pete Postlethwaite.'

'I liked Pete Postlethwaite.'

'Yes, but YOU DON'T WANT TO FUCKING LOOK LIKE HIM, DO YOU?'

She stayed in a foul mood for most of the journey, her snuffling punctuated with doomy bongs from the TomTom. The top of the dashboard was a model version of the flat's living room floor, strewn with fag packets, lighters, empty cans and severed hair accessories.

On the far hills was a wind farm, the rows of grey sails turning slowly. Next to that, an advance of pylons marched towards the motorway. On either side of us, trees were silhouetted against the drab sky of the early morning, the kelpish fronds of their branches swaying, suspended in the air. A flock of crows flew across a field, black and featureless, like patches torn out of reality. Nothing was to scale.

Tyler fiddled with the tape deck. She had four tapes, home recordings from CDs long ago. The Saddle Creek stable: Bright Eyes, Azure Ray, Rilo Kiley. Music from the homeland. She rammed a tape into the deck with the heel of her hand, wound down her window and lit a fag. When it was lit she indicated, swerved into the fast lane and took a long drag.

I watched the hard shoulder. 'Pheasant,' I said. 'Fox. Ooh, magpie, that's a shame. You don't see many magpies.'

'Do you have to do that?' Tyler said.

'What?'

'*Announce the roadkill?*'

'Sorry.'

She sniffed and winced.

'Do you want some Sinex?' I said. 'I think I might have some in my bag.'

'DON'T GIVE ME THAT VOODOO!' She veered across three lanes onto the sliproad. The collection of objects on the dashboard slid rapidly from one side to the other. 'I tried some earlier and it felt like my entire head was on fire. I'd sue Vicks if I had the strength.'

'Well, it *is* designed for colds . . .'

'It's designed for *blocked sinuses*. And ninety per cent of people with blocked sinuses do not have colds. Ask anyone who works in Boots.'

Boots. Strip-lit treasure trove of my formative years. In my teens I'd skipped round most Saturdays with a basket, gathering make-up and tanning cream and divinely inspired shaving products. Fiddle-de-dee! Now it fulfilled something closer to its traditional pharmaceutical role: a place of healing, or prevention. Tyler had once been buying her 'weekend kit' (Sinex, Night Nurse, ibuprofen, balm-soft tissues, chewable multivitamins) and pulled her Boots Advantage card out of her purse to release a magician's cloud of the previous week's remains. I stood behind her, clutching a Fruit Corner, watching the damning puff of powder sprinkle onto the lino. The girl on the checkout smirked at Tyler with a look of darkest collusion and processed the transaction without a word. *One of us*, Tyler said on the escalator out, jerking her head back in the girl's direction. *After all*, everyone *uses their Boots Advantage card. Either that or their gym card. It's our last stab at irony on the edge of the abyss.*

She swerved into the car park. It was almost midday and the wedding village was busy. We drove round the one-way system for five minutes without success.

'There's one!' I shouted, spotting a space.

We got closer and the painted yellow wheelchair became visible on the tarmac. 'Typical.' Tyler hauled the car down the next row. 'Disabled people get all the luck.'

We eventually parked, car parks away, and walked back to the wedding store across row after row, Tyler with her shades on even though it wasn't sunny, rubbing her nose and walking in the way of moving cars out of spite.

Inside the store, a sales assistant caught sight of us over the rails of dresses.

'That woman's looking at me,' Tyler whispered. 'She's looking at me.'

'She's a shop assistant,' I said. 'Eye contact is part of her training.'

'You're going to have to deal with this.'

The woman came over. 'Are you looking for anything in particular?'

'Something quick,' I said.

She smiled uncertainly. 'Well, see if anything takes your fancy and you can try it on upstairs. I can get you ladies some fizz, if you like?'

Tyler brightened at this, took her sunglasses off, and gave the shop assistant a broad smile. 'Come on, Princess Bride,' she said, tugging my sleeve. We snatched a few random dresses and went upstairs. Tyler sat down on a red velvet chair and picked up a newspaper from a curved plastic coffee table. I dumped two dresses on the chair next to her, went into a changing room, slid the curtain across and started taking off my clothes. I could hear Tyler drumming her fingers to the beat of the William Tell overture on the table. Like I said, *educated*.

The dress was too small and I couldn't zip it up over my boobs. I held the top part over my bra and slid open the curtain a little way. The sales assistant was walking towards us across the store, carrying a tray with two wine flutes on it.

'Now remember,' she said when she got close, 'we offer a full alterations service. We don't expect anything to fit right at first.'

I nodded and looked at Tyler. 'So what do you think?'

Tyler made a baffled pig-face.

'Try and imagine it without my body in it.'

Tyler frowned. I looked at the sales assistant. At the wine. At

Tyler. At the wine. The sales assistant said: 'Would you ladies like your fizz while you deliberate?'

'YES,' we said.

She handed us a glass each and took the tray away. I took my drink into the changing room while I put on the next dress, which this time fitted around the top but not the hips. I waddled out to see Tyler halfway through the paper.

'There's another Austrian girl been held hostage by her father in a basement,' she said and patted her nose, winced. 'I'm such a loser.'

'Now now,' I said, 'it's all relative.'

She didn't look up. The top of her head was a dark vortex. 'Well, it's all rela*tives* if you're Austrian . . .'

'What about this dress?'

'Oh, it's awful.'

'Great. I've only got one left to try then we've got to go and choose some more.'

'Fuck me,' she said, folding up the paper. 'What a thoroughly intolerable process. We should have brought some mandy along for this. Seriously. It's sending me under.'

She clicked her fingers. The sales assistant, over by the stairs, jerked her head and started to walk over.

'Tyler!' I said 'Do not – I cannot believe you just – '

I retreated and hid inside the cubicle, listening to Tyler saying, 'Look, we're going to be spending an obscene amount of money in here (*Pretty Woman*) so be a doll and go get that bottle of Asti Martini, would you?'

'It's Hardy's.'

'No shit.'

When I emerged in the next dress, Tyler stood up and proffered me a full flute. She circled me, trailing the fabric with her free hand. 'Yes, okay,' she said. 'So this is a lesson I suppose in terms of What We Don't Want . . .'

I looked at the bottle on the table and saw half of it was gone. I necked my flute and held it out for her to refill.

'You know what this needs to be?' Tyler said, waggling her finger up and down the length of me.

'What?'

'RED.'

'Look around you, Tyler. It's wall-to-wall white in here. It's like John and Yoko never moved out.'

'Now there's a cool couple.'

'A cool *married* couple.'

'Don't start.'

I'd been batting back with a list of modish marrieds every time she fronted me with the 'marriage just isn't *cool*' line of argument. Tim Burton and Helena Bonham Carter. Neil Gaiman and Amanda Palmer. Tom Waits and Kathleen. Johnny Depp and Vanessa Paradis (even though they'd split up). Now I could add John and Yoko.

Tyler looked unconvinced. 'Uh oh,' she said, 'here comes the cavalry.'

The sales assistant was walking towards us with an armful of dresses, followed by another assistant freighted with netting and frills. 'I'm sure there'll be something you like here!' the sales assistant said brightly, which translated as You'd Better Fucking Buy Something After Having So Much Wine.

There wasn't anything I liked – but that didn't stop us taking our time with the next onslaught of options whilst working our way through another bottle of sparkling something or other. Soon, Tyler was trying on dresses, too – dresses that, predictably, all looked much better on her.

I stared at myself in the full-length mirror. 'I look like I'm in fancy dress.'

'Now you're talking,' said Tyler, wine sloshing from her flute onto her collarbone as she almost tripped over the train of the dress she was wearing – a pearlised number with puff sleeves. 'Hey, that's what you should do! You should be a ZOMBIE BRIDE. I'll do your facial lesions. There are tutorials online . . .'

The sales assistant appeared by the cubicles. 'Anything you ladies like?' she said, looking at me.

'Another one of those, please,' said Tyler. She'd put the empty wine bottle upside down in a vase of silver twigs.

The woman began: 'I'm sorry but . . .'

'Fuck's sake,' Tyler said, hitching up her dress and waddling into the cubicle. She reemerged after a few seconds proffering a crumpled tenner.

'I'm afraid you don't understand,' the sales assistant whispered. '*This isn't a bar.*'

'If it were a bar it would be a very shit one,' Tyler said. 'I would give it one beer mat out of a possible ten and that would be for the free parking.'

The sales assistant looked at me.

'Okay,' I said, channelling my mum, 'I'm going to go away and have a little think. Tyler, take some photos of me before we leave.'

I paraded a few ill-fitting monstrosities around the fitting area while Tyler clumsily snapped away with her phone. 'Send one of those to Jim, would you?' I said afterwards, one leg in my jeans, trying not to fall against the closed curtain. 'The most flattering one, if such a thing exists. Just so he thinks I'm doing something pro-active.'

'I don't have his number stored.'

'Oh.'

'What's he wearing for the wedding, anyway?'

'Probably just one of his work suits.'

'So why are *you* making all this effort?'

I took a breath. 'You know, it tears me up when you and Jim do this.'

'Do what?'

A hotel bar in the Lake District. Me, Jim and Tyler on our first and only holiday together. Jim and I had only been together a few months but I knew it was serious enough to warrant an introduction to my best friend. *We should all go away together!* I thought. Somewhere clean. The Lakes seemed like a good choice. I booked us two rooms at The View by Ullswater, and Jim drove us there in his new hatchback.

We'd had a long dinner with lots of wine and by the time we adjourned to the residents' bar we were pretty much wedding-drunk (an ironic observation now . . .). Things had been going okay. Jim and Tyler had slowly relaxed after scoping each other out with questions about their upbringing (Jim to Tyler) and favourite poems (Tyler to Jim). I was feeling very hopeful about everything, like a well-oiled axle between two shiny wheels that would speed me joyously through the rest of my life. Easy to be happily morbid when you're drunk in good company. I kissed Jim on the cheek and he squeezed my knee under the table.

'Look, there's a piano,' said Tyler, nodding to a barkish old hulk propped up against the wall. She looked at Jim. 'There's a piano, Jim.'

Jim looked. 'I can confirm that that is a piano, Tyler, yes.'

Tyler let her thumb glance off Jim's elbow. 'Well, you should play it then. You being all piano-y.'

I laughed nervously into my drink. Jim looked at me and took a swig of wine. He'd told me it happened a lot, people asking him to play (*If I was a plumber they wouldn't say,* Go on, do something with a pipe, *would they? But musicians are constantly on call* . . . I thought it a little churlish of him. A little). Then he stood up and walked over to the geriatric instrument, pulled over a chair from a nearby table and sat down. Tyler sat back in her seat, pleased.

I tensed. I'd heard him play the second-hand Steinway upright in his flat a few times drunk, but never anything in public. The concerts he'd played so far had been abroad and it had been too early for all that. I was worried what Tyler might think, what – dare I think it? – what *ammo* it would give her. She didn't like how often I was staying over at his. She'd brought up the matter of rent a few times, swiftly dropped it. Still.

Jim ran his fingers along the keys in opposite directions. The room filled with noise – a good rhythm and a cascade of sounds. He turned to look at us. 'It's not quite tuned but it's not as bad as I thought,' he said. His fingers were hitting the keys as he talked. 'Hang on . . . almost got it . . .' His fingers fluttered, up and down, in ever decreasing breadth until he was down down down to one note which he struck struck struck with a DONK DONK DONK. 'There,' he said, and grinned. 'Found the room.'

My pelvic floor twitched.

'What do you mean, *found the room*?' said Tyler.

Jim, playing again, up and down and up and down, smiled at her – bizarrely in that smile he'd *reminded me of Tyler*, as though something had in that moment been transferred – and said, 'There's always one note that makes the room resonate. It's something you want to avoid.'

Tyler rolled her eyes, raised her glass and struck the side with a flick of her middle finger. The glass sounded with a short ping. 'Look, I found it, too.'

Jim turned back to face the piano. 'Anyway, now I've got it . . .' He launched into a casually glorious, soaring, swelling, hell *perfect* rendition of 'At Last' by Etta James.

'Fuck,' I said under my breath.

I looked around to see the bar staff standing by the door, rapt. I looked at Tyler. She was watching Jim, her glass poised midway between her mouth and the table, her face a crisp twist of angry awe. It took a lot to make Tyler forget about her drink.

'French onion soup!' Tyler declared. 'That's what we need to recover. Soup and a pint of real ale, like the ursines drink.'

We walked from Salford – where we'd abandoned the car post-Cheshire – to one of our favourite pubs, a Victorian chophouse that was tiled like a swimming pool and staffed by bartenders in bowties. The onion soup there was the best in town – rich and murky as pond water, served with a dumplingy cheese crouton the size of a baby's fist. Tucked away in the slats and canopies of the beer garden, we dissected the day over ale and then red wine.

'I've got the decorators in!' Tyler said loudly, raising her glass. It was a phrase I'd told her was a traditional English toast for whenever you were drinking red wine. As a gag it had enjoyed a remarkably good innings.

'Just get a normal dress from a normal shop,' Tyler said. 'That place was heinous.'

'I know,' I said. 'It's almost as if they want to put you off.' I swirled my wine. The legs lingered in thin, filmy waves on the sides of the glass and then retreated back to the pool at the bottom.

'Why ever would they want to do that? Put you off a barely evolved pagan ceremony for needy morons?'

'I'm not a needy moron. Well, maybe I'm needy sometimes, but aren't we all?'

'I'm not.'

'Yes, you are.'

'I'm not.' She grabbed my wrist. 'Tell me. Tell me I'm not needy, Laura. Say it. Say you're not needy.'

I picked her hand off my wrist. 'No.'

She drained her glass. 'I just don't get it. What is this need for *a special dress*?' She said 'special dress' in a little-girl voice.

80

'Why don't you just wear your favourite dress – the maroon lacy one? It's not as though we're the kind of people who take photos of ourselves all the time when we're out in a desperate need to document our lives.' I thought of the photo I'd sent earlier to Jim. 'I think it's so fucking tragic when people do that. What, so they can sit there when they're eighty, pointing through albums mid-air with a virtual-reality glove, saying *And here's another glorious moment I failed to participate in because I was too busy taking a fucking photo*. Wear the maroon. In ten years you'll have forgotten you didn't buy it especially. And you know what, Lo, it's *your fucking wedding.*'

This one was from Tyler's friend Agnes, the only friend from Crawford she'd ever kept in touch with – although Agnes had recently 'gone over to the dark side' (childrearing). Apparently Agnes had been so bombed on speed at her own wedding that when the photographer and members of her family were hassling her to get out of her room to have some photos taken Agnes had emerged enraged, her train hitched halfway up her legs, stood at the top of the grand central staircase and roared at the foyer of assembled guests below: 'LISTEN UP, PEOPLE: IT'S MY FUCKING WEDDING.' Tyler, boshed on the same speed, stood on a chaise longue and applauded. The phrase had since been applied to any situation where you were going to do something your way because it was your thing.

'The whole idea of marriage *is* preposterous, though, in the modern age,' Tyler went on.

'Everything's preposterous when you look at it too long,' I said. 'Especially the word "preposterous".'

She swigged more wine and banged her glass down on the table. The glass base hit the wood with a jarring crack. 'But there's no ceremony for *friendship*, is there? Does friendship mean nothing in this world? Nothing to *you*?'

I lit up a cigarette and took the first drag back hard into my throat, so hard it made my eyes water. I looked at her. 'Take a day off from this. An hour, even.'

'Why? Because you know it's true?' I looked at her. She looked back. 'If you go ahead with this wedding then you realise that what you're actually saying is that your friendship with me is not meaningful and durable. That,' she sipped her wine victoriously, 'is the logical conclusion.'

'Believe me, if I could marry you too, Tyler, I would.'

Would I? Probably not.

'Did you know there are now as many unmarried parents as married parents in the UK? Things are changing. You don't have to fuse the nuclear family any more.'

'I don't want to fuse the nuclear family.'

'So why marry Jim at all? Why this insistence on upheaval?'

I looked at her and kept looking at her as I brought my glass to my lips. I had to make light of it, had to. 'I dunno, *variety*?'

'You're ruining my life for variety's sake?'

'I'm not ruining your life! There's more to your life than me! And I'm marrying Jim because I love him, I do, and this feels like . . .' I couldn't say 'adventure'. ' . . . progress.'

She smacked her forehead with her hand. 'Progress? What about our hard-earned system? Have you forgotten about that? Isn't marriage just another example of everything we've always fought against, as in the shit people do because they think they should rather than because they actually want to?'

I held her chin and turned her face to mine. 'Listen to me, Tyler. I want to marry Jim. I have not been coerced or conditioned – '

'But how would you – ?' She looked like a Cabbage Patch doll, her mouth squished in my hand. I released her.

'And I want to be part of a team against the world again. When I was a child – '

'Oh, the formative anecdote . . . Come on then, Fred fucking

82

Savage, let's have it.' She looked into the middle distance, made her eyes all dreamy. '*That was the day I realised . . .*'

I slapped her arm. 'When we were in his van going out on a Sunday my dad used to say *We're the J-Team!* Like the A-Team.'

She nodded. 'I am aware of *The A-Team*. It's one of my people's cultural gifts to the world.'

'So I want to be part of a new team against the world.' I quailed at my own schmaltziness but I knew it was true – the idea, at any rate.

'Teams are awful. Families are awful. People are awful. Why perpetuate the awfulness?'

'So why don't you live alone? Why have me around?'

Neither of us said it but it was there, unspoken. It flashed in her eyes at the same time it went through my head but I was afraid of saying it and I knew she was, too. *We used to be a team.* She lit a fag.

I reached for the fag packet and lit one up, too. 'You can get a new housemate.'

'Who? I don't know anyone else. I don't like anyone else.'

She wiped her nose on the back of her hand. Two jackal-faced men came out of the pub and perched on the seats at the end of our table without asking. It irked me but I didn't say anything. Tyler picked up her phone, read something and put it back down on the table. The men didn't speak to each other, and I saw them clock Tyler with interest. She registered them, too. An audience.

'So I was at this party the night before last in an old mill,' she began. 'That was where all the trouble started. I was fiercely bored as I so often am in this weary little city.' Curls had snapped out from the kirby grips above her temples. Her fingernails were filthy where they were missing polish, all coal seams and saffron crescent moons. 'Around 2 a.m. someone put a metal pole through the amp – '

'Doormen,' one of the men piped up.

Tyler didn't look at him but she nodded sagely, acknowledging the suggestion. 'There was talk of sabotage.'

'Rival clubs,' the man said again. 'This town's run by them, you know.'

'Anyway,' Tyler said, still without a glance at the men, 'that was exciting for all of five minutes but the upshot was that there was no music.'

'Whereabouts in America are you from?' said the other man.

'What has this got to do with us?' I said.

Tyler glanced at the men. 'The Midwest. Where the twisters are.'

'You don't look American.'

I sighed. 'I really think we should finish our conversation.'

'I don't want to. I want to tell you about last night.'

I dragged on my fag and exhaled, frustrated. 'Go on then.'

'So we sat around in a circle on the floor of the club, talking about sex.'

'Your suggestion, I presume?'

She took off her sunglasses and tugged a stray hair out of the hinge. 'Well, what the fuck else? Charades? You need a bit of stimulation at that point. You need a good fuck or a good fight or a good sing-song.'

'Want some weed?' said one of the men. I looked at him holding out his soggy joint and shook my head.

Tyler batted the offer away with her hand. 'No. Hate pot. Too slow.'

'What's the matter, love?' the man said to Tyler. 'Is your body too bootylicious for me?' The other man laughed.

'Bored,' said Tyler, 'my body is too bored.'

I drained my glass, anticipating our imminent departure. I hoped this wasn't going to turn out like the time a man had overheard us talking about drugs in a queue for a cashpoint and said: *I thought junkies were meant to be thin?* She'd punched him.

84

She lit up another cigarette. 'And some reprobate,' she said exhaling, 'posed the question: *What's the worst thing someone can say to you just before sex?*'

The men froze. You could have heard a joint drop in that beer garden.

Tyler went on: 'So people started putting forward their suggestions, you know. *Put this horse's tail butt-plug in . . . Call me Uncle Mo* . . . I won of course.' She tapped her fag in a leisurely way and smiled like a boar, pink wine-tusks disappearing into grin-folds.

'Go on then,' I said. 'Let's have it.'

She made me wait a few seconds. Dragged on her fag. Sipped her drink. Leaned in, tongue lolling in her bottom lip. 'Make a face like you don't understand.' She reclined, victorious.

The men stood up and went inside.

'Shall we get another drink?' I said.

'Yes, more drink. More everything. There's a party going on not too far away if you fancy it. New friend of mine. An artist. I've got something in my pocket.' I looked at her. Of course: the whole conversation had been an elaborate preamble. Tyler *was* good: talking about parties made you want to party. I felt like it by then – I felt as though (oh, the justifications, they come like flying monkeys through the window) getting lost somewhere together might be good for us.

I said: 'I need at least ten hours' sleep in the next forty-eight hours.'

'Baby, that's so feasible that it's verging on *Logic*.'

THE COWPAT AND THE PSYCHIATRIST

Nick the Artist opened the door and held his arms wide at the sight of Tyler. His hair was hairsprayed into a tsunami of a side-parting.

'I'm so glad you came!' he said, and looked at me like he wasn't so glad.

'This is my friend Laura,' said Tyler.

'You'll have to excuse my informal attire,' I said. 'I was planning on coming in a wedding dress but I just couldn't find one that fitted . . .'

Tyler laughed – not her usual laugh but one that got her by socially sometimes. 'Come get a drink,' Nick said.

We walked through the crowded studio and people didn't move to let us pass, we had to say excuse me a lot and walk sideways with our hands up like crab-claws around manbags and jutting elbows. The studio was in a semi-derelict building just behind Oxford Road and through the grey-paned windows the grey city towers loomed like tired totems. Everyone at the party seemed to be wearing the same thick, black-rimmed glasses. The party was a private view – a launch for Nick's new collection. He'd invited Tyler the previous night at the mill. *Before or after your sex-face story?* I asked. *Oh, after,* she said. *But he'll be disappointed if he thinks he's in there. Too prissy for me. He'd be making a face like he didn't understand because he wouldn't actually understand.*

'Annihilations' consisted of cushion-thick canvases hung from the walls at daring intervals. Splodges of dark oil paint on darker backgrounds, clumsy blobs and squares – they looked to me like large versions of micro-bacterial slides that a monkey had attempted to replicate with handfuls of baby shit. We reached a trestle table that didn't look strong enough to support the two ice buckets teetering on its gummy surface. Tyler fished two beers from a bucket and opened them with her teeth. She had a tiny curved scar on her top lip – I imagined this was from removing a bottle-top inexpertly at some point. She handed me a beer and whispered: 'Let's not stay long. It's all rather austere.'

I clawed up a handful of peanuts from a bowl on the table and sprinkled them into my mouth.

'What are you doing?' said Tyler. 'Do you not know that there will be hipster urine particles in there?'

I shovelled in another handful. She pressed a wrap into my other palm.

'What's that?' I said, spraying nuts. The affectation of innocence was such a comfort sometimes. Still. The wrap was like a gauntlet, a glove thrown down, a dare.

When I was secure in a cubicle I uncurled my palm. What was this? As I carefully picked open the wrap I saw it was a flyer, the words gradually revealed. I jiggled the crystals around to decipher it in full.

THEMES OF THE EMBITTERED HEART: A Talk on W.B. Yeats by Professor Marty Grane, Goldsmiths University, London. Join us for a lunchtime lecture about the later works of the great Irish poet. The Georgian Library, Mosley Street. 4th May. 1 p.m. Free.

I stared at the words. Had Tyler done this on purpose, as a joke? This was going to be difficult. I could hardly bear to, it was so desecrating. I say *hardly*.

As I handed it back to her I said: 'Was that flyer especially for me?'

'What flyer?'

'The one you're using as a wrap.'

She looked confused. 'I picked it up off a stack on the counter at work. I didn't even look at it.'

'Oh. It's for a talk on Yeats in Manchester next month.'

'Your favourite!'

'Fancy it?'

'Sure.'

Approximately twenty-three minutes later I was in the corner of the studio dancing by a tinny stereo to a song I didn't know and didn't care that I didn't know, it had a beat and that was enough for me. I could work with it. I could work with anything. Tyler was eyeing up two boys and I have to say boys, they were doing their utmost to look like boys, in tight jeans by the window. She went over to them and I heard her shout: 'What is it with young men and this knock-kneed flamingo stance? You clearly haven't got enough Vitamin *Me* in your diets. Straighten your legs. Straighten your legs right now.'

There was a woman next to me, running on the spot, smiling. I ran with her, keeping my arms and legs in time with hers and in time with the music.

I saw that Nick the Artist was by my side. He started dancing with me. 'That's Caroline,' he whispered in my ear, nodding towards the running woman. 'Old Hacienda head. It's like she went out in 1992 and never went home.'

I looked at her. Maybe she did go home, I thought. Maybe she found something that made her happier than a semi in West Didsbury, or a semi in someone's fat mam.

'Ever tried your hand at art, Lisa?' Nick said.

Tyler came to join us. She heard me saying no to Nick and asked what I was saying no to.

'I've never chanced my arm at art.'

'Yes, you have, tell him about your dirty protest.'

'Okayyy . . .'

'We need another drink for this,' Tyler said, dragging us over to the trestle table, where a few lonesome beers bobbed around in the dirty ice. I looked around the room. Ten or fifteen people remained. How long had we been there? An hour? Longer.

'I was about seven years old, and I needed the toilet, you know, and the teacher wouldn't let me go until break-time,' I said. 'So by that point – '

'She'd crapped her pants!'

'I crapped . . . my pants, yes. So I hobbled to the loo at break-time and when I got there . . . Well, it hadn't exactly remained in one piece.'

'It was like a cow pattie!' said Tyler.

'It was like a cowpat, yes. Anyway, I thumbed what I could into the toilet bowl and flushed – but then, well, what to do with the rest?'

Nick was looking around the room but I wasn't deterred.

'So I took my knickers off, stood on the toilet seat and wiped the inside all over the cubicle walls. I really got into it by the end, doing wild strokes, emphatic arcs.'

Tyler slapped her thigh with her spare hand. 'Tell him what the headmaster said!'

'And so the next day in assembly the headmaster said: *Well, the caretaker had a nasty surprise last night* . . . and he told everyone about the thing in the toilet and a few of the teachers started casting aspersions and he had to say *No, no, Mrs Jennings, this was the GIRLS*.'

Tyler doubled up like a penknife. Nick was regarding me with a look of appalled concentration.

'I was an anxious child. Pulled my eyelashes out. Threw up a lot.' My phone vibrated in my pocket. 'Oh, that's my fiancé.' I read the text. Jim had just got home.

'You're *engaged*?' Nick said.

'Do not call him,' Tyler said, straightening herself. 'Just text him back. Remember The Rules.'

When I was twelve my parents took me to a psychiatrist who they said was a doctor but I knew better. Prof. E.G.L. Daubney's name was affixed in solid silver letters on his door.

'Eggle,' my mum said as we waited on the chairs opposite. 'That's a funny name, Eggle.'

We were half an hour early. I'd vomited on myself in bed the night before and could still smell it on my hair. I stroked the tip of a cheeseplant leaf between my thumb and index finger. On the wall clock the minute hand slowly fell to half past.

My parents waited outside when I went in. The psychiatrist didn't have a couch, which was disappointing. I sat on one of two chairs at the back of the room. He waited until I sat down and then made a big show of asking me to sit on the chair next to his desk so there were no barriers between us, so that we were just two people sitting having a chat together and that was nice, wasn't it. I wondered whether he was a paedophile.

He sat down, clapped his knees and said: 'Well, it must have been a relief to find out it's not anything physical, eh?'

They'd had me in for tests the previous month at the other hospital, thinking it might have been triggered by some latent tropical disease. Not one of the doctors seemed deterred by the fact I'd never been anywhere tropical.

'Yes,' I said. I didn't want him thinking he was a bad psychiatrist.

'How would you describe yourself as feeling, generally? Happy? Sad?'

I thought. Quickly. 'Pressured.'

'That's an interesting word.'

'Thanks,' I said, because I knew how to accept a compliment.

He looked at me until he realised I wasn't going to say anything else and then he said: 'Where do you think this pressure comes from, Laura?'

I wondered whether he could smell the sick on me. I'd vomited in bed because I'd had a dream where I was balancing on a football of rock in outer space holding a spoon. The spoon could shoot out hard bolts of lightning that created a temporary bridge for me to walk across to the next football of rock. I knew this was going to go on for ever.

'I think it comes from me,' I said, because I wanted to give the right answer. Professor Eggle nodded.

I woke to find a warm, recently vacated dent in the bed next to me. Jim's bedding. Jim's room. Morning.

Fuck.

I'd gone to Jim's.

This was bad of me. It was one of our new rules: not turning up at Jim's late at night. Yeah. Try telling that to yourself when you're goulashed. Times like that, everything seems like a fine idea. Contacting that person you fell out with? Why not? A capella karaoke in a taxi queue? Oh boy! Leapfrogging over a postbox? You betcha . . .

Shafts of sunlight cut through the blinds, scoring celestial rents on the floor. By the look of it, it was about nine. Outside, I could hear the post-dawn weekend soundtrack: tidal traffic, descending planes and the postman's squeaky cart making its way along the street. A flock of geese flew overhead, honking. It was a sound that always cheered me. The town hall clock started to bong. That was a cheering sound, too. I lay still and counted ten beats. I could hear Jim down the hall in the kitchen – in the distant inside, sharp and dull sounds: of metal on pot, of pot on metal, of glass on glass. I listened to the creaks of the waking flat, its pipes warming the walls, like blood bringing something back to life, and I felt an ancient nostalgic feeling in my guts. The hollow expanding into a sort of hunger, not pleasant or unpleasant; a rich, savoury hopelessness. The old yearning for yearning. I put my hands down my knickers like I often did to comfort myself, making a triangle with my thumbs and index fingers. I turned my head to one side and smelled my breath coming back off the pillow: the acrid scent of just-used emery board; of something grown dead and burned. I was thirsty. I pulled my hands out of my knickers and sat up. There was a pint of water on the table beside the bed. I reached for it and looked inside, swooshing the water round. One of the only times Jim had stayed at mine I'd woken in the night and grabbed a glass of what I thought was water from the top of the laundry box only to hear Jim shout NOOOOOOOOOO! It was too late. I'd drunk his contact lenses.

I pieced the memories of the previous evening together: I'd left Tyler with Nick in a tiki bar on Stevenson Square around 2 a.m. They were in a hammock sharing a fish-bowl cocktail. She'd tried to stop me from going over to Jim's. *He's hounding you with these text messages!* I'd ignored her like I'd been ignoring him.

I got up and walked along the hall. The kitchen was a shock of brightness. Jim was at the sink, topping up a glass of iced orange squash with water. He liked orange squash and I liked watching him drink it. When he drank he held his free hand (usually his right) close to his chest and clenched and unclenched his fist. A relic from toddlerdom. I'd vowed never to tell him about it. Through the window the day looked clear and not overcast, the city turning in the distance to green, to height, and the grey-pelted humps of the Pennines. I went and looped my arms around him from behind and squeezed his back against my chest. We stood like that for a while and did a slow little silent dance. I pressed my head on one side between his shoulder blades. He was wearing a vest so thin I could smell the night on him; the slow-leached losses of his dreams, the unrealistic fabric conditioner. I looked to my side and noticed that the LED display of the tumble dryer was flashing with a little orange message: *Clean Door Filter*. It had been flashing all night, unnoticed, and I felt sorry for it. I pulled away from Jim and switched the dryer off. He pulled me back towards him. I kissed him, holding the back of his head, my fingers splayed, thumbs spasmed. I liked the look of them when I looked.

We got dressed and walked to the shop. He took my hand and tutted at the dirt beneath my fingernails.

I looked at him – his hair, his skin – and I felt thick and bloody by comparison, pink and bulgy in my tight t-shirt, like vacuum-packed meat. A chill in my chest.

'Do you remember what you said to me when you got in?' he said.

I couldn't remember getting in as such. 'No.'

'You said you weren't sure you wanted to move into the flat. You said we should look for somewhere new because you weren't sure my place could ever feel like home.'

'Oh.'

'Is that true? Because if it's true then we need to have a proper talk about it.'

A *proper talk*. It sounded like a work meeting. This was what the wedding was doing to us. Making us professionally involved.

'I think I was probably just talking shit.'

'Right,' he said. 'Well, you should watch that. Probably.'

I thought I might vomit. Was there a bush I could run behind? There was not.

'Look,' he said, 'I don't want to give you a hard time, especially not today, but I need to know this won't keep happening. I don't want this to be my life: not knowing what time you're coming in, what state you're going to be in. I couldn't get back to sleep last night after you said that.'

I stopped walking.

'What's the matter?'

I didn't speak. He shook my shoulder.

'Why are you just staring at the ground?'

I looked at him. I was aware of my movements.

'Jesus,' he said, 'don't make *me* feel like the bad person.'

I gave him a firm nod. The week's miseries were in the post: Teary Tuesday, Weepy Wednesday. For now: Silent Sunday. 'I'm tired, that's all. Let's walk.'

He took my hand. 'Apology accepted.'

As we approached the shop I felt a flutter of nerves. The woman in there had caught me off-guard not so long ago. She'd put the contents of my basket through the till – sausages, thick sliced bread, tinned macaroni cheese, Tia Maria – and said: *Got kids, have you?* I didn't want to get into it. I was abominably hungover for a start, so in the moment I said: *No, but I'm expecting.* EXPECTING! Where did this shit come from? It wasn't as though this was a shop in St Ives, or Knutsford even. This was Jim's local shop, where I went almost every week, at least once. For booze and fags. I'd fucked it. Totally fucked it. I didn't know how I was going to sustain this fabrication – whether I should shove cushions up my top, gradually increasing in size for the next nine months, and then borrow a baby off someone when I went in after that. Whose baby, though? Shirley was the only baby I knew and she was in London. I lingered on the threshold.

'Do you mind if I wait outside?' I said. 'I fancy a fag.'

He looked at me. 'Course,' he said, and went in the shop. By the time he came out I was myself again.

Back at the flat we made eggs and sat down in the living room.

'Have you thought about drinking less?' he said.

Oh not today not today I thought you said not today.

94

I put my cutlery down, unhungry. 'Yes,' I said, 'in the morning usually. Then by the evening I change my mind.'

He looked at me. Oh. Give me a glance between two lovers on any day and I will show you a hundred heartbreaks and reconciliations, a thousand tallies and trump cards. And still there is something that survives beyond the sham of domesticity, beyond the micro-promises and micro-power-shifts, and *that* is the motherfucking miracle.

'I find myself wondering more and more how we're going to stay on a level in the precious time we get together.'

I was unable to speak. In this, paralysis. The past reviled; the future threatened.

'I'm just trying to be realistic in terms of both our needs,' he went on. 'I didn't mean to put you off your breakfast.'

I held on to the sofa. 'You didn't. I've had enough.' He looked worried then and I liked it so I let him worry a few more seconds before I said, 'Of the eggs.'

He put his plate down. 'I forgot to say, my folks want to invite a few extra people to the wedding.'

'How many?'

'A few friends. Ten max.'

'Imagine having ten friends.'

He laughed and the room relaxed.

'Can I invite an extra, then?' I said.

'Who?'

'Kirsten.'

'Kirsten?'

'She's a no-nonsense person, isn't she?'

Kirsten was a cellist with the Hallé. We'd had a long night together after a concert the previous year. She was a pert, bitchy-shy blonde who looked like Kirsten Dunst or maybe I just made that association because of her name. The three of us were the last men standing at the afterparty and ended up smoking on a bench down by the Irwell until it got light. Kirsten had grown up in Stockport with her mum, who was just eighteen when she had her. They'd lived in a refuge for a month when they first got away from her dad. Kirsten could remember it vividly. Her dad had tried to break into the refuge one night and one of the other mothers, a woman who smelled of weed (Kirsten knew it was weed, she was seven), had hidden her in a kitchen cupboard while her mum shouted at her dad and her dad tried to drag her mum out. Kirsten said at the time she'd wanted him to drag her off so that she could be done with both of them. She said she used to fantasise about being an orphan, like Annie. *A fresh start.* That's what she said. *I must have been the only seven-year-old in Stockport who wanted a fresh start.* We'd texted each other a few times and then the connection had waned. I thought about her sometimes. I'd dreamed about her a couple of times – we were always running away from something together. Sometimes I thought about calling her, in the small hours. I still had her number.

'I dunno,' Jim said, 'I've invited enough people from the orchestra. It's going to get complicated if I start asking those not so close.'

A surge of peevishness. 'So your parents are inviting people I've never met but we can't invite people I *have* met and liked?'

He rubbed his forehead. 'This is exactly what I didn't want. Stress. Maybe today isn't the best time to discuss it.' A significant look. 'But we get so little time together at the moment . . .'

I looked down at my feet. They would always be my feet. That was a shame. I looked at Jim.

Looked at him.

In the bedroom he said: 'Let's not use a condom.' Something about this appealed, in the absence of alcohol, in the rip and flick of quickly undressing: to just have a good old-fashioned unabandoned *fuck*. I felt better as he belted my wrists to the bed frame, felt his frustration, allowed him it, and loved myself for that allowance. I punished him, too, in that fuck. I gave him nothing to suggest I was enjoying it or not enjoying it. I made a china doll of myself. A cold pose. An abandoned shell; uninhabited. The night is a zoo and the next day is its museum.

A text arrived from Tyler as I was lying in bed, untied, the shower spitting in the bathroom.

TURNS OUT NICK DOES UNDERSTAND IF HIS FACE IS ANYTHING TO GO BY

I wondered whether we'd been fucking simultaneously in beds across town, our lives in split-screen. I recalled a conversation we'd had at the beginning of our friendship.

'Define love,' Tyler said, her hand dropping onto her forearm as we sat relighting saggy rollies. She'd spent the previous ten minutes doing CPR on a pack of ancient Golden Virginia. It was 6 a.m.

And I said: 'True freedom.'

She thought about it.

'So you're talking unconditional,' she said after a while. 'Not romantic. Agape as opposed to Eros.'

'Okay, then: maximum contact with maximum freedom.'

'That's not love,' she said, exhaling with a gurn, like Popeye. 'That's a tampon ad.'

AN INSPIRING ENCOUNTER THAT CAUSES
OUR HERO TO SLEEP UNDER A BUSH

At lunchtime on the 4th of May I stood waiting for Tyler outside the Georgian library. It was raining half-heartedly, still enough to make the smoking of a cigarette unpleasant. I had to keep relighting my fag after tapping it too hard and losing the hot end to the glossy pavements. Overhead, a plasticky lid of cloud sealed the city in a thwarted dream. The windows of passing trams were beaded with condensation. Outside the Sainsbury's over the road, gloomy groupings of students queued by the cashpoint, eating packet sandwiches. I waited twenty-five minutes and at five to one I called her.

'Tyler, I'm at the library – it's that Yeats talk, remember? I reminded you yesterday.'

'Oh shit. Look, Lo, I got blackout-drunk last night. I feel like if I move I'll vomit electricity. Can we take a raincheck?'

I looked at my shoes. They were wet through. I'd come straight from a nightshift and hadn't anticipated the weather.

'Course.'

I threw my dimp towards a grid and made my way inside the library, up three sets of winding stairs, to the main room where the ceiling rose in a stained glass dome. It wasn't a large space, a square twenty metres, but it was airy and light and had the vast tranquility of libraries that's a lot like being outdoors; you feel like there's more air in those places. I inhaled at the sight of the dome above and exhaled dry-mouth tobacco taste. Books held together with yellowing strips of masking tape lined the walls, spliced with dark-wood shelving. A few people milled around the large room, their hair wet, their faces amiable. In the middle of the room were five or six rows of chairs and, beyond, a lectern backed by a series of concertina'd screens pinned with what from a distance looked like charcoal drawings. There was a table of red and white wine at the back of the room – free, and at lunchtime! I thought, *I should really make an effort to come to more literary events.* I took a white wine and sipped it – it was tepid and acidic, curving my stomach with windy cramp but relaxing my limbs, my mind. I tucked myself away by a back window and peered over the wide wooden ledge to the sill and beyond. The tops of umbrellas, parked cars, empty taxis, beneath the steaming rain. The library itself – its poise, its stark lighting – reminded me of a girl I used to be friendly with before I got close to Tyler. Maud the Painter. Her face was drawn to a point – I always thought of Yeats' *beauty like a tightened bow* when I saw her. *Not natural in an age like this.* And she wasn't of the age, not at all. She went through friends like she went through cities, never settling, leaving in a blaze of fire and offence. *A person of dubious evolution* was how Tyler (jealously) kissed her off. I wondered where Maud kept herself these days, these nights, in the small hours; whether she had found love. Had babies. Joined Facebook.

I pulled my t-shirt out of my armpits. What had I done to deserve such a generous quota of sweat glands? I went up for more wine, looked around. There were barely twenty people in the room and the talk was due to start any minute. The wine-to-people ratio was looking good. A woman walked up to the lectern. A fountain pen dangled on a cord round her neck and I smiled to see it – this place was comprehensively antiquated. 'Welcome, ladies and gents!' By her side was a man – the professor, surely. He had a hobo sort of look about him: mid-forties, Americana beard, denim shirt, black knitted hat worn slightly too far back from his face, wire glasses, thick little lips. I thought, *You look like Richard Dreyfuss in* Jaws. He nodded and the thin arm of his spectacles glinted like gossamer.

'Thanks for coming,' he said. An accent without geography, each vowel free, each consonant its own continent. 'Please, take a seat.'

I took a detour via the drinks table and then sat at the end of a row three from the back, in case it lasted too long.

As it turned out, it wasn't long enough.

The professor talked about what had brought him to Yeats, first for his thesis and then to complement his teaching. *I tried to love other people, really I did, but something kept bringing me back – especially these later poems, which are at once so deeply personal and so evasive, so desperate and defiant* . . . Yes, I thought. Yes and yes and yes. This is a fine ambush. I kept looking down and finding I had wine to drink. An hour passed and I didn't notice.

Suddenly: sparse applause, and the woman was there at the front again, saying thanks to everyone. I glanced at the wine table as I clapped – plenty left, great, great. When would be acceptable to get up and get another glass? I was having such a good time.

And then another thought budded and began to uncurl. *I should go up and thank him.* I should do this because he has reminded me of so many things. Also it makes me look less like a freeloader.

I downed a glass of wine standing next to the table and then I took another glass down to the front where the professor was standing, coat on now, bag on shoulder, talking to the woman from the library. I stood there a few seconds feeling conspicuous. When my presence became suitably oppressive, when the atmosphere in the room felt like it just about to crack and I was just about to leg it, they turned to look at me.

'Hallo!' said the woman.

'Hi,' I said, and then, to the professor: 'I just wanted to thank you. That was very inspiring.'

He smiled and I wondered whether he thought I was drunk. Was I drunk? I was not. Maybe I was. Either I was or I wasn't.

'My pleasure,' he said. 'Glad to be of service.'

'Are you a member?' said the woman.

No penis jokes.

'No.'

'Are you interested in becoming one? I can give you some literature to take away . . .'

'Okay.'

And off she went.

The professor stuck out his hand. 'Marty.'

I shook his hand. 'Laura.'

'You said "inspiring". So you write poetry yourself then?'

'Oh god, no, not poetry. I mean, I'd like to. Wouldn't everyone?'

'Would they?'

'All writers, I mean.'

'I'm not sure.'

'Aren't you?'

It was perhaps a little early to do something like disagree but I couldn't help myself. I was having fun. He raised an eyebrow, acknowledged interest, opened his mouth to speak –

The woman was back. She handed me a slim stack of white and blue sheets of paper. 'If you're interested, just fill in the membership request form and drop it in.'

She stood there, waiting for me to walk away. What she didn't know was that I was waiting for *her* to walk away.

'Hester,' Marty said, 'do you mind if I sit in your lovely anteroom an hour or so while I wait for my train? And do you mind if I take a bottle of that leftover wine in there with me?'

'With pleasure, Professor!'

He looked at me. 'Do you like wine, Laura?'

Hm. Hm hm hm.

The anteroom was sentinelled with heavy-legged tables and lit by standing lamps with Christmassy shades: emerald, crimson, gold. As in the main room the walls were thickened with dishevelled bookshelves. It felt cosy and clever. We sat down opposite each other at a table for four. He enjoyed his teaching job well enough, he lived in Islington, his book, *Widening Gyres*, had been published ten years ago to little effect. We drank two bottles of wine. We were halfway through the second when he said: 'You're engaged, aren't you?'

'How do you know?'

'Because you're not wearing a wedding ring and I'm only ever attracted to irreversibly attached women.'

I burned for that. I was engulfed. Ambush No. 2 of the day. I topped up our glasses for something to do. The second bottle was empty. I set it down. *Stop shaking.*

'So you said not poetry, but you are writing something?'

For once I was glad of this particular conversational trench. 'A novel.'

'Got a title?'

'*Bacon.* Why is that funny?'

'I'm not laughing. What's the story?'

'It's about a priest who falls in love with a talking pig.'

'Why?' His mouth was slightly lopsided, his features untidier, the wine showing on him. Good.

'He can't help it.'

'No, why do you want to write?'

I dismissed Moira Shearer, pre-fantasia: *Why do you want to live?* He leaned forward and his teeth flashed, or something in his mouth did, and looking at his mouth even briefly felt very inappropriate. I composed myself and said solemnly: 'How else to rage around the dark mansion?'

'You know I'm going to kiss you if you keep talking like that. What does your fiancé do?'

I should have sat back, should have objected, shouldn't have acquiesced by ignoring that thing he said but – I failed the test. I didn't care.

'He's a pianist.'

'A penis? Great.'

The wine. The wine was making him slur.

'So I take it you're not married?'

He laughed like I'd asked him whether he played the spoons or did topiary on his pubes. 'No no no. Too selfish. Too much to do.'

'Girlfriend?'

'No one that regular.'

I felt it, then: a tremor down my spine; a cold spot at the back of the courtyard. A cat lying in the shade, flicking a caught bird with its claw over and over and over. He felt me feel it. A bolt of recognition. He drained his glass and without looking at his watch said: 'I should get to the station.'

'Thanks for the chat, Marty. It was – '

'Yes, you too. All that. Don't suppose I can take your number?'

I shook my head. He smiled, saluted, left.

An undrunk blob of wine, like a glass eye, stared at me from the hollow where the stem met the bowl. I felt the need to talk to Jim. I pulled my phone out of my bag. Three long, flat rings and then he answered. 'Hello, you.' A rush of air on the line said he was in a moving car.

'Where are you?'

'Dubai. Where are you?'

'A library in town.'

A pause. 'Have you been drinking?'

'A bit.'

Another pause. Was there some kind of satellite delay?

'Is Tyler with you?'

'No, she stood me up.'

'You know, if she was reliable she'd be dangerous . . .'

'Jim.' He tutted. 'Don't tut at me! This is driving me fucking insane.'

'All right, all right, calm down. There's no need – '

'DON'T FUCKING TELL ME TO CALM DOWN.'

'You're shouting now. Are you in a library, shouting?'

'I DON'T GIVE A FUCK, EVERYONE'S A – .'

'Take a breath.' I almost hung up. Oh, white wine. White wine. I was so excited and so angry and so myself. I took a breath. 'Look, why don't you invite her over for dinner or something when I get back? *Does* she eat, or do any of the other normal human things?'

I didn't say anything to that. He'd invalidated his gesture. He didn't deserve praise.

'I'll cook. I'll even buy the wine.'

I maintained a haughty hush.

He said: 'I had a really good wank this morning thinking about you.'

This was more like it. 'Tell me.'

'Later.'

He hung up. As I focused on the phone screen the room bulged in my peripheral vision. I put on my jacket one arm at a time and walked carefully through the library, smiling at the woman on the desk as I passed. She didn't smile back. I walked down the stairs like a toddler, one foot then both together, next foot then both together, holding on to the wall and then the handrail.

Outside: rush hour. How had four hours passed? I weaved along Portland Street, past the all-you-can-eat Chinese buffet, and waited to cross the road on the corner. I wanted Tyler. Tyler, with her eyes and elbows, could have easily guided me through the heartless scrum of 5.30 p.m. The lights took too long to change so I crossed anyway, dispatching an elaborate double bird to a honking hackney cab, and carrying on up the street, where the Odeon cinema used to be, now just a fly-postered deco wreck with peeling paint and, I imagined, dusty staircases and huge vaulted rooms inside, like a run-aground liner. Someone banged into me as they passed, not on purpose but they didn't say sorry, I turned to see him turning his brief-case back round to his side. The impact of his arm or case or whatever had struck me and knocked me sick and I had to veer towards the wall, to the side of the Odeon building, and place my palm flat on the peeling blue paintwork for a moment, breathing deeply until the air pumped all the nausea out. I did not want to be sick at rush hour. Once, at a boutique music festival, I'd been walking along with Tyler when she emitted a neat curve of projectile vomit onto the grass in front of her and just carried on walking, resuming what she was saying exactly where she'd left it, barely missing a beat. I don't think she even wiped her mouth. It was an adept expulsion – not so impressive for the twenty people sitting at picnic benches outside a food stand, wooden cutlery held aloft, unable to finish their falafel. We'd christened it the 'walk and puke'. It was the epitome of styling out. I wasn't up to it. All I wanted to do was lie down.

I walked through St Peter's Square, past the Midland Hotel, down Peter Street towards Deansgate, a nonsensical, higgledy, mindless route, walking for walking's sake. Only when I got to the Free Trade Hall building did it dawn on me that a) I was making my way to Jim's and b) he wasn't there. Just before Deansgate there was a place called Lion Bar, built beneath an old Methodist church with an organ and, according to *Most Haunted*, who had investigated in 2005, a disapproving ministe-rial spirit. Previously, Lion Bar had been a club called the Red

Room. I'd worked there for a few months in my early twenties and had started refusing to go upstairs after another waitress, Jacqueline, saw a mop bucket fly across the abandoned church of its own accord. She was always helping herself behind the bar, but still, with that and Yvette's findings . . .

I'd had a laugh with Jacqueline. The club had a regular fetish night and one night I'd almost swept up a gimp on the mezzanine. There was all sorts to clean up after those nights. They turned the downstairs area into a dungeon complete with nets, chains and a corrugated cardboard 'rock' wall we put up with a staple gun. The interesting thing to me was that hardly anyone drank there; all we really sold was diet coke. I guess you have better aim when you're . . . anyway. I was sweeping away, stacking chairs, dragging tables, working my way from the steps to the back corner. As I tried to sweep the broom into the corner it struck against something hard. I pulled the broom back and peered into the darkness, thinking it would be an upturned chair or forgotten handbag. It was a shoe. Or rather, a patent leather socklike thing. Up from the shoe was an ankle, and, following on, ankle bone connecting to leg bone, leg bone connecting to knee bone, etcetera, etcetera, until the shape of a whole adult person was discernible, crouched like a frog. I screamed. The gimp scurried out from the corner, and this was someone who had gone full-gimp, zipped up to the chops, and ran down the stairs and almost through the glass front door. The door was locked and the gimp began bashing the glass with its fists and Jacqueline had to abandon her dish-washing duties to release it. The gimp scarpered down the street, patent leather flashing orange under the streetlamps. I wondered what that gimp was doing for nights out, now that Red Room had become a cocktail bar. Suburbia, I concluded. Suburbia would offer gimps something. And what about Jacqueline – what was she doing now? We'd always got on. I still had her number in my phone. I'd scrolled past it a few times when I was drunk and thought about her for a moment. If I was on Facebook I wouldn't have to wonder about these things. But then, if I was on Facebook I wouldn't have to wonder about these things.

Where the dual carriageway began there was a series of roundabouts over which a small viaduct split the sky. At the side of the viaduct were a few outcrops of green – fast-growing trees, spiky bushes that had ensnared windswept litter, scrubby defiant grass – elevated from the street on tilting brick embankments. Almost impossible to climb. Almost.

I jumped and grabbed the top of the sloping wall, put my trainers flat on the bricks and slid down a little. The wall was slippy. I gripped tighter with my fingers. One foot found purchase on a cracked brick. I nipped the toe of my other trainer into a gap in the mortar. Tested it with a little bounce. It would bear my weight for a few seconds while I found my next foothold. I moved my other foot, lost my balance, ended up scraping my knee and hurled myself upwards, laddering my tights and nicking my shin. At the top of the wall I rolled onto my back and lay there, panting. Above me leaves, just leaves. I got onto all fours and crawled under a bush, out of sight of the pavement and passing traffic. Wide, flat ivy covered the ground in a sea of tongues. Between the ivy, skeletons of sycamore seeds lay pale and brittle like moth wings. I heard footfalls and a man's low laughter. I turned onto my side like I did in bed, into the foetal position that was slowly eroding my left shoulder. I closed my eyes and listened to the tidal ebb and flow of traffic.

Where were my allies? My sad captains? Those moonsick girls I drank with over long winters behind the bowling alley, driven there in cars we didn't know. Those times when we were all strangers and everything was so far away but all we needed to

107

do was run towards it. I had not grown much. I had not reached anywhere. I was still running. When I wasn't lying down.

I opened my eyes and saw leaves above me, flickering in the wind.

THE IMPORTANCE OF QUESTIONS

Something slimy by my hand. I threw back the duvet (my duvet, my room) to see a chicken carcass, grey and sunken-ribbed, crouched on a dinner plate. Chicken jelly had gathered around it. I retched. A sound in the hallway.

'Hello?'

The door opened and hit the clothes rail. 'Fuck!' Tyler's arm appeared round the door and shunted the rail over.

'Is it morning or night?'

'Night.'

It all came back as it always did: in shards and splinters and burning arrows. I remembered waking under the bush and walking and buying a hot roast chicken, getting back to the flat and getting into bed with the chicken.

'How are you?'

'*My mouth has been used as a latrine by some small creature of the night.* How are you?'

'Pretty stoked actually. The talk was amazing.'

'Can't have been that amazing if you're using the word "amazing".'

I lifted the plate off the bedsheet and held it steady. Tyler peeled the end of a nail off with her teeth and spat it onto the floor.

'Jim says he wants to cook you dinner,' I said.

'Are you getting me in practice for seeing you *in situ*?'

'Oh, just come and have some fucking spaghetti.'

'But will he let us drink in there?'

'*He*'s buying the wine.'

He bought good wine, too. Rioja. Two bottles. I saw Tyler glance at them in the middle of the dining table when she came in and then look away. I wondered whether we should have asked her to bring a date to even things out. Jim poured two glasses of wine and a pint of lime and soda for himself. We sat down.

'I almost came in your place for a coffee yesterday,' he said to Tyler.

She was loosely blowing on a Medusa-like forkful of spaghetti. She stopped blowing. '*My* place?'

'The coffee shop.'

Personally I think it's insane that people ever try to eat and talk at the same time but this is the situation you often find yourself in at dinner parties and restaurants. Not that this situation was either, of course: we were just three friends sitting together having dinner. Still, I wished we were on the couch watching TV with our bowls on our knees.

'You should come in sometime,' she said. 'I'll give you a free shot. Of syrup.' She raised her glass of red wine. 'I've got the decorators in!'

'You know that means you're on your period,' said Jim.

She looked at me and tipped the glass into her mouth.

All things considered, they did a reasonably good job of barbed civility until dessert, when Tyler said: 'I haven't asked you, but are you two having a first dance?'

It was an odd thing to hear her say. *I haven't asked you.* Like she was a stranger or a not very good friend. I looked at the table. The red cloth was splodged with cream where Jim had spilled the trifle.

'We've discussed this,' Jim said. 'We talked about having lessons at one point, put on a bit of a show.'

'A show.' Tyler's teeth were dark and grainy from the wine. We were halfway through the second bottle.

'We decided against it,' I said, getting up to smoke out of the kitchen window. 'I'd bottle it on the day, I know I would.'

'Just get some drugs in you,' said Tyler.

I was afraid that if I went to the bathroom they might kill each other. I turned the lever on the window and pushed the pane open. Cold air whirled in. I got up on the counter and pulled over the ramekin I used as an ashtray at Jim's.

'It's a drug-free occasion,' Jim said. 'Has Laura not mentioned that?'

'I was just kidding,' said Tyler.

'Just so you know. Charlie's not invited. Or any of his illegal friends.'

Silence. I exhaled. I thought, *They're actually going to leave it there. Thank fuck.*

'Weeeellllll, of course you know they shouldn't *be* illegal in my opinion. But for the sake of what this pathetic government deems "legal" for tax purposes, I'll respect your frankly patronising request.'

My hand shook as I held my cigarette.

'The libertarian in me wants to agree with you,' Jim said. 'But it's not as simple as legalise drugs and they become safe.'

'It's a start. Out of interest, are you presenting this as a health issue or an organised crime issue?'

'Both. Besides, people on drugs are wankers. Especially coke. Coke is the worst.'

Tyler emitted a squeal. 'How do you NOT KNOW I'm on coke right now?'

'Because you're asking me a question,' Jim said. 'Ever noticed how someone on coke doesn't ask a single question?'

I thought about making coffee and taking through Jim's big shiny cafetiere and the pretty little pastel cups.

'I'd better get home,' Tyler said. 'I'm up at six.' She got up, put on her jacket and looked at me. 'You're staying here then?' She smacked herself on the forehead. 'Of course you are. Sorry, force of habit.'

'Let us call you a cab,' I said.

Oh, that 'us'! She flinched and I instantly regretted it. I made a point then of saying 'I' in every subsequent sentence. *I'll go get my phone. I do have a number in here somewhere. I'll come outside with you. I'll meet you at the station after work.*

'Have a great time in London,' Jim said. 'Look after each other.'

'Oh, we will. Shame you can't make it, but don't worry, I'll be your stand-in.'

'You're welcome, Tyler,' Jim said, turning to stack the dishes.

I stood in the road smoking long after the cab had gone, thinking about her travelling through the city towards the opposite outskirts, the streetlights sliding over the window in front of her peering face.

TO LONDON!

Tyler was waiting for me outside Piccadilly. Shades on, smoking, reading a paper, a carrier bag by her boots. As I reached her, a sports car screeched away from the drop-off point, tyres searing the tarmac. I jumped and dropped my bag. 'Oh no stop please come back I simply must have sex with you,' Tyler said, folding the paper. She was in a good mood.

On the train she emptied the contents of the carrier bag onto her tray table. A quarter bottle of vodka, four cans of diet coke, two pork pies. 'We need to get these in while we can,' she said, unsheathing a pie. 'Jean has turned practically macrobiotic. There will be nothing to eat except beansprouts and dung.'

When we arrived at Euston we sat down for a smoke at one of the wooden picnic tables in front of the station. I was enjoying my London cigarette. I'd never been one of those Northerners who hated the South. Big cities comforted me: the cover, the chaos, the hollow sympathy of the architecture, the Tube lines snaking underground. London could swallow you up, in a good way. There were times when I'd been broken and being subsumed into a city had made me feel part of a whole again.

A copy of *Nuts* magazine had been left on the table. Tyler picked it up and began flicking through. 'Oh this is abysmal. Abysmal! You know what this country needs? Another world war. Something on the doorstep to knock things back into perspective. A recession clearly hasn't been enough. *This week's stripper is an air hostess!* An AIR HOSTESS! Get her in a nuked-up plane over the Middle East – see if she feels like whipping her norks out then.'

'I thought we agreed it was wrong to slam individuals for the perpetuation of – '

'Oh, you think her real name's "Vikki"? She's a symbol! An allegory! That's all we have, and people celebrate these symbols as though we don't need a complete economic restructure. I despair, I really do. It's all completely fucked.'

'You watch porn!'

'Well, that's different – that's already there, like meat. You might as well.'

She tore the magazine in half and threw it to the ground. I sat down. There was a woman reading a book on the other side of the table. She looked at me and went back to her book. Tyler pushed the fag packet towards me. I pulled out a fag and sparked up. 'Let's get a drink before we head to Jean's. These station pubs are hideous, though. Threadbare seats and homemade vodka. It's like capitalism never happened. Let's finish these and go somewhere louche en route.'

A wasp zigzagged past my fag and I jerked backwards. The insect landed on the table and began crawling towards a sticky patch of something. The woman across the table quickly shut her book and bashed the insect to a pulp, hitting it ten times at least. Tyler watched. When the woman had finished, the wasp was a mass of black and yellow on wood. Tyler tapped her fag in the parasol hole. The woman recoiled, as though a cigarette was worse than a wasp.

'NOT A BUDDHIST, THEN?' Tyler said.

I loved her. I did. Sometimes.

We stopped at a pub called The Approach in Hackney, sat out back smoking and sharing a bottle of rosé. The wine was disgusting – every time either of us sipped any we gagged.

'Why do we keep trying with rosé?' I said.

'Because it feels like a compromise when you don't know whether you want red or white. Rosé, you think, it's the natural choice, straight down the middle. But it's not, it's fucking shit.'

The barman came and cleared some glasses off the table. 'I'll bring you ladies an ashtray. You'll have to move your bags, they're blocking the fire escape.'

Tyler looked at him as though she was imagining the true horror of a blocked fire escape. She leaned down and gave the bags a few bashes until they were flush with the chairs. The barman stood over us, clutching a spray of dirty pint pots. 'What's in them, anyway?'

She looked at him. 'Blow-up dolls and ketamine.'

'You're lucky this isn't an airport,' he said. 'Oh talky hand, you're doing a talky hand at me, well *that's* polite.'

We had another bottle before we left – rosé again. (Tyler: *Might as well, I can barely taste the fucker any more.*)

By the time we got to Jean's in Bethnal Green we were somewhere between wedding-drunk and wake-drunk. *Christening-drunk* – a new one, I thought to myself joyously as Jean opened the door with a lint roller in her hand. The baby peered from her side, squinting in the crook of Jean's arm like her dark half.

'Lola!' Jean said. No one had called me that for years. It reminded me of nights out with Jean, years ago. The two of them singing to me in stupid English accents: *I met her in a club down in Old So-ho.* I hugged Jean carefully around the baby. 'Whew!' she said. 'You guys smell of . . . fun.'

'We stopped off to refresh ourselves,' Tyler said.

'Where?'

'The Approach.'

'Great,' Jean said, but she didn't look as though she thought it was great. I started to feel self-conscious. I was staying at her house: was it rude to turn up drunk now she had a baby? The baby. It was staring at me emotionlessly. I thought of Lisa Bonet's baby in *Angel Heart*. Yellow eyes and pointing . . .

Tyler released a heraldic fart as she crossed the threshold.

'Oh, do please try and contain yourself, Tyler,' said Jean.

'Jean's a shadow of her former glory,' Tyler whispered loudly. 'They don't even chill wine around here any more. They keep it in a rack so you have to plan ahead if you want any.'

I stepped into the hall. Jean closed the front door. 'Everyone's in the kitchen,' she said. On our nights out, now deep in the past, she'd lasted the longest despite being the youngest. In Nebraska she'd dated a man who cooked crystal meth in his garage (*Your whole brain gets pins-and-needles and you don't sleep for days*), and she'd been living in New York on 9/11 – had run away there after the meth-chef dumped her for her best friend. Got a job at a gallery in Chelsea. Was always in work early. That day she was in for eight. *What was it like?* I'd asked her, the ghoul in me elbowing past the human. 'Oh, I was heartbroken at the time,' she deadpanned, 'so it sort of passed me by.'

I followed Tyler down the hall. Photos in odd frames were hung on the walls, like you found in so many of the new Manchester bars ('quirky taxidermy bars' as Tyler called them); a forced eccentricity that had dismally mutated into conformity. I didn't imagine Jean and Tom had collected the frames so much as ordered a job lot on eBay (I chastised myself for this thought, trespassing on their hospitality, but I couldn't help it). *Desperately random, like the elaborations of a bad liar*, I thought and wondered where it was from. The answer (*Silence of the Lambs*) came to me as I entered the kitchen to see Tyler's mum seated at the table and Tom fishing about for something in the down-scaled green Aga. A warm domestic scene. People smiling, eating, drinking, happy in each other's company. I thought of my parents' living room, of Jim's bed, and I thought Yes, Okay. All right. I'll have some of that.

'Here they are!' Tyler's mum stood up at the sight of me. I kissed her on the cheek.

'Hi, Ro.'

I loved Tyler's mum, with her flamboyant openness and heavy clothes, all that academic lingo she used so effortlessly. She walked over to the fridge, her thighs stretching a houndstooth miniskirt. 'I put some wine in to chill for you,' she said. I loved Tyler's mum, really I did. She poured two large glasses.

'Make that three,' Tom said.

'Four,' said Jean. 'Shirley's on formula.'

This information was for me, in case I'd forgotten. I hadn't. I'd admired Jean's attitude to not breastfeeding, relayed to me via Tyler. Jean had taken formula and bottles in her bag with her to the hospital, this after pre-booking an epidural. *There are plenty of times in life when I'm going to feel pain*, Jean had said. *When I'm in a building full of anaesthetists is not one of them.*

'You can do what you like,' said Ro.

'Wellll . . .' said Tom.

I hoped the dynamics didn't intensify or I was going to have to make a break for the bathroom. I looked out of the window. A pug was playing in the small, neat garden. The garden was green and brown, strong solid colours in definite shapes like someone had painted it by numbers. It made me think of a nuclear testing site. The pug picked up a partially deflated ball and trotted across the garden, neck arched proudly, like a miniature show horse.

Shirley was sitting on Tom's knee, sucking her cuff. 'She's beautiful,' I said. It was what you said about babies.

'Remember what Dad said about me when I was born?' said Tyler. The room stiffened. 'He said I looked like a tortoise without a shell.'

117

Ro handed me a glass of wine. 'I remember you having a liking for Chenin Blanc,' she said. I shrugged, smiled and took the wine. Ro had a constantly delighted face. Plump little jowls hanging lower than Tyler's, falling round into the solid bowl of her chin. A vision of gravity's better effects. Whenever I saw her looking slightly older, always the case due to our sporadic meetings, I got a rush of few-times-removed tenderness, like when I saw a favourite actor in a new film.

My phone rang in my pocket. I pulled it out. Jim.

'Back door's unlocked,' Jean said.

I lit up a fag and then answered the phone as the door closed behind me. A trellis was nailed to the wall. On the trellis a clematis plant was starting to bud.

'Where are you?'

'Hong Kong.'

'What's it like?'

'I've only really seen hotel rooms.'

Diddums. I stopped myself saying it. Roaring silence. Background radiation and white noise. I inhaled. Exhaled.

'Did you book the DJ?' he said.

That sound again.

'Laura?'

'No. Sorry.'

'It's okay – that's why I'm asking: my parents know someone. DJ Pete from Halifax.'

'DJ Pete from Halifax?'

'They just want to help. Be a part of it. I'm an only one so it's a big deal for them.'

I thought about it. Did I *really* care about the DJ? No I did not. 'Sure.' I said. 'Fuckit.'

He laughed. 'Well, yeah. Speaking of which, I've been enjoying what we've been doing or rather not been doing.'

I liked the abstract riskiness of it more than anything. What if I *was* pregnant? Unlikely, but what if? I had no idea where I was up to. I shut the thoughts down and right then it was easy. 'You know,' Jim said, 'something for us to think about in the future is the fact that you have more chance of conceiving if you . . . never mind. Enjoy tomorrow!'

I finished my cigarette before I went back in, trying not to blow smoke on the foliage. There was nothing in cigarettes for plants.

Later, in bed, after Tyler had fallen asleep, I took out my laptop and Googled the fuck out of Marty Grane. Googled him hard, all night.

The next morning I woke early to see Tyler already up and sitting at the dressing table in the corner of Jean's guest room.

''Eyyyyyyyyyyyy,' she said, holding a comb by the side of her head. She was dressed and fully made-up – liner, shadow, lippy, rouge. The chocolate-y mole on her left cheek was more prominent that usual, highlighted by foundation and a liberal twist of kohl.

I raised myself onto my elbows. 'How long have you been posing with that comb?'

She glanced at the clock on the bedside table. 'Twenty-eight minutes.'

I stuck my tongue out wide and exhaled fruitily. Parched. I was so parched. 'I feel terrible,' I said. 'It's all your mother's fault.'

'That old chestnut. Hey, want to go for a walk? London can be picturesque in the morning if you choose your route wisely.'

'Is your brain on already?'

'*Bam bas bat bamus batis bant.* Seems so.'

'Why is it that the memory cells are the hardest ones to kill?'

'Come on now, get your legs moving. Your blood will renew! Your liver will rejoice!'

'Maybe you could just push me round a park in a bath chair, like Heidi with Clara.'

But we didn't have time for a walk in the end. We had to be at the church for midday. I'd forgotten to hang up the dress I'd brought, so it was creased all over and the thin grey fabric hung off me like the skin of an octogenarian elephant. I'd taken three Nurofen Express and felt altitudinous. Tyler was wearing her fish-scale top and one of Jean's trouser suits. We stood out on the street smoking, waiting for the cars, jacking up our morale by blowing smoke rings and headbutting them. Soon a minibus and a beautiful big white car turned the corner. I whistled. The car soared along, like a plane.

'Always wanted to drive a Rolls,' said Tyler, twisting her heel on the end of her fag.

'No,' said Jean firmly, taking her by the arm and leading us towards the minibus.

Stepping inside a church felt, as always, like an ornate form of excavation. The statues, the dust and the wood; alien archaeology, with signs and symbols to be sought and interpreted. I walked down to the front and sat and waited while Tyler and her family stood greeting people at the door. I sang the hymns gutsily, not sure who or what I wanted to notice me. After the ceremony I snuck outside and went round to the side of the church, disappearing behind a tree. I sparked up and wondered what to do with my dimp when the time came.

'Are you a friend of the family?'

I turned to see the vicar standing by a small door. A dog collar under a black turtleneck. Creature on creature on creature.

'Yes,' I said, looking guiltily at my fag.

'Don't worry about that. I often nip out here for a joint after funerals.'

I looked at the floor. It was littered with jack-knifed joint-ends. I said: 'That was a lovely service.'

'That's what they all say.'

She looked young. Mid-twenties. Fresh out of vicar college. She had long dark hair and the big silver cross round her neck looked like she'd kept it from when she was a goth teenager. I felt suddenly close to her, as though she could help me.

'You were looking round the church a lot,' she said. 'Are you a Christian?'

'I don't know,' I said. 'My dad was raised Catholic but I also know I'm happier outside once I've got in.'

'I like that feeling, too. But then I never feel truly alone. I suppose that's what brought me to God, that sense of solidarity.'

'I never feel alone either. Sometimes I can't eat a *banana*, know what I mean?' She did but she didn't say. 'So do you go in for the whole omnipresent schtick?' I realised as I said it that subtext had always been masturbation. 'I write,' I explained, 'I'm just thinking about how I always feel the need for that audience – and I'm not sure whether that makes me a better writer or just a narcissist.'

'I don't think you should worry so much.'

Ha. 'Without the worry I wouldn't write at all.'

'Then try trusting the audience you most want to impress.'

'And make sure they're as drunk as you.'

'Do you know the Serenity Prayer?'

The first time I'd read it, I'd thought it was a joke. I rattled it off before she could. '*Grant me the serenity to accept the things I cannot change, the courage to change the things I can, and the wisdom to know the difference.*'

Her eyes blared as she smirked. I cursed myself. Church was school and I was damned like always. I thought of my dad, who saved everything; conversations included. 'Here's one for you,' I said. 'Higgs boson walks into a church. Priest says, *Thank God you're here, we can't have Mass without you!*'

The vicar laughed. She had lovely teeth.

NEAR-DEATH IN A SUBTERRANEAN BAR

Back at Jean's I sat on the end of the sofa near the door so I could get in and out without disturbing anyone. The house was full, with a queue halfway down the stairs for the bathroom, and smalltalksmalltalk everywhere. I looked from face to face, trying to spot couples, looking for matches in expressions and mood, like I was playing a kiddies' card game. Jean was standing by the wall talking and holding Shirley. The baby's long white dress trailed to the floor while the black plastic aerial of the stereo system was positioned on a shelf just behind Jean's head in a squarish halo. I remembered wanting to see Jean when she was pregnant, to map the changes on her; the mystery of life going on inside. I wanted to see whether any of that mystery showed on her face.

Tyler came over with a glass of Cava. My own glass was empty. She tipped half of her drink in. 'Thanks.'

'Eh, *mi Cava es su Cava!*'

'Fancy a fag?'

'Boy, do I. I just made the mistake of reading the christening cards.'

I sipped my drink. My hangover was receding. The hair of dog theory held, depressingly. We walked outside and stood on the street. I shook two cigarettes out of my pack.

'*Welcome to the club*,' Tyler said, taking a cigarette. 'That's what they all say. Welcome to the club!' She exhaled. 'You know what the "Baby Club" is? The Baby Club is one of those godawful discos in Leicester Square: starkly lit, tacky and full of tourists.

The décor is dated and you can't get a decent drink, and every time someone new walks through the door everyone who's in there smiles manically with this huge relief because they're just so glad someone else walked into their shitty club after they paid twenty quid and can't leave.' She went on: 'But I'd never say that to them, you know, *Stick your shitty fucking club – I've got better places to be.*'

I wondered whether to tell her that Jim and I hadn't been –

'Are you worried you're getting too old to have a baby, Tyler?'

'I'M TWENTY-NINE!'

'Thirty in two weeks.'

'Still. Fifteen years at least before I need to freak. I know you think I'm pissed because I didn't get my invite to the baby party yet. But I'll tell you something, my friend, I'll tell you something. If I do decide to do it then it'll be something I just do and not something I try and sell as an exclusive event when in fact it's anything but. I have my definitions, my developing theories, and I will never live without a lonely hungry longing in my soul, never.'

We smoked in silence.

'Listen to that,' Tyler said.

I strained my ears, my neck.

'Hear it?'

'You mean the distant rumble of Time's winged chariot with its massive fuck-off spike on the front?'

'Just behind that.'

I listened again. 'Mm, not sure.'

'Precisely. Nothing. The sound of the suburbs. They sell it as peace but it's actually death, closing in.'

Irreversibly attached. *Irreversibly.*

After the party Ro went up to bed. Shirley lay asleep in her Moses basket in the corner with one hand above her head, index finger extended, like a little despot who had fallen asleep in the middle of giving an order. The chairs had all been brought in from the garden. I stroked the dog under the table and felt the bones along its back.

'This is the first time I've been properly drunk since having her,' Jean said suddenly. 'I'm so much happier not being drunk very often. So much clearer on everything.'

Tom nodded in approval and gave Jean's shoulder a squeeze. I felt Tyler bulging and popping.

'You treasure your flesh when you're pregnant,' Jean went on. 'You consider every cell. The time things take to grow.'

On top of the enamel bread-bin was a pestle and mortar I recognised from one of Jean's previous abodes – a night when we crushed pills in it and snorted them. Then she forgot to clean it and made a tagine. That tagine had gone down well. Best. Cumin. Ever.

I was still stroking the dog's head but I must have stroked too hard because it moved away. I thought, *Jean's drunk and she's trying to sound all wise and in control for Tom.* I didn't care if she used me for that. I thought, *Zen is possibly the way to go here.* 'There are many roads to happiness,' I said. 'I'm glad you found yours, Jean. Today was – '

'There are many roads to hell, too,' Jean said. 'I worry about you two.'

The mood of the room changed. A fall in atmospheric pressure. I looked at Tyler. She was growing purplish.

'She's always been more wilful than me,' Jean said, to Tyler, via me.

Bathroom, bathroom, how could I get to the bath –

'You know you can cut down, if you want to. I know some places – '

'I don't need your *places*,' Tyler said.

'You might need to grow up a bit then,' Jean said. 'Sorry, Lola, no disrespect, but – '

Tyler snatched for the warm wine bottle in the middle of the table and poured. When she got to Tom he held his hand over his glass and she poured wine over his hand until he moved it away. 'I've warned you, Jean,' she said.

'It's a case of mind over matter, I find,' Tom said, wiping his hand on his trouser leg.

'Last time I checked my mind was attached to my matter,' said Tyler. 'Furthermore. I like what my mind and matter do to each other. And I can stop. And as long as that's the case, I'm not changing a fucking stroke. Just because your mind and matter fell out, Jeannie . . .'

Tom raised his palm and looked upwards, like a saint. I remembered something Tyler had told me, something she shouldn't have, late one night. Tom had confessed to seeing a prostitute not long after he and Jean started dating. Jean was aghast. *If you ever see another prostitute I will cut off your balls with a butter knife* . . . Tyler, in the wreckheaded re-telling, was not aghast – or rather, she was more aghast at the fact Jean was morally outraged rather than jealous. *There's no sense of the other woman in this situation*, Tyler said. *Let's think about that.*

'So you're just going to wait until you collapse in the street or get cancer?' Jean said. Her voice was louder. Higher. I flinched at the word and I could tell Jean was sorry for saying it.

'You bet your fucking bottle of shitty Chardonnay in the boiler closet I am,' said Tyler.

A boiler closet. That sounded like a nice place to be. It would be dark and warm and quiet. I put my hand over my mouth and supported my head that way.

Tyler said: 'The world is over-populated. Way I see it, I'm saving the fucking planet.'

'Some people would argue parenthood is the most adventurous thing you can do.'

Tyler slammed her glass on the table. 'Well, they've got to, haven't they? It's one of the great unspoken rules. *Never admit how resentful you feel towards your children.*'

'Know what I think, Tyler? I think you stayed too long at the fair.'

'Know what I think, Jeannie? "Wilful" is a word that should be reserved for horses.'

I calmed her down in the bathroom. 'You know, you have to let people choose their own adventures.'

She stopped brushing her teeth, pulled the toothbrush out. 'What are you not telling me?'

'Nothing. Come on. Spit.'

'No, you spit.'

There was no point –

'Jim and I haven't been using protection.'

It sounded very formal.

'You're fucking kidding me?' Blobs of toothpaste gathered on her décolletage as she spoke. 'IS NOTHING SACRED?'

'It doesn't mean I want to get pregnant.'

She wiped her mouth with the back of her hand. 'But it does mean that you might.'

'So I'll have an abortion.'

Gotcha. I saw her thoughts follow mine and hit the wall I had her up against. I kept her there, watched her wriggle. Then I sat down on the side of the bath. 'Is anyone ever sure, though, when they really think about it? What kind of fool would think, *Know what I'd like? Less sleep, less money, less privacy* . . . Best-case scenario is it happens by accident.'

She put her toothbrush carefully into a free hole in the holder. 'I don't know why I expected to be involved. My bad.'

'Don't be like that.'

'Nah, it's too late. You're on the track.'

The next day it was still frosty between us but frostier still between Tyler and Jean – the basis of comparison, of lesser evils (like the eternally sobering sight of someone drunker than you regardless of your own state), rendering the conversation we'd had in the bathroom almost forgotten. I heard Ro talking to Tyler in the kitchen while I was smoking in the garden. *Don't you dare drag her back into anything, you hear me?* We left as soon as we were showered and dressed, around noon.

We took a tour of London pubs and museums, ending up in a pub by Euston around six with a plan to catch the first off-peak evening train. I followed Tyler towards the bar and then over in the corner of the pub I caught the eye of someone recently familiar. Recently very familiar. Intimate even.

Yep.

He waved. I waved back.

'Who are you waving at?' said Tyler, following my gaze. 'No fucking way.' I looked at her. Her face split into a grin. 'MARTY?'

He was halfway across the room. '*TYLER?*' Adjusting his glasses as he ran. 'Tyler *JOHNSON?*'

'MARTY GRANE, AS I LIVE AND BREATHE!'

They hit each other like footballers in a chest-hard embrace. I stood there, boggling.

'Hang on,' said Marty, stepping back and looking at me. 'You know each other?' Lots of fast pointing – you, her, you, her. Tyler looked at me.

'Marty did the Yeats talk at the library,' I said. Then to him: 'Tyler's my flatmate.'

'Landlord.'

'Whatever.'

They embraced again. I moved to one side and ordered a large glass of white wine. Typical. Just. Fucking. Typical.

'Look at you,' Tyler said, flicking Marty's collar as she pulled back. 'Luckily I know the insidious truth beneath the dandy veneer.'

I took a large swig of wine and swallowed.

'You look exactly the same,' he said. 'Exactly.'

I let my head fall back and I looked at the ceiling, my mouth hanging open in a silent howl.

'Marty and I did our Masters together,' Tyler said. 'Then he defected down south. And now I hear you've gone all Romantic? Fuck you!'

'I fell in love with another! Allow me that, you pebble of a girl.' Tyler cackled. 'I still remember every line anyway.'

'I should think so. You were the Wife of Bath.'

Marty loud-whispered: '*I have the power durynge al my lyf upon his propre body, and noght he . . .*'

They laughed. Oh, the loneliness of ignorance. It was lonelier than genius because you didn't even have your knowledge to keep you company. I picked up my wine and tipped all of it into my mouth. Ordered another.

'Make that two,' said Tyler.

'Come and join us!' said Marty. 'We're just over there.'

I looked over. A man and a woman were sitting at a table, regarding us cautiously. Tyler flew towards them, jacket tassels flapping.

'Americans,' Marty said, watching her. 'Don't you just adore them? They're like basking sharks, running at life with their mouths open.'

I paid for our wines.

'Well, this is random,' Marty said. (*Desperately random, like the elaborations of . . .*) 'What brings you two to London?'

'Tyler's niece's christening.'

'Tyler has family? I thought she came out of The Pod.'

'Hard to believe, I know.'

'How's the novel?'

I pretended I hadn't heard and walked past him with the wines. As I put them down on the table I caught the edge with my hand so that the man's pint spilled a little. I chastised myself for my obviousnesses, my elaborate social effort. *You do not possess the normal micro-movements of politeness.* 'Sorry.'

'Sheila Jones and Michael Perrin,' Marty said, catching up. 'Old friends from Oxford.' (Wooo.) 'They've just set up their own independent publishing house, so we're celebrating. Tyler Johnson, who I studied with for my Masters in Manchester. Laura Joyce, who I met there last week.'

Hello. Hello hello hello.

'Masters courses are the greatest,' Tyler said. 'You get just deep enough before you get bored and the seminars are like dinnerless dinner parties where everyone shares the same interests. If I ever get any money I'm going to spend my whole life doing one after another. I'd do one on Modernist architecture, one on 1960s French cinema, one on twenty-first century European history . . .'

Her dad had paid for the last one – same time he'd paid for the flat.

Before we lived together I went round to hers unannounced one evening. I was twenty-six, she was twenty-three. It was mid-December, dark and sleeting, and I was surprised to see the bottom door of the block wedged open with a half-empty bottle of mineral water. I bent to pick up the bottle as I opened the door and then tucked it back in as the door closed, in case someone who was fixing or cleaning something had left it there so they could get in and out. The motion detector strip-light on the low ceiling flickered to a buzzy glow. Then I heard it – a blare of words from a few floors above. Her floor. Her voice.

THE FUCK OUT MY HOUSE.

A soft bump from the same place, a person falling against a wall, a shoulder charge, hard to tell much in terms of damage or intended damage.

She said it again, slower, louder.

THE FUCK. OUT. MY HOUSE.

I was on the first landing by now. I thought, *She's being robbed or worse.* I couldn't move quick enough. A pale man, late fifties, checked shirt and cheap jeans, passed me on the last flight of stairs. He was sore-shaven, his whole face red apart from his eyes, which had a vague, milky look. He didn't look like a robber. A lover? I already knew Tyler's sex life was a broad church. I still wished I'd taken more time to look at him, to retain more of his details. I'd always been curious. I was still so curious. But he was past me in seconds, and by the time I reached Tyler's floor I heard the main door slam shut below.

Tyler was standing at her front door in her kimono and a skullish clay facemask. It was hard to tell what her face was doing but her hand was up to her nose, her first fingers stroking her philtrum as she heavily breathed.

'Are you okay?'

'Yes, of course.'

'Who was that?'

The mask had gone all patchy under her nose – she looked like a very shit white rabbit. 'Three guesses.'

I knew then. I also knew that I'd known as soon as I'd heard her shout. 'What, here? In England?'

'Biggest mistake I ever made, letting him pay for this hellhole.'

I'd brought a bottle of wine with me. We didn't talk much as we drank, every now and then she'd have a one-sentence outburst like *I'm bigger than him now*, and *Fucker's shrinking*. When the wine was finished I suggested going out to a bar but she shook her head. 'Don't fancy it. I'll drink more in here, though, if you don't mind the trip to the store.'

'I don't mind.'

'Mull something over while you're walking, why don't you.'

'Fire away.'

'Move in with me.'

I didn't need to mull. I was living with my parents. 'Okay.'

I'd drunk half my wine by the time I sat down.

'Laura's writing a novel,' Marty said.

'Oh, now and then, you know.'

A slight twitch to his nostrils, where a brush of fine hairs protruded. He was drinking whisky, I could smell it. Something stirred in my stomach, something that usually nestled there. I reddened.

'You must send it to us when it's done,' said Sheila. I nodded. Burning burning I was burning. I sat down. 'We're focusing on novels, with perhaps the odd short story collection and poetry anthology.' She leaned towards me. 'We're trying to get Marty to let us publish some of his old poems.'

'I bet they're all *Baby this baby that ooh ooh ooh* . . .' said Tyler.

'Now now,' Marty said. 'No need to get personal.' He was blushing then, too, and I felt my own face cool. Saw it all in a flash. The *Writers' and Artists' Yearbook* for Christmas, rejection letters pinned for posterity on the wall of his poky room in halls, the summer job in the bookshop, the full-time job in the bookshop, the retreat back into academia . . . Other Observations: a dimple when he grinned and a gap between his two front teeth that would have marked him out as village idiot if he hadn't been so smart. Different Clothes: denim shirt, red knitted tie, black cord jacket, the shirt tucked into his jeans, jeans held up with a blue belt with a gold buckle.

Don't look at his belt buckle.

Tyler did most of the talking, disagreeing with things I said, sharing a private joke with Marty, telling her own (superior) anecdotes, or her (superior) versions of mine. I felt myself retreating. Competing for attention with Tyler was futile. She didn't just change the temperature of rooms, she changed their entire chemical make-up so that anyone in the room would only be aware that the room was an extension of her and she was the thrumming nucleus. As I embarked upon my third glass of wine I noticed that Tyler had gone to the toilet and Marty had quickly followed her. I tried to make conversation with Sheila and Michael but I couldn't help but be distracted. After too many wrong-footed intonations, too many quizzical glances to see if I was listening, I made my excuses and went to the Ladies. I heard Tyler in a cubicle, sniffing and rummaging around, and then she came out and said, 'Hey, Lo, wanna bump?' She was holding a baby-blue wrap, sugar paper. *London*. I looked at it and frowned. 'Marty's.'

'Marty has coke?'

'As you see.' Proffering.

'Hm.'

She handed it to me. 'I think he likes you. In the worst way.'

'What makes you say that?'

When they called last orders Sheila and Michael said goodbye and left the three of us to it.

When they kicked us out we danced down the street and down a side alley. Tyler wiped a stone windowsill with her sleeve. Marty opened a wrap, nudged out some of the contents and racked up three lines. I looked around. A single rain-hooded tuk-tuk meandered slowly past on the main road.

'Here,' Tyler said, handing me the note. 'Atta girl. Just like a Dyson.'

My phone rang. Jim.

'NO,' said Tyler, taking the phone from my hand and dropping the call.

I snatched it back. 'You shouldn't have done that! We don't drop each other's calls. He'll be worried.'

'Send him a text and say the reception's bad and you'll call him back in the morning.'

Marty said: 'Where now?'

'I know just the place!' said Tyler. 'A Spanish drinking den!'

She grabbed our hands and marched us back up the alley.

Criss-crossing streets, roads, cabs beeping, we arrived at a wooden door. Tyler rapped on a little window within the door and it slid open.

'*Sí?*' The shape of a man's head through the mesh. Loud music thick with drums and shouts tentacle'd out into the air.

'Are there any ice skaters in for my guest tonight?' said Tyler. 'I was promised ice skaters.'

It wasn't her accent. She sounded like Joan Crawford.

I just wanted to get inside and down to the music and the drinks and the writhing darkness and some way to keep moving rather than just be standing there. The window slid shut and then the whole door opened. We stepped inside. Tyler nodded at the man behind the window as we passed. I grinned. He jerked his head towards the stairs. We made our way down flight after flight of narrow stairs, each landing turning and twisting into another flight. They seemed to go on for ever, the music getting louder, the temperature hotter. Eventually we arrived at another door. Above it, the amber disc of the emergency light was full of dead flies, dark like sunspots. Tyler opened the door. An assault of sound and smoke. The room was long and thin, lightless apart from a few neon signs hung crookedly on the walls. The furniture consisted of upturned crates – everyone sitting on them had their knees almost round their ears. The ceiling was low, so low that several taller men were stooping where they stood. We made our way to the far end of the room where there was a bathtub full of ice, beer and wine. The labels from the bottles had all washed off. Next to the bathtub there was a large punchbowl and a stack of plastic cups. 'DON'T DRINK THAT,' Tyler said. She skittled three cups in her fingers and pulled a bottle of wine from the bathtub. I looked around the room. People were staring at us, there was no doubt about it, paranoia notwithstanding, so I grinned and moved with the music to try and blend in. In a nearby corner four men stood holding cups of punch. They were dressed in conquistador costumes with ruffled shirts open to the waist. A band from a Spanish restaurant who had clocked off early. In the other corner two men were sitting playing flamenco guitar, punch cups down by their feet. One appeared to be passed out, slumped over his instrument, with only his fingers still moving. Nobody was smiling.

'Everyone in here is fucked,' I said.

Tyler handed me a cup of wine. 'Yu-huh.' She raised her own cup and began whooping and stamping out of time. I had a faraway feeling that we might be better not drawing attention to ourselves. Marty sat down on a crate and I sat next to him, Tyler on the other side. The light shifting, my eyes tripping, Marty looked younger, younger than me, or no age at all.

'Do you still write poetry?' I said.

'Sometimes, late at night. When the ghosts come knocking.'

I looked at him. Sincerity. How refreshing. I felt his leg come to rest against mine. I moved my leg away and wished I hadn't. Jim would have flirted while he was away. I wasn't dead inside. Far from it.

'Fast little drinker, aren't you?' said Marty.

I looked at him. I hoped he was going to get *really* antagonistic now. I hoped I was in some Real Actual Danger. I kept my face very straight. 'It's only because I'm a woman that you even see my drinking as a feature. No, hear me out on this. There was a pop concert in Manchester last year. Boy band from the Nineties.

It was mostly women in their thirties who went – you know, because they'd liked them first time round.' He nodded. Was I rambling? Fuckit. 'So, that was the demographic. And the press went for them – I mean, *went for them*. They were "vomiting in gardens, clogging up A&E, wearing unflattering pink outfits at their age", you know. This all coming in the wake of all the binge-drinking stories that the media had been using to demonise women, especially young women. Why? Because women's bodies are not seen as their own. They are *birthing machines*. Are you laughing?'

'Absolutely not.'

'Do you think A&E was any busier that night than after a football match at Old Trafford? No. It wasn't. I checked. Tyler and I both checked, because this shit matters to us.'

I looked round at Tyler. She was watching the dancing.

'So,' Marty said, 'you're just *expressing* yourselves with your little revolution show? I hate to break it to you, missy, but the alcohol and tobacco companies are owned by the capitalists responsible for sustaining the very system you want to crack. But by all means, revolutionise away. Just make sure it's fun.'

'It's about choice. I choose to do everything I do.'

'Wanna bet?'

Missy. Motherfucker. Inside me, a chorus line of devils in tutus did a fast little cancan. I pulled my fag packet out of my jacket pocket, lit three fags and handed one to Marty then reached across to hand one to Tyler.

Something afoot. She had a beatific grin on her face, and when I followed her line of sight I saw a beautiful young man dancing in the middle of the room. The man kept glancing at her and making his moves more fluid, as though he was enjoying Tyler looking at him that bit too much . . .

I looked around the room. Two handy-looking girls were standing by the far wall, holding punch cups so tightly they had buckled in their hands. One of them looked at the man and then back at me, then at Tyler, and then back at me. Her eyes were full of rage.

'Tyler,' I said, leaning over Marty, 'I think he's trying to make his girlfriend jealous.'

'Fuck her,' Tyler said, still staring.

The girl started walking towards us. My feet twitched and I gripped my cup so hard that wine spilled onto my knee.

'Tyler.'

The girl was over in seconds. She bent down and spat a few words in Tyler's ear. Tyler didn't look at the girl, didn't move her gaze from the man or alter her expression, just raised her hand very slowly and tapped her fag in the girl's drink. Twice.

The girl didn't do anything at first, just looked in her drink, then back at Tyler, then at me (I looked away, then at Tyler). Tyler sucked on her fag but otherwise didn't move a muscle, just kept smiling at the dancing man. *She's fronting this out*, I thought. *Oh Jesus, this is it. This is actually it.* I didn't want to die underground, holding a plastic cup. I thought of Jim, how ashamed he'd be at the funeral. Could I run? No, I couldn't leave her. I sat there waiting to die. The girl stood by Tyler for another few seconds and then moved away. I half-expected her to come back with her pal and pulverise us, but the two of them just stood by the wall, glowering. The man danced on, oblivious or enjoying the tension. I allowed relief to dribble over me. I swigged my wine, and was about to turn and engage Tyler in conversation when –

There was a commotion over by the door. Tyler broke her gaze to look over. I looked, too. A girl had come in – coiffured and classily dressed in a black bodycon dress and red boat shoes. *Hola!* she was saying. *Hola!* She knew everyone. The music quietened and an air of reverence came over the room. The girl walked through the crowd, waving and nodding and kissing people. Someone handed her a drink, someone else a cigarette.

Marty emitted an audible gasp. 'WHA – ?'

I looked at him.

'I can't allow THIS!' he cried, throwing his fag down and stamping on it. He handed me his drink and stood up. Before I could stop him he yelled: 'WHO IS RESPONSIBLE FOR THIS CHILD?'

The club swivelled. Liquid horror and terror and multiplying mortifications.

'No, Marty,' I said, 'no, she's – '

But it was too late. He marched across the room. 'PUT THAT CIGARETTE OUT! PUT THAT DRINK DOWN! HOW OLD ARE YOU, GIRL?'

The music had stopped. The dancing had stopped. As Marty stood there, looking down, I saw his face change. He clapped a hand over his mouth.

The dwarf looked impossibly fucked off.

Someone behind me cracked their knuckles. People who had been sitting on crates began to stand up and move towards us. *We're going to die*, I thought, *going to die going to die*. I threw the drinks down, grabbed Tyler and dragged her towards the door. I presumed Marty was following.

FIRST LIGHT

We ran until we had to stop, ten or eleven streets away, Marty behind and behind him, nobody.

'I think the safest thing is to go back to mine,' he said, out of breath. 'We can get a cab. It's not far. And I've got a cellar full of fine wine.'

'Mayb – ' Tyler began.

'No,' I said. 'I've got work tomorrow evening.' I was still shaking, sober or at least felt like I was.

Tyler looked at me. She rolled her eyes and then nodded. 'All righty, don't freak.'

Marty licked his lips. There were clumps of white granddaddy spittle congealed at the corners of his mouth. They went stringy as he spoke. 'We should swap numbers at least,' he said. 'Keep in touch.'

Tyler said: 'My phone's dead. Swap with Laura.'

I pulled my phone out of my pocket. When numbers had been exchanged Marty bade us goodnight. I kissed him on the cheek. 'Thanks,' I said. I thought, *I will never see you again.*

We watched him get into a cab.

Tyler said: 'Way to let the drugs get away, Lo.'

I laughed but I didn't enjoy it, I could feel my bottom jaw moving with the laugh like a ventriloquist's dummy.

'What time is it?'

I looked at my phone, still in my hand. 'Two.'

'Three hours until the first train.'

'What shall we do? Fancy another drink? A coffee?'

She linked my arm. 'Let us wander the streets and at first light press our noses up against the window of a Poundstretcher whereupon I shall recite Sassoon in a solemn voice . . .'

In the end we just sat on the picnic table outside Euston, fending off stag dos. London was a jungle full of lonely hunters and I felt old in it – gummy, declawed. 'Have any of you got any drugs?' Tyler kept asking people. 'No? Then fuck off.'

As I smoked I scrolled through my phone contacts – I still had Jacqueline's number, and Kirsten's, and Maud's.

'I fucked him, you know,' Tyler said. 'Back at uni.'

I looked at her. 'Why does that not surprise me?' I felt like I might throw up and knew it would be fine if I did, which helped stop me.

'He was dirty. *Really dirty.*'

'I don't really want to think about it.'

'Sure you don't, Little Miss Spanky.'

When I was ten and Mel was twelve she and I used to play a game, the objective of which was to take it in turns to catch and spank one another hard. Of course, we got caught, in spectacular style, in my bedroom: me bent over my bed, Mel behind me, braced one foot behind the other, whacking away merrily; me pretending to cry but loving it. My dad, walking past to the toilet, was so uncertain about exactly what was going on (and I could tell, even then, that he just didn't want to even *go there*) that he didn't speak – just ran over, dragged Mel off, hurled her into her room and slammed the door on mine. He couldn't make eye contact with either of us at teatime. The only person I'd told the story to was Tyler. She'd hooted. *Explains a lot! A whole lot! And so British!*

How different the winding, stony path of the morning to the straight, solid road of the night. The sky was pigeon grey. The way the day begins decides the shade of everything.

We disembarked at Manchester just before nine. On the platform my every step felt like a decision. I was full of spinning magnets attracting and repelling their own poles: walk, sleep, drink, call, don't call, eat, sit down, don't sit down. I stopped to pick up a stranded worm off the pavement and throw it into a tub of primroses. A little further along I saw a bee, almost motionless on the pavement but still with the solidity of moving blood and air keeping it upright. It was alive. I looked around for a twig. Found a scrap of paper. Coaxed the bee on. Back to the primroses I went, knock-kneed as an apprentice plate-spinner, balancing the bee. I held the paper over a flower and nudged the bee on with my finger.

'Come on,' said Tyler.

'But there's a dying bee.'

'Oh, the karma bank, the karma bank. It'll just fuck us over, you know, like all the rest.'

When the bee was safe I pulled my phone out of my pocket. Three missed calls and two texts from Jim. He was home, at his. I could collapse there. Fuck the rules. I couldn't cope with any more surprises.

'Tyler.' She stopped walking. 'I'm going to Jim's.'

She looked at me. 'Suit yourself.'

On Oldham Street I passed shop fronts shut up and not just for the night. Cash loan exchanges, pawnbrokers, boarded-up newsagents. Down past the CIS, the half-built Co-op. Victoria Station. The cathedral. The dripping-moss bridge. Knew I was almost at Jim's when I heard the ragged sound of the metal sign spinning outside the laundrette on the corner. I thought he'd probably still be in bed, jetlagged or just lying-in.

I slithered along the main hall and fumbled my key into the lock. A scratch as the key bit. Once I was inside, I attempted to undress. It was as tricky as unlocking a door. At the sound of a creak, I looked up, half-naked, to see Jim standing in the doorway of the bedroom.

'I thought this was going to stop.'

I hopped backwards, one leg still in my tights. 'It is,' I said when I came to a standstill.

He went back into the bedroom and in the time it took me to gather up my clothes he came back out with an armful of bedding. 'This way,' he said. I followed him into the lounge and watched him make up a bed on the couch.

'You serious?'

'Yep.' He kissed me as he passed. 'Sweet dreams.'

'Jim!'

'Nope.'

I lay on the sofa, feeling my heart pounding in my chest. I got up. Went to the toilet. The window. The kitchen. The lounge. I watched the red fireflies of the entertainment system's standby lights. I went back to the couch and got back under the covers. I listened to a lawnmower.

Jim got up around noon. I was lying on the sofa, Pterodactyl-style, my hands up like claws near my chest. I was watching a cookery programme that was making me feel sick but I couldn't move to find the remote to turn it over. Instead I was wincing every time the presenter said 'boil' or 'butter'.

'Morning.'

'Morning.'

'Good time in London then?'

'All right.'

'You know that shit comes into the country sewn into some poor bastard's leg.'

He was holding a mug of something. I swung my legs round and sat myself up. Jesus. All the warning lights across the dash of my forehead were flashing. 'What are you drinking?'

'Coffee.'

'Is it fairtrade?'

He looked at me. 'Don't you dare.'

'No, don't *you* dare. All I've done was have a little holiday with my friend when I never go fucking anywhere and it didn't even turn out that great, and on top of all that I'm so fucking worried about my dad.'

The Dying Dad Card. I played it.

'I know you are. That's partly the reason we're doing all this so quickly.'

I looked at him. He'd actually said it. Trumped me. He looked down, ashamed. Softer: 'What happened?'

'Just . . . I didn't have the greatest time, Jim.'

He came and sat next to me, put his arm round me, kissed my neck. 'You stink,' he said into my ear.

'Mm hm.'

'I sort of like it.'

'I know.'

I kissed his neck and his chest, working my way down to the top of his boxers and then pulling them down, using my mouth. He moved onto his side and tried to pull me up and turn me round, but I kept facing him and said from the plateau of his belly 'I need a shower', then moved back down with my mouth, finished him so I could also be sure – You know. I didn't know where I was up to.

After, he said: 'I'm playing Stockholm a week on Sunday. Why don't you come?'

'It's Tyler's thirtieth.'

'What, all weekend?'

TWO FRIENDS

It didn't seem to want to be summer any more. Late June and the leaves on the trees were tugging at the branches. Some of them had even managed to wrench themselves free, landing on the ground shiny and curling at the ends, like dying fish. I stood outside Jacqueline's house in Chorltonville for many minutes before I plucked up the courage to walk up and ring on the bell (the handle of which hung from the ceiling of the porch like the whistle-blower on a steam train). There were two pairs of pristine wellies by the side of the mat.

Jacqueline opened the door. She was wearing a floral tea dress, leggings and thick-soled sandals. Her toenails were painted black. 'Laura! How nice to see you! Won't you come in?'

She kissed me on both cheeks and held my hands for a moment. I squeezed her hands, shaking them. I don't know what I was hoping for – something to be conducted between us: prehistoric camaraderie, maturity, contentment. Nothing came. I followed her down the hall, closing the front door behind me. Jacqueline's house was cool and calm. Everything was magnolia and lemon and pine. She led me into the lounge, where a toddler was sitting on the rug in front of an unlit wood-burning stove. The toddler stared at me, a teddy drooping in its hand, and started to cry.

'Now, now,' said Jacqueline, walking towards the toddler and picking it up. The baby stopped crying but hid behind her shoulder. 'This is my old friend Laura. Are you going to say Hello? Say, Hello Laura!'

Awkward silence. The baby didn't look old enough to talk.

'Hello,' I said.

More crying.

Jacqueline tutted and bounced her hip. 'She's a mard-arse,' she said, 'just like her daddy.' She nodded to the wall above the wood-burner. There was a wedding photo on a shelf, in between a posh candle and a record that had been made into a clock. On the photo, Jacqueline was wearing a big white flouncy dress and the man standing beside her had closely clipped hair and narrow glasses, his mouth open in a downward smile, the smile of forced glee. He looked like a children's television presenter.

'Bore,' said the toddler, pointing down at the floor.

'Ball,' said Jacqueline, 'that's right – where is your ball?'

'Bore,' said the toddler again, looking at me.

'What's her name?' I said.

'Daisy.'

'Cute.'

'Thanks. Do you want a brew?'

'Please. Hey, do you mind if I use your bathroom while you put the kettle on?'

'Go for your life. Top of the stairs and left.'

On the first-floor landing there was a *Never Mind the Bollocks* poster in a gilded frame. As I sat on the toilet I held on to the wedding invite in the pocket of my jeans so that it wouldn't fall out. I read the backs of three shampoo bottles.

Back downstairs, Daisy was bashing coloured blocks together on the floor. She stopped when she saw me, looked at Jacqueline, and wailed. I looked away and sat down, ignoring her the way I ignored Zuzu. Daisy stopped wailing and the sound of block-bashing began again. I looked at Jacqueline. She picked her tea up from by her sandals and pointed to a mug down by the side of my chair. I picked up the tea and took a sip. Scaldy-hot. I took another sip.

'So when did you leave the Red Room, then?' I said when I could.

'Not long after you. Four months, maybe five. Those 3 a.m. finishes! They're a killer. What have you been up to since?'

'I work in a call centre.'

A pause, then: 'See, much better hours, you know what I mean. Neil's an accountant so we get something like a normal life at the evenings and weekends.'

'Well, my shifts are pretty unpredictable. It's a twenty-four-hour service. Credit cards.' I didn't know why but it was almost as though part of me was enjoying making out I did the worst thing in the world. I think I was trying to embarrass her or convince myself or both.

Jacqueline's maggoty toes hunched in her sandals.

'Don't get me wrong – I still overdo the vino on a Saturday night sometimes!'

'Yeah.' I looked towards the shelf over the fireplace.

'Are you married?' she said.

'No.' The corner of the invite was spearing my thigh.

'Kids?'

I shook my head.

'But you want them?'

'Not sure. Less and less, to be honest.'

Jacqueline looked crestfallen, as though a childless woman was The Most Tragic Thing she could think of. The spinster aunt of fairy tales. The witch of modern society. I sipped my tea. It was still too hot. I let my body shudder with the pain.

'I want *loads of kids*. Loads of boys,' she said.

Don't say it. *Do not* say it.

'A whole football team.'

I thought about pouring the tea over my head. Silence as we both worked our way through a few more stifling gulps.

'Neil thinks we should wait a bit before the next, but as a

woman you've got a biological window, haven't you?' (*A euphemism.*) 'I've tried talking to him about it but he just looks at me like some kind of stupid dog. And the thing is I want to have another baby before I'm thirty-five . . .'

I tried to picture them having sex: Jacqueline homicidal with productivity, him rigid with generosity. Neither of them speaking, before, during, or after. The Inarticulate Conception.

'How did you know you wanted a baby?' I said.

She looked at me.

'I mean, did you feel it as a desire that was totally yours? Or was it a case of feeling like some sort of failure if you didn't? I'm sorry, I just – I'm so curious about this. You know all the language around pregnancy is so against us from the start – you *lose* a baby. You fail at life somehow if you don't manage it. But it's just a physical state, isn't it, so why is there a value attached? Or did you love her, Daisy I mean, when she was *in there*, did you feel that? Because that changes things, I'm sure. I suppose I'm just scared of not knowing why I'm doing what I'm doing.'

Jacqueline said: 'I think I felt like I might be missing out on something.'

I paused. I knew what she meant, sort of. Still. 'Isn't that just the brat in you, though, wanting everything? Because that's no good, either. I'm not judging you, by the way. I'm a total brat.'

She looked at me. Looked down.

'Hey,' I said, regretting everything I'd said – *what was I doing here?* – 'I still use your White Piss Good; Amber Piss Bad rule. Like almost every day.'

Jacqueline brought her hand to her mouth, looked to one side, racking. 'Did I say that?'

'Yeah, I mean, I think it was you.'

I could still see her face as she said it, the bar's reflected optics lighting the shafts of peroxide in her hair.

'Do you remember the gimp?' I said, desperately.

She thought for a moment. 'Oh yeah! The gimp. We got all sorts, didn't we?'

Lying. These things you treasure, how often they're somebody else's trash. I looked around. I felt sad as fuck in that little showroom. I looked at my phone. 'Oh!' I said, 'I've got to get to work . . .'

'It was nice to see you, Laura,' said Jacqueline. 'Wasn't it, Daisy? Say, Bye Laura.'

Daisy looked at me. 'Bye, Daisy,' I said.

'What you up to this weekend?' Jacqueline said.

'Oh, I'm probably going to go out and take lots of drugs.'

She did a coughy laugh. 'You serious?' I smiled. 'God, I haven't taken drugs for years.'

She looked down at the baby on the floor and kicked it, gently, with her foot.

On my way to the office I posted the wedding invite into the grinning maw of a black metal bin. When I got to my desk I accessed my personal email (*Verboten* but fuckit), and dropped Maud the Painter a line.

My phone rang that evening about half past eight. Tyler picked it up and handed it to me. 'Unknown number,' she said. She reached for the remote to turn down the TV.

'I'll take it in my room.'

She narrowed her eyes as I backed out and closed the door. I waited until my bedroom door was closed before I answered.

'Maud!' I said, swigging wine. 'How are you?'

'Oh, you know, drunk.'

'Me too.'

I wished I'd brought a cigarette in, to smoke.

'Are you okay?' she said. 'I thought there might be something wrong when I got your mail.'

'Oh no, I'm fine, just, you know, been a while.'

'Ten or twelve years.'

'What are you up to? Are you still painting?'

'Yes. Are you still in Manchester?'

'Yes. Are you still in Bristol?'

'No, St Ives. I moved to Somerset, then Penzance, and then here in 2006 to be with Ann. I'm still here, somehow. Ann's a gallery owner. I know what you're thinking.'

'I'm thinking it's really great you're still painting.'

'And it must be handy to be fucking a gallery owner, right? Especially when all I do is peddle cowardice fluffed up as *truth . . .*'

'No, Maud, I – '

'None of it stands up, though, does it? Are you still writing your stories?'

'Sort of.'

'I've Googled you a few times but I couldn't find much.'

'That's not surprising.'

'And you're not on Facebook, are you? I mean *I'm* not on Facebook but I go on sometimes at night in stealth mode. Ann says I should set up an artist's page but I'm not the sort of person to do that, know what I mean?'

'Mm.'

'Otherwise she won't help me. She hates my art. Everyone hates my art.'

'Fuck them!' I said, trying to be supportive. 'You always did okay in Manchester.'

'No, I didn't. I ran out of things to paint in literally five minutes.'

I thought, *That's because you painted your own floor, walking backwards. And now you're on tiptoes in the corner.* But I was never honest with Maud, that was part of the problem – the problem ultimately being we merely used each other as a spittoon for catharsis.

'Say, I really thought there must be something wrong with you when I got your mail. I was going to offer you somewhere to stay.'

'No, I'm fine. I'm – '

'I thought you must be heartbroken or losing your mind.'

'No more than usual. I was born that way, remember? Brokenhearted.'

She laughed at this. I wanted to kill myself.

'You should come visit me,' she said, 'that'd make you feel better about your own life. Come and see this fucking awful situation I've got myself into.'

'I might have some time later in the year.'

I would not.

'Well, you've got my number now.'

'I have. Thanks for calling, Maud.'

Well, what else is there to do sometimes except fall back on politeness and get the fuck out? I sat for a while, my legs dangling off the end of my bed, feeling dried out with smashed exhilaration, the internal post-funeral dunes. Both of the day's encounters had left the taste of ash in my mouth. There was just something so sickening about that sparkless reanimation – and you didn't know how sickening it would be until you tried. Like sucking on a gone-out cigarette.

A knock. I sat up, guilty.

'Jim's on *my* phone for you,' Tyler shouted from behind the door.

I got up, slid the clothes rail to one side, and opened the door. She handed me the phone.

'He said he couldn't get you on yours.'

She closed the door but I knew she was still there, listening.

'I've only got five minutes,' Jim said. 'Sorry to stalk you.'

I cleared my throat. 'I think you get special dispensation where stalking is concerned.'

'Are you moving some stuff over to mine tomorrow?'

'Yes.'

He laughed. 'You'd forgotten, hadn't you?'

'No!' I had. 'Hey, Jim – I meant it when I said ask Kirsten to the wedding.' I whispered. 'Who cares if it puts a few noses out of joint. It's our fucking wedding and I like her. She's . . . proper, you know.'

Worth a shot. A floorboard creaked behind the door.

'I'll ask her.'

YOU CAN'T HANDLE VERMOUTH

When I heard a shriek from the living room I dropped the bin bag I was holding and slung aside the clothes rail.

'SHE'S TURNING INSIDE OUT!' Tyler screamed.

It didn't look good. Zuzu had a strange, squishy lump on her anus. At first Tyler thought it was a winnet but after several wrenches with a tea towel it became apparent that the object was attached to Zuzu on a far more fundamental level. When Tyler finally got a hold on the protrusion she tugged hard, only for it to stretch two inches out of Zuzu, prompting a shriek from the cat, who scarpered away, mystery appendage trailing.

'We've got to get her to the vet's!'

Tyler managed to catch the cat and bundle her into her cage. Zuzu thrashed around and bit the bars, gagging on them, backing up and retching with fury – we could hear her still doing it even when Tyler put her jacket over the cage. The cab driver was perturbed. *That cage is waterproof, right?*

When we got in the vet's there was a heavy-breathing Rottweiler on the other side of the waiting room. Zuzu went quiet. The three of us regarded the dog as we waited. When our turn was called we stood up and Zuzu let out a thin mewl. I looked at Tyler. She had tears in her eyes. 'I hate to see her like this,' she said. 'So *resigned*.'

In the consulting room the vet inspected Zuzu and looked at Tyler. 'Has she been alone for any amount of time recently?'

'Two days. I was down south.'

'You do know that's too long to leave an animal unattended?'

'What's wrong with her?'

'She seems to have resorted to eating hosiery.'

'Hosiery? I don't keep hosiery.'

The vet motioned to her assistant, who came over and held Zuzu while the vet gently took hold of the protrusion and pulled it gently. Zuzu let out a low howl but didn't move. The vet held the offending item up in all its glory. It was a glittery stocking. Jim's most sexual gift.

'That's mine!' I said. 'That's why I could only find one when I was packing!'

The vet looked at me.

Back in the waiting room Tyler put the cage on the counter and pulled a packet of toy mice off a display stand. 'Do these have catnip in?' she asked the receptionist.

'Yes,' the receptionist replied.

'Good. I'll take five packs. She deserves them.'

At the flat Tyler released Zuzu and went to the toilet. I went into the kitchen and started unpacking the bag of cocktail ingredients she'd bought to cheer us up.

'Give her a mouse!' Tyler shouted from the bathroom.

I opened one of the packets of mice and threw a blue mouse down the hall. Zuzu looked at me, then at the mouse, then back at me. She scissored her legs and began licking a splayed back foot. 'She won't play,' I shouted.

'How are you doing it?'

'I dunno, throwing it.'

'Drag it along by the wall. You have to make it seem as though it's looking for shelter. Cats love that shit. My dad used to say that their pleasure in cruelty showed a certain level of intelligence. We had about ten of them living around the ranch. Feral but dignified. He found one of them dead on the porch one winter, frozen solid. He picked it up and carried it round the back of the house and rapped on the kitchen window with it. My mom said it was stretched out completely stiff, like a baguette.'

The toilet flushed. She came out into the hall.

'How did that go?'

She grimaced. 'Slugs in jelly. It's the stress.' Zuzu started vigorously scratching the carpet, looking at Tyler. 'Yes, you're so good at scratching. Really, I have raised a magnificent little show-off. I could not be more proud.'

The cat jumped up on the window, looked out at the rain, turned back to Tyler and howled.

'Yes, yes, dearest,' Tyler said, walking over to Zuzu and stroking her. She turned to me. 'I can't go away again. I can't abandon her like that. To her, I am God. Look, see, right now she's saying, *Turn the big light back on, would you?* I control her food, her warmth, her entertainment. Why would I not be in control of the sun?'

'That's the beauty of pets, I guess. They never outgrow you.'

'Too true. She will never look down on me and say, *You fucking mess.* She will always be in awe. Now how about a martini? I don't think I can handle any more packing today.'

I looked to where she'd been sorting books. There were barely ten in a pile I supposed was mine. I stared at them for a few minutes and then shrugged and followed her to the kitchen. She took two different-sized martini glasses from the cupboard and put them in the fridge. She rinsed a jam jar with vermouth and poured it out into a bowl. Shook vodka with ice in the jam jar and prepared to strain it with a cheese grater. Tyler made great martinis. *That's right, I sold my soul for mixology skills. So who's the big fool? Satan, that's who! SUCKER.* She hooked up her phone to the digital radio to play music through the speakers and put on one of her favourites: 'Cocktails for Two' by Spike Jones & His City Slickers.

She handed me a martini. The song giddied up with a whizz and a pop. 'I've been thinking about my birthday.'

My mind flicked to Stockholm and back again.

'Jeannie was going to come up for it and get a break from the baby but she's been back in rehab.'

'Fuck.' I put my cocktail down. '*Fuck.*'

Tyler slurped her martini. 'Best place for her. I think the christening sent her under.'

'So it'll just be me, you and Nick.'

'Nick?'

'Yes, he's one of us, don't worry.'

'I didn't realise you'd got so close.'

She tilted her head. 'Oh yes, I quite like him. He treats sex like it's a race. He just fires ahead and says *That's me!* when he comes. Then he rolls off. But I'm onto him now, so I go for it and shout *LOSER!* in his face when I beat him. It feels like a really honest transaction.'

My phone beeped in my pocket. I pulled it out and looked at the screen.

Kirsten can't do it but says thanks x

'Oh, that's a shame,' I said.

'What is?'

'They can't get organic ham for the buffet, only beef.'

She started making a second round of martinis. I drank half of mine in one gulp. Bliss, there, for a second, in the unsullied alcohol. I felt my blood being exchanged for vodka and was glad. My phone beeped again in my hand. I looked at it, thinking Jim might have sent the message twice by mistake or be following up – but no.

A picture message.

A pink-grey thing, for which interpretations rolled and wrestled within my mind's back-catalogue of similar objects – balloon animals, raw sausage, *Nessie*? – before the undeniable truth.

A Penis.

More specifically An Erect Penis.

More specifically Not Jim's Erect Penis.

Marty Grane's.

I stared at it, too shocked to even blink. I was transfixed. On a distant planet somewhere, Tyler was shaking the jar again.

The photo had been taken from above. It looked as though Marty was sitting in an armchair, around which variously patterned fabrics – hoisted plaid shirt, Persian rug, chintzy upholstery – ringed the main event. His trousers were down to his knees. His balls were quite bald compared to Jim's. Possibly shaved. Imagination caught the pass and ran with it: Marty, naked, foot up on the side of the bath, beavering away with a Gillette Venus . . .

Could it be a mistake? (*Oh HI, my good angel! Been a while!*) Could Marty have confused my number with one of his 'non-regulars'? If so, then any minute he'd realise and I'd receive a mortified follow-up that would be almost as messy to field. I couldn't bear the thought of having to console him about this.

'You know what they give you at Alcoholics Anonymous in the States, to mark your progress?'

Someone somewhere was talking to me.

'Laura?' I looked. At Tyler. 'You okay?'

I turned my phone off. 'Mm-hm.'

'Poker chips.'

I felt every passing second keenly – knowing that, even if he had meant to send me the photo then every second of my non-replying would intensify his shame. He'd be pacing right now, beating his chest, his horror reducing, reducing, reducing down to one single word. *WHY?*

In the background, the song played on. I stashed my phone in my pocket.

'What's the matter? Is it Jim?'

'No. I – '

'You get a different-coloured chip for however long you last.'

'Um.'

'Know what colour the last chip is, the Ultimate Chip, to say you've been sober a year?'

'Pink?'

'No, dummy. Black. Don't you think it's strange, though, referencing another addiction? I mean, what do they give you at Gamblers Anonymous, shot glasses?'

BANDITS

'You sure you can't see my nipples?'

Friday night. Her thirtieth birthday. The balcony of a first-floor champagne bar off Peter Street. The monstrous blade-phallus of the Hilton Tower in view.

'They're fine,' I said.

'I don't mind the general thrust being perceptible,' she said. 'I just don't want areola contours, you know.'

She was wearing a cowl-necked gold lamé dress that stuck to her curves like plating. Backed by the twilit city, with her gold eyelids and bronze lips, she looked like something *made*.

I'd come straight from the call centre after getting changed in the toilets. My work clothes and make-up bag were in a carrier bag under the table. I kept nudging it with my foot so I wouldn't forget it. I kept thinking about the flight I had to make. I hadn't yet packed. But it would be fine, totally fine. I had a whole morning to do it. I didn't have to be at the airport until noon tomorrow.

The waitress came out to take our order.

'Vodka-tonic, please,' Tyler said.

'Same for me, please.'

The waitress nodded. 'We only serve doubles – is that okay?'

Tyler looked at her. 'BANDITS.'

The waitress went inside.

Tyler plonked herself in a chair and lit a fag. The fabric of her dress folded into ripples above her lap.

'How's your day been?' I said.

Her arm shimmered as she placed the lighter on the table. 'I had two croissants this morning to line my stomach, like a true sophisticate. A liquid lunch. And then an afternoon of domestic drudgery.'

'You haven't been doing housework, have you?'

'Jesus, no. But first off Jean called to wish me Happy Birthday and told me she felt high from cleaning the shower in her rehab room with Cillit Bang. I pretended the line was bad and hung up. Then, when I was doing my eyeliner, someone cold-called me to ask what brand my washing machine was.'

There wasn't a washing machine in the flat.

'What did you say?'

'Well, it's the first time I've had to spell H-I-T-L-E-R.'

Our vodka-tonics arrived. I took a large swig and crunched an ice cube in my teeth. The bar was busy and loud, blasts of commotion making us turn and look whenever anyone came outside to smoke. At one point someone fell over inside and the bouncers rushed to drag them out.

'Amateur night,' said Tyler. 'Almost as bad as New Year's Eve.'

My phone beeped. I looked at it. A text from . . . bracing, bracing . . . Jim.

'Is he keeping you in check?' Tyler said. 'Coordinating my birthday from afar? The audacity of the man. This is weapons-grade passive-aggression, Lo, and you mustn't stand for it.'

'Hush. He's just looking forward to seeing me, that's all. Now, do you want another drink?'

The door swung open and a man came out carrying a tray. He looked familiar. I scanned his face. The android screen locked and flashed. Identity confirmed. Nick.

'Hey, cutie,' Tyler said. I looked at her. At him.

On the tray there was an orange ice bucket with a green bottleneck protruding and three shiny flutes lying on the ice like fish. Nick did the honours – the cork firing off towards a nearby table and causing someone to dodge it like a bullet. He poured us all a flute. I downed the remains of my vodka-tonic in anticipation. He handed a flute to Tyler and she pulled his hand further up to her lips and kissed his knuckles.

They smiled at each other. I necked half my glass of champagne. Look on the bright side, I told myself, you can leave early now.

Nick said: 'I hope you're both proud of me. I have managed to store something special all week in the medicine cabinet. It's burned a hole in the fucking wall, let me tell you. Every time I've gone for a shower or a piss I've nodded towards it and said, *Soon . . .*'

My stomach fluttered, a minor thrutch. A dog responding to a bell.

Tyler took his hand under the table and went to the bathroom first. Nick brought his flute to his lips and sucked back champagne in a long, smooth inhalation. His eyes were very very black. Whatever Tyler was being introduced to in the bathroom, Nick had been acquainted with for quite a few hours.

'How's the exhibition going?'

'Well, thanks. Looks like we'll be taking it to Berlin in autumn.'

'Congratulations.'

'How's the wedding coming?'

I wondered what Tyler had divulged. These drunken indiscretions, how often we mistake them for intimacies.

'Almost ready. Just a few loose ends to tie up.'

'I heard that the ham's been problematic.'

I drained my flute. Nick refilled it.

Tyler barged back out onto the balcony and took a seat. 'Fuck's sake,' she said, grabbing her champagne and tipping it down her neck. 'It's like a fucking *roux*.'

Nick smiled. 'It's worth it, don't worry.'

I watched it possess her. She became a metal shell of purest night. 'Jesus,' she said. 'Where did you . . .?'

Nick poured more champagne. 'Don't leave Laura out.'

She passed it to me under the table. I slipped it into the side of my bag and made my way to the bathroom. But when I got into the cubicle I found I couldn't do it, didn't want to. I rubbed the little bag and thought – well, the word that came to mind was, hilariously, *fuckit*. I could see the future too clearly. The memories we'd make tonight would not be new ones even though they might look like it on the surface. Given the same stimuli the brain makes the same connections and distracts you with emotion so you feel like they're new. I liked distraction well enough. I also liked the idea of free will.

I went back out to the balcony and passed the bag back to Nick. While he was gone, Tyler said: 'Why not?'

'Don't fancy it.'

'It's really fucking good.' Her voice was claggy.

I stayed with them drinking, watching their disintegration, and before long it was all talk of the past week's social triumphs accompanied by clumsy footsie.

'Look, do you want me to go?' I whispered as Nick charged to the toilet for the fifth time. Who had it? I'd lost track of their clandestine pass-the-parcel.

'No,' she said, 'stay.'

I tried to distract myself by watching the people coming and going inside the bar, trying to work out how they knew each other, how much they cared. An hour or so later, a woman walked in who I thought looked familiar. The woman was about forty judging by the speed at which she moved, skinny and nervous, but her face looked much older, with sunken cheeks and deep crow's feet, stringy hair coiled into a knot high on the back of her head. She made her way over to the bar, followed by a pair of men in their twenties in jumpers and jeans. As I turned to Tyler to ask whether she recognised her I saw that her face was ashen and she had started to slide very slowly under the table. Nick was watching her, none the wiser.

'Tyler,' I said, 'isn't that – '

Tyler didn't say a word, just kept sliding. When she was fully under the table she looked up at me and nodded. Mouthed *MARIE*.

I put my legs forward to obscure her, in case Marie looked over to the window and could see beneath the table. I looked over at Nick. 'Nick,' I said, 'don't make it obvious but there's someone just come in that we really need to avoid – that Tyler especially needs to avoid.' He nodded. *Yeah, and?* I went on. 'So the best thing to do is look at me as though I'm saying something really interesting and possibly even slightly funny and let's hope that they either leave or move to a place where we can get Tyler out without them seeing her.' He nodded again. Stopped nodding and laughed uproariously. 'Okay, don't overdo it. We don't want them to look over at us specially, but if they happen to glance at us we need to look as though we're utterly engrossed in each other rather than pretending that somebody isn't hiding under the table.'

I prayed that Marie or whatever she was called wouldn't recognise me. I'd been round to hers once with Tyler – a terraced street in Belle Vue so forgotten that it was practically a study in post-industrial melancholy – and waited outside, trying not to look through the front window's slipped nets. Beneath the table, Tyler had her hand around my ankle, squeezing gently.

'She's asking the barman something,' Nick said, smiling. He was doing well, considering. Clearly he was enjoying a mission.

'Right,' I said, smiling back. 'Is she buying a drink? Don't look for a bit but . . .'

'No,' Nick said, gazing lovingly at me, 'no, she's turning around.'

'Okay, stop looking.'

'She's walking out.'

Through gritted teeth: 'Stop looking!'

'She's gone.'

A cold wash of relief. 'How about the boys?'

'Gone.'

I looked down to Tyler. She climbed out, sat down and emptied the bottle.

I went to the bathroom to cool down. It was tiled like a Parisian subway, all Fifties emerald and cream. There was a bank of four butler's sinks along one wall, big rectangular bowls and arching taps. I put the plug in to get a nice little pool to cool down with, but the water was so inviting I had the urge to get closer, to lap at it.

I told myself that I would go back to Tyler's for a polite hour and then head over to Jim's.

As we walked to Hulme I went ahead at every corner to check that Marie and her henchmen weren't waiting. After fifteen minutes we reached the bridge over the Mancunian Way. I stopped to spark up. A taxi went past, engine clattering. The noise of the traffic on the motorway below was terrible, like something huge that was breathing too hard. I looked ahead, and saw Tyler and Nick walking arm in arm. A feeling of relief washed over me. As though I could slip away and leave them to it.

A few weeks after I'd moved in with Tyler I woke in her bed to find her gone. As I strained in the darkness I heard the front door click shut. I got up and went to the door, opened it, and heard the main door slam downstairs. I went down, barefoot, my pyjamas loose and letting the cold in. I hugged myself as I opened the main door and stepped out into the night. She was walking twenty metres or so ahead. I followed her down the road and then right along the next road towards town, past the chicken-wired scrubland. It was the very middle of the night – that exact point between late and early – when everything is poised, waiting, and not a bird or an engine breaks the stillness. I had to be very quiet. I thought she might be sleepwalking and you know what they say about waking sleepwalkers but also I didn't want her to stop. I followed her to the bridge, stopping when she stopped and concealing myself behind the base of a streetlamp. She started to climb, stood on the third rung, her boot heels biting the steel and hooking her on. She raised her arms like a warlock and tipped back her head. She stood there for a long time, fifteen minutes or so, just balancing. I knew she was awake. I left when I saw her start to get down, went back to the flat and got back in bed, pretended to be asleep.

Back at her place she poured us each a glass of wine and then smeared the remains of the night onto a CD case. She did. He did. I didn't. There was blood on the note they were using. Tyler noticed and said, 'One for the wash.'

Nick lay across the sofa (a true gent) and I sat on a cushion on the floor by the coffee table, tapping my fag in a dead beer can. Tyler brought out the jar from the ice-box, too, chucked some of that down for good measure, and stood in the middle of the room talking. Whenever Nick or I tried to interject she interrupted and talked over us until we ceased; surrendered to the Mighty Goddess of Birthday. I checked my phone. It was 1 a.m. I could leave soon.

I looked at Nick. He seemed oblivious to everything except Tyler's tits jiggling in her dress. Saucer-eyed, rubbing her rigid arms, rocking back and forth, she looked like a T. rex having a mild epileptic fit. She jiggled over and took a fag from my packet. Took my lighter and jiggled back to her position centre-stage. Put the fag in her mouth. 'I can't be doing with it,' she said, around the cigarette. I stood up and walked towards her, turned the cigarette in her mouth the right way round and lit it.

'What's that?' I said.

'Oral.'

I looked at Nick. He was looking at Tyler. How had they got onto – ?

'What, not at all?' Nick said.

Jim's. Bathroom, then Jim's.

'Nah. It's frustrating. It's like some fucker hovering with the lighter or the note. I feel like saying, Put a cock in it, love.'

'Typical,' said Nick. 'You spend decades telling us you're not getting enough – '

'Try centuries sweetheart and who is this "you"?'

' – and now we're doing it – '

'It's not me this "you" I know that much.'

' – too much. There's no – '

'Be specific that's the first rule of argument you silly boy.'

' – pleasing Women.'

'Oh whinge whinge whinge you know I'd have a lot more sex if I didn't meet so many fucking whingers and ditherers last guy I slept with was down there for hours I wanted to say look my friend I appreciate the effort but the sensation went a while ago.'

'Hey, Tyler,' I said, 'I'm calling a cab.'

'So this is a length issue?' Nick said. A wonky smile at his own mangled cleverness.

'Not so much as a variety issue.'

'Tyler.'

Any minute now he's going to start asking her for tips. The conversational orgy going back to basics; Tyler taking advantage: Hey, maybe I can just show you, that'd be quicker. On your knees, pilgrim!

She looked at me.

'I said I'm calling a cab.'

'A cab? Where?'

'Jim's. I've got my flight tomorrow afternoon.'

'So you're leaving?'

I looked at her face. Crushed and spoiled and hole-punched near the top with two nocturnal-woodland-creature pupils. She was six years old with two people at her birthday party. She was a worm, drying out in the sun . . .

'I am if you keep talking about your sex life.'

She looked at me. I looked at Nick. 'Jesus,' she said. 'I was only talking.'

'We were only talking,' Nick parroted.

Tyler seemed to remember she had a cigarette in her hand and looked at it with a sort of strained, Botox-gauche surprise-delight (one eyebrow half-involved, forehead struggling to catch up), and took a drag. 'So there was this one time me and Lo were at a festival and we got home and she had a shower and this insect fell out of her *vagina*.'

'It fell out of my *pubes*.'

'Whatever it was, a fucking tick or something – '

It was a tick. Bloated and slightly frilled round the edge, like a broad bean. It had been living in the crease of my groin and I hadn't noticed because for two days I'd only taken a piss in a long-drop toilet, in the dark – barely wiping, never mind inspecting myself.

'Really, Tyler, I thought we agreed to save this anecdote for dinner parties . . .'

' – so she had to shave off all her pubes like for a Hollywood or Shirley Temple or whatever the fuck they call it and when she came out the bathroom I was there and I said *JESUS LO THAT HAIRCUT'S TAKEN YEARS OFF YOU*.'

It took Nick a minute. Well, five seconds. It felt like a minute. It felt like a fucking *age*. Then he burst out laughing and had to sit himself up on the sofa so he didn't choke. Tyler was dancing to what I could only presume was the sound, in her head, of her own wit resonating off the walls. When he'd finished laughing, Nick said: 'Why are you freaking out? It's barely Saturday.'

'I'm not freaking out.'

Fucking artist. Who actually called themself 'an artist'? Did he have business cards with his name, colon, 'Artist' on them? Was Tyler actually going to fuck him, again? His eyes were all pupil. If he managed to get an erection tonight then I'd eat my own pussy. Lengthily.

'You need to chill your beans,' he said. He looked at me. Tyler laughed. I knew what this was. I looked at the CD case. Hackles rose on my neck and back, accompanied by a sudden recollection of a sibling roughhousing. Melanie screaming on rollerboots, smashing her temple into the brake-light of my mum's car as I spun her round, rage-fast . . .

'Give me that fucking note.'

So: first, honour – and then a bigger balloon expanded inside: brazen exhibitionism. I ran into my room to get my laptop. Ran back. 'I'm going to read you the beginning of my novel.'

'Here's to that,' said Nick, raising his glass.

In all honesty I was starting to like the guy.

At 4 a.m. I told myself 5 a.m. was my absolute cut-off point. 5 a.m. would be totally fine.

'Have you ever listened to the Beach Boys?' said Nick. 'I mean, really listened? There's never a pause. There's always something upfront. The Beach Boys never stop.'

'Fuck *that*,' I said, 'who wants to hear some Yeats?'

At 9 a.m. I said ten was fine. Fine. Absolutely. I could always have a shower when I got to Stockholm, at the hotel. All I had to do was pack, which was easy. I could even go straight from Tyler's – no need to go via Jim's.

At 11.30 a.m. the Fear and Horror hit me. I ran in and out of my room, flailing, grabbing at random items of clothing.

'DON'T PANIC!' Tyler said.

'I'M NOT PANICKING!'

I called a cab, grabbed my barely packed bag and ran out of the flat with half my jacket on. I heard Nick's laughter resonating all the way down the stairs.

The taxi company sent a minibus. Of course they did. The drive lasted four hundred thousand years. At the airport I checked in and then went to the Ladies before security. I emptied out my handbag, checking and double-checking each compartment of my purse. I made eye contact with the security staff once each and no more. I walked like an innocent. I bought a diet soft drink from a machine and drank it in a corner by the gate until my flight was called. On the plane I adopted the brace position, made it my own.

BUSKERS

Jim couldn't meet me at Arlanda due to rehearsals so I took the airport bus to the City Terminal and walked to the tunnelbana. I stood by the entrance of T-Centralen station listening to a solo violin rendition of 'Smoke Gets in Your Eyes'. The busker finished the song with a flourish, a dreadful sort of deadening *Wogan* chord, and struck up another I didn't recognise. I bought a ticket, dropped a coin into the plush hollow of the open violin case and moved into the dirty-warm air down the stairs.

Stockholm is a city of islands. The old town, Gamla Stan, is a maze of winding pedestrian streets packed with shops where you can buy fripperies or stop in a café for a 'fika', that Swedish ritual of afternoon coffee and cake. We were staying on a floating hotel, a refurbished cruise ship from the Fifties, anchored at Söder Mälarstrand. A little blue bridge connected the boat to the dock. Checking in, surrounded by wood and russet leather, felt like stepping into an Agatha Christie novel. On the far wall, the side of the ship, small gingham curtains were bunched either side of six or seven porthole windows.

After I'd checked in I dropped my bag in the cabin – which I was relieved to see had a double bed; I'd been dreading some unromantic bunk-bed situation whereby jokes about who got to go on top could have only alleviated the disappointment for so long – and brushed my teeth in the cubicle shower-room. I washed the holy trinity.

I had a wander en route to the venue. Scandinavian design

seemed almost utopian. The whole city hummed with the promise of telepathy. I walked round admiring the buildings, the strange familiarity of it deepening – I tried to think where it was in the world that Stockholm reminded me of. Where had I been that was similar? Then I realised. Stockholm reminded me of Jim. I loved him. I did. Sometimes.

At the concert I was seated in a box alongside the venue manager and his wife. I had learnt the Swedish for 'Thank you' ('tack') and said it repeatedly, like an imbecile, whenever either of them looked at me. I'd decided not to have a drink before I saw Jim but the urge to dash out to the foyer and buy one before the concert started was strong – especially when I saw the venue manager and his wife attacking a bottle of champagne. I resisted, and found myself resenting my own resolve. It wasn't as though Jim would mind. Would he? I wasn't sure. I deliberated too long and the lights went down.

When Jim walked onstage I saw him look for me and I did a little low wave near my chest so he'd see it just above the front of the box. He held my gaze a few seconds, which was all he ever did in concert situations. *If you get nervous just imagine me naked* I'd said to him the first time I'd gone to see him play. *I don't get nervous, but I will anyway.* He walked to the piano, flicked out his coat-tails and sat. The restrained applause faded to a few last-minute coughs, and then there was silence. He began – briskly, baroque-y? *Is it Mozart?* I thought, *I should know this by now.* I watched his fingers moving, his torso held strong and still, his head tipping and shaking, the parts of him not adding up to the sum. There were things in him I hadn't quantified, might not ever quantify, and yet he made no sense without them. I had forgotten what he looked like from a distance. I had forgotten how good he was at what he did. I wished he didn't know I was there so that I could watch him, innocent of the knowledge of my presence. I wanted to see what he looked like when he was alone. The recesses that gave him his shape. I should watch him sleep more often, I thought.

The aftershow was up in the venue's polished wooden-floored café. I fetched two orange juices from the drinks table and waited by the dressing room door. The juice was from concentrate, oily, and tasted vaguely of the afterburn of vomit.

Jim came out, freshly changed, a bottle of water in hand, and was accosted by the venue manager and wife – champagne-giddy and both of them tactile now – before he could get to me. I smiled and looked into my drink. Half of it was gone. I didn't want another. I'd have to make this one last. I sipped it in greasy little mouthfuls until he came over.

'Well?' he said.

'Very good.' I held his chin, kissed him.

We stood together, holding hands, as a stream of people came over one by one to congratulate him. I thought, *Isn't this lovely, just being together, celebrating Jim's talent in a beautiful city? I am a lucky wretch.* After half an hour or so the well-wishers slowed, the odd one bursting forward for a handshake on their way out. I thought absurdly of microwave popcorn.

And then we were alone. We walked a little way down the corridor, towards the door.

'How was the orange juice?' Jim said.

'Delicious.'

'You're a shitty actor, you know. You'll never play the Dane.'

'Fuck the Dane. I was Aladdin.'

'Aladdin?'

'Upper-fourth Christmas panto, December '91. A ginger, female Aladdin. And they say the North is backwards.'

He stopped. I stopped. 'You look tired,' he said.

'Must be the travel.'

'How was Tyler's birthday?'

'Fine! Cool.'

'You look as though you haven't been to bed.'

'Stop scrutinising me,' I said and turned away. Oh don't cry don't cry you fucking baby, fucking idiot.

'That's how much this trip meant to you, is it?'

I took a breath, unsure how to proceed.

'Oh, have a drink for fuck's sake, Laura,' he said. 'You might as well. You're not going to be much company like this.'

I opened my mouth to say *I thought I was doing pretty well until you turned the Manson lamps on me*, but then I stopped, because Kirsten walked round the corner.

'Oh hello!' she said. She was carrying her cello and she didn't put it down when she reached us. Agonies of awkwardness! I hadn't seen Kirsten for months and now to bump into her here, like this! It was so obvious there was an atmosphere, too. She didn't know where to look.

'Kirsten!' I said, trying to sound normal. 'How are you? I didn't know you were in Stockholm! This is a nice surprise!'

I sounded like someone who was learning the English language.

'Oh, I'm playing here tomorrow with Joanna Newsom. I just bumped into Jim in the foyer earlier . . .'

I liked the way she said 'foyer'. It was a good, Northern way of saying 'foyer'. I wanted her to say it again so I could close my eyes and savour it.

'You weren't at the concert, then?'

'No, we're rehearsing downstairs in a minute.' She widened her eyes as though remembering something. Kirsten glanced at me, met my eye, and away. 'I'd better go . . .' Killer. What a thing to step into.

'It's a shame you can't make the wedding,' I said.

'Yeah.' She edged past with her cello and ran to the end of the corridor.

Jim looked at me and frowned. Disapproval. Something else in his look, too: annoyance. The wedding. Every time we saw each other all we talked about was the wedding. 'Let's go outside,' I said, desperate for air.

We walked along the water to the hotel. A group of teenagers were swimming off one of the piers, screaming and jumping in.

'Idiots,' said Jim and I realised what I really wanted to do was accuse him of having lost his sense of adventure, which wasn't really fair. Hadn't I fallen for his fixedness, his pin-like regard, as I'd sprayed around that scruffy bar like a Catherine wheel come off a fence? Was that what happened: the things you fell in love with became the very things that repelled you, in the end? (In the *end*? Where had that – ?) There had been a time when the idea of me wilding it might have turned Jim on. No more.

We sat down in the bar at the hotel. I blinked, the tiredness taking over me. 'I might have a whisky,' I said. And then, before I really thought: 'Have one with me.'

He smiled and shook his head. 'I was wondering if you'd manage it.'

Bet you can't get back inside that bottle, genie.

This was the perfect time to turn into Tyler – and furthermore, dearest, *up with this passive-aggressive bullshit I will not put ...* But instead I said: 'I bet I fucking can.'

He dipped his fingers into his shirt breast pocket (he kept notes there, like a bus driver – a detail I'd immediately put in the sacristy of my heart when I'd first spotted it). 'I'll get you whatever you want,' he said, standing up. As he pulled a ten-euro note out of his pocket his passport came with it.

'You keep your passport in there, too, now?'

'Might as well.'

I cried then and he sat down and put his arm around me.

'I'm sorry. I don't know what's up with me.'

'You've just used up all your serotonin.'

'I'm sorry I didn't save you any serotonin.'

'You know,' he said, hugging me closer. 'If we're going to have a baby you should start respecting your body. I dread to think what you're like inside.'

I stopped crying. I felt – well, fucking furious actually. Before I knew it I unleashed a torrent. That's the thing with honesty I guess, once you break the seal . . . I hadn't known how much I'd been holding back but as I spoke I felt like I'd pulled my finger out of the dam and fuckit fuckit drown them all and watch them die. 'Your conversation has never been up to all that much,' I said, 'but this is really scraping the barrel. Constant nagging and talking about babies like some moany little bitch with no ideas. And you're shit in bed since you stopped drinking.'

Of course, we went straight to our room then and fucked, hard and porny, lots of looking. Sometimes tenderness was the way, other times you had to take it all out on each other. I felt a deep, sunless fury in him, swirling round the things he hadn't said: the times he'd been at a bar or in company and craved a quick fix (had he always resisted?), all the times he'd sat alone in his hotel room sober and bored and unable to sleep (somehow this was my fault, why was it my fault?), the encroaching wedding with its myriad inanities. What did I have to hit him with? Guilt from the weekend; the fact that all I wanted to do was write and yet I never did when I sat down to do it; the pressure to do the next thing even though we weren't even done with this one; my own cowardice at bringing none of this up. I got on him and went harder and then, because me coming first didn't feel like enough, and I was determined not to give him anything that could be construed as a compliment, I pushed him out, got on my knees and held him down my throat. When I heard him about to come I pulled back. I hawked and spat on his cock. Hawked and spat again. Turned around. 'There.' I clenched, intensifying the grating physicality. Like chewing a lollystick, it was nicely un-nice. It was another experience, surely one of the few remaining now, that said You Are Here – ho yeah, definitely mostly *there* right now. He shuddered as he came but made no sound. The porthole window in the opposite wall was misted.

(Tyler in my head again – would she always pop up like this, for ever, wherever? *Isn't that just the term you use when you do it with precisely the right lighting and music?*)

As we lay in bed I listened to him falling asleep, his breathing slowing and deepening, until his snores rose regularly to questioning snotters. I felt the soreness of myself and took a righteous pleasure in it. I thought about killing Jim, how I could do it with a pillow.

Some not entirely unpleasant embarrassment as he left the next morning. I was on the toilet, dispatching a dirty rag. He opened the door and leaned in to kiss me. 'Text me when you land.'

'Shall do.'

'There's money for a cab on the bedside table.'

He squinted. I squinted back. I said: 'I've got a subway ticket.'

I left his money as a tip for the maid.

The plane was delayed and we sat on the runway waiting to take off. I turned my eyes from tray table to window and round again, over and over. I thought I saw Tyler standing on the scrubby grass across the tarmac. I looked back and she was wearing a werewolf mask. I looked back again and she was on all fours. I laughed and then remembered there was a man next to me. I looked at him and he was looking straight ahead but too concentratedly. How did he always end up next to the raving weirdo – on buses, planes, trains, in the cinema? I looked away and bit my lip. Tyler had gone. After half an hour they offered us a free drink and the man ordered a gin and tonic and I copied him. We took off an hour later. Every time the man ordered a drink, I ordered one – he bought me a few, too. Four doubles in, he started crying about his loveless marriage and eventually fell asleep on my shoulder. I looked out the window. The sea below was dark and blue and glittery, like just-mopped lino. I took out my notebook and held a pen lightly over it, fantasising, as I always fantasised on planes, of a sudden explosion, fire cascading down the cabin, of burning, of falling, of everything falling away. Would there not be relief in that, just for the briefest of moments, before the end? How much longer could I spend all of my time thinking, *How does this fit? How does this fit? How does this fit?* and then when clarity came – rarely, and only for a split-second – feel as though it had arrived before it set off (it was so bleeding obvious!). Was deliverance not just a trap? Something pre-ordered? Had I been too compliant with Jim? My detachment hadn't come out of nowhere – it had hobbled and straightened and crept to a canter. How had I not noticed? Had I got some twisted kick out of becoming what someone wanted me to be? Embody someone's desire and you feel powerful: giving them what they want; knowing how. But the emptiness that screams in when you realise you are merely a creation. Everything I was I had allowed myself to be. I was so good at beginnings, so good at beginnings. Hadn't my writing shown me that? All those perfect false starts. Maybe beginnings were all I was good for. Maybe my life could just be a series of beginnings, and that would be fine, that would be *best*, in the end. I looked down at the table and saw I had written three words over and over down the page of my notebook.

Killing

The

Changes

I closed the notebook as we commenced our descent. The

man next to me woke when the wheels juddered out, reached into his trouser pocket and twisted a silver ring back onto his finger. 'Terribly sorry about that.'

'No worries. I finished your drink.'

He was all admiration.

THE MASTERY OF AVOIDANCE

I opened the front door and heard the TV on. Tyler at home at noon on a weekday. Something was wrong.

I ran through the kitchen, down the hall, into the living room. 'Tyler?'

She turned, her face revealing itself in classic cinematic style, millimetre by millimetre, centimetre by centimetre, millennium by millennium, until . . . I gasped. Her eyes were insolent but there was a carnation-sized purple bruise across the left, from brow to bag.

'Shit! What happened?'

'They followed us. They fucking followed us. Marie and her work-experience henchmen. They waited outside and when Nick left they knocked on. I thought it was him, I thought he'd forgotten something. And I was still fucked, you know. I shouldn't have answered. That's the mistake I made. Answering.' She brought her right hand up to her nose and squished the knuckles of her first two fingers into her nostrils, grimaced, and pushed them in harder.

'Jesus, Tyler!'

'Don't flip out.' She sounded like an adenoidal robot.

I ran to my room, grabbed the bin bags I'd been packing and pulled them to the living room. 'Get your necessaries,' I said. 'We're getting out of here. Where are your car keys?'

She muted the TV. 'What are you talking about? I've been here twenty-four hours on my own and I'm absolutely fine. They got what they came for. It's done.'

'She's a fucking psychopath! Who knows when she's "done"?'

Her hand dropped from her nose. 'Lo, I'm not running. I am not afraid.'

I ran into her room, pulled her hold-all out from under the bed and started throwing clothes, shoes and underwear into it. All the toiletries in the bathroom I could see.

'Turn the TV off,' I said, coming back into the room. 'I've got our things. Now all we need to do is ask someone to feed Zuzu tomorrow and leave my keys with them . . .'

She stood up. She winced as she put the weight on her feet. I dreaded to think whether she had bruises on her body. 'No need,' she said. 'They took the cat.'

I fell to my knees.

'They took *Zuzu*? Why would they do that?'

'To break my heart, little did they know. She said they'd take care of her. I said they could kill her for all I cared. *Make a fucking stole for yourself, Marie. Cover up that turkey neck.*'

I couldn't take it in. 'Car keys. Where?'

'I've told you I'm not running.'

'You're just going to wait for them to come back and kill you? Come back and kill *us*? I can't stay here, Ty, and I don't want to go to Jim's, and it wouldn't be fair on my parents – come on, just get in the car, would you?'

She staggered round the sofa and picked up a bag.

'Save me, then, Lo. That way, you get to blow your load with the notion that you're kind. But you're not kind because there's no such thing as kindness, there's only pity and stealth.'

I didn't care what she was saying as long as she was moving.

'What about Jesus?' I said, putting her arms into her jacket and pushing her towards the door. 'And Father Christmas?'

'Angling for fans.'

In the car, at a red light, I turned to inspect her. 'Fuck you. And anyway, what about that time you saved *my* life?'

I'd been choking on a pear drop and she'd given me the Heimlich manoeuvre (courtesy of a Beanz coffee shop first-aid training day).

She sighed. 'Well, it *was* my fault you were dying . . .'

We'd been watching a documentary about Simon Weston and she said WOULD YOU LOOK AT THIS WHINING TORY CUNT.

At Lancaster Services I called Jim. 'We're having a little holiday together, Tyler and I.' I only thought of it then but we were already on the ring-road heading north somehow, so it made perfect sense: 'We're going to Edinburgh. For the festival. For inspiration.' I almost said *Think of it as my hen do!* to bolster it but for some reason I couldn't. I couldn't tell him about the black eye, couldn't tell him about Marie.

I pitched the idea of Edinburgh festival to Tyler in the car.

She shook her head. 'Chinless drama graduates haranguing me to go see some "really cool improv" at every turn? No sirree.'

'There's literature,' I said. 'And comedy. You like comedy.'

'I like watching comedy on TV so the people who made it can't see me *not* laughing. Now hand me the keys. You are relieved of your duties, blessed saviour.'

'Fuuuuuuuuck you.'

LAURA AND TYLER FLEE NORTH

We stopped in Wasdale, a deep back-pocket of Cumbria, tucked away to the West amongst the highest mountains, as good a place as any to hide. The Wasdale Head Inn was at the end of a dirt road. Tyler's car shuddered over a cattle-grid and onto the final stretch of track. On either side of the mounds of green ferns on our right, the purple depths of Wastwater loomed, backed by slopes of scree, lunar-like in their colour and lifeless-ness. The whole side of the mountain looked to be sliding down into the water, grey rocks and pale bushes in a sad, slow descent. Small waves scuffed the surface of the lake. As we turned a corner we came across a flock of foamy grey Herdwick sheep who turned to stare at us with identical expressions. In the distance, the word INN was painted on the side of a white building in large black letters.

Call me masochistic (no, call me it *harder*) but I'd asked Tyler to drive past the wedding venue in Patterdale, to see what it did to me. The View was a shuttered, tilting Seventies hotel. Long ago, so it felt, I'd fallen in love with the shabby tragedy of the place – its drab corridors like something out of *The Shining* and its background fizzling bleakness – but when we pulled up outside it that day I was dismayed to see it looked as though it had been refurbished. I leapt out of the car and ran into the foyer.

'Hello!' said the man behind reception.

I looked around. The lobby was bright and clean and smelled of wet paint. I put a hand over my mouth.

'Are you all right, madam?'

I looked at him and my hand fell. 'When did this happen?'

'Oh, a few weeks ago! We wanted to get it done before the weddings. We have a lot of weddings coming up.'

I heard Tyler's voice behind me. 'Hers is one of 'em.'

The man raised his hands. 'How wonderful! You must come and see the new function room . . .'

We followed him. Something was different about the bar, as well as the new décor, something else, something missing. The piano. The old piano was missing from the corner.

'Where's the piano?'

'Oh, we got rid of it. Decrepit old thing, really. No one ever got a decent note out of it. Well, there was this one fella once, he did all right, must have been a professional or something . . .'

I zoned out from listening and did an about-turn, pushing past Tyler. I started crying as soon as I was inside the car. She got in and rubbed my back. 'Look, we can do Edinburgh tomorrow, whatever you want.'

Two hours later we arrived in Wasdale. We sat opposite each other in the snug. A bottle of wine spoked the dark-wood table between us. I studied Tyler's face – the made-over bruises, the mole on her left cheek defiantly steadfast in orbit. The scar on her top lip a lonely scar no more.

'Damn beer bottle,' I said.

'Yeah.' She picked up her glass. 'Motherfucker.'

She looked at me and there it was, the final mystery between us, stretched and stuffed with bright new beady eyes. Oh, I'd known, though, hadn't I? I'd seen her so many times, in my dreams, under that vast Midwestern sky, eight and twelve and fifteen years old, waiting for the storm to break. It swept through the house with slammed doors and slung bottles; it retreated with beds unslept-in, phone calls from her mother's sisters. (The way the day begins decides the shade of everything.) She looked away. Knew I knew. Did she know that part of me also envied her dark causality? Oh god, no. Not there. Not yet.

'Cigarette?'

Dusk was falling and swallows flitted around the inn's fascias. The moon was a steady spotlight over the fells. On the nearby campsite a group of campers were sitting in folding chairs, dividing a box of wine into plastic goblets. There was the sound of laughter, ebbing and flowing like water or music.

'Define happiness,' Tyler said.

'Peace,' I said. 'Calm. Something like that.'

'Didn't you always hope it would be something more?'

'Yes. Maybe that's why we fuck things up – so that peace, when it comes, feels like enough.' I thought of Ezra Pound but I didn't say it, it was too sad too sad: *And the days are not full enough, and the nights are not full enough, and life slips by like a field mouse, not shaking the grass.* The great tragedy of not being remembered is the time you waste worrying about it in advance.

The inn was done out like a saloon with leather-set booths, a long bright counter and three-quarter-height slatted doors swinging into the kitchen area. Tankards were hung along a picture rail and, beneath these, a row of chalkboards detailing the day's specials. Gammon and pineapple. Vegetable lasagne. On the other walls were framed photos of mountaineers standing in heroic poses.

'Let's go ringside,' Tyler said and we sat up at the bar on a pair of high stools with torn red leather cushions.

There was a group of big, strong-looking lads by the bar. Quiet, less sure hikers and campers drank pensively at tables, reminding me of sheep.

'My people, my people,' Tyler said, nodding. 'Livestock handlers all.' She smacked her lips.

'Maybe you should chew on a piece of wheat,' I said. 'Just so they know you're one of them. It might get us free drinks.'

'Oh, they know,' Tyler said. 'They can *sense* me.' She took another swig of wine and put her glass down nicely. Then she let out a long whistle. 'Oh boy. I think I just ovulated.'

'What?'

'Constitution of an ox, two o'clock.'

I waited a moment, sipped my drink, discreetly turned to look. 'Oh *boy* is right,' I said. 'Way too young.'

'He's not! He's at least twenty-one. And a half.'

'He's a child.'

'Look at his hands. He would cup my butt. He would cup it. Capably. Seriously, I am getting the major fanny gallops.'

'Tyler.'

'Don't worry, I'm not going to go over there and start fisting him.'

'Oh god please really.'

'Fisting's too good for kids.'

'You take my point, then.'

'He is ripe for the picking. Seriously. They should put up pictures of him in IVF clinics. He looks like he could fertilise you just by looking at you.'

'Let's hope not.'

Close up he had soft blonde hair along his jawline and a mouth that never quite closed fully. His name was Larry For Short.

'What happened to your eye?' he said.

'I'm a Thai boxer,' Tyler replied. 'Pendlebury Pythons. I've got the kimono upstairs if you want to see.'

At nine o'clock one of the three boys made his excuses and left and I wondered whether there had been some unspoken nod, some agreement at the urinals pertaining to how this was all going to pan out.

'You know what I think,' Tyler said while we were outside smoking. 'You might as well.'

'Tyler.'

'All I'm saying is to dismiss possibilities is to – '

'To not dismiss possibilities is immoral.'

'Big talk for a – '

'You know what stops me making this even slightly – ?'

'It might just be a simple case of – '

'The thought of Jim eating rice.'

'Huh?'

'Jim loves rice. You should see his face when he's eating rice. I couldn't do anything when I think about him eating rice.'

'Rice-fan Jim is probably fucking every flautist in Finland as we speak.'

'Stop.'

I'd once watched a chat show with my mum, the topic of which was 'Affairs – Could Your Relationship Survive?' One of the experts on the panel kept saying how it was wrong to use words like 'unfaithful' and 'infidelity', that you should use the term 'concurrent relationships' instead. My mum scoffed at this. Concurrent relationships. But I'd always wondered about how practical monogamy was, especially once you had longevity in the mix. The night had flung things my way and I'd taken them more than once, usually towards the end of a relationship, I did console myself with that. Not that it provided much in the way of self-charming when you were on a commuter tram with a turned-off phone and bruises on your thighs and a hangover so bad you felt as though you'd been shat out of Satan's own starry arsehole. Catalysts, that was how I categorised those briefless encounters, confirming to me that things had changed irrevers-ibly from love to not-love. One-night stands spawned of begged cigarettes and night buses to nowhere. It was my way of cementing the death of feeling. If you could do that then you didn't love someone, not when you had a pact that didn't allow for Other People. I wasn't judgmental where other people's relationships were concerned (other people's relationships, like sex, had always been one of my least favourite topics of conversation). Swinging was fine if you both swung (always visions of chandeliers, of lines of unfathomable cocks awaiting legs-akimbo acrobatics. Sometimes I thought my imagination was constantly on drugs . . .). But if you had an agreement to be monogamous, if you believed in the holiness of (not marriage, but) sexual exclusivity, i.e. you are free to be many things to many people but you are only *that* to me, then there was a line, and once you crossed that line it was all over. It was just rags and bones. Shit and sawdust.

His name was Sam and he had some interesting views on what constituted 'proper books' (crime fiction, thrillers, murder mysteries). He also kept going to the bar without asking what everyone wanted and buying pints for himself and Larry and halves for me and Tyler. When I said I was going outside for a cigarette he said *I finally managed to get my mum to stop smoking last year*, to which I said *Teenagers these days.*

Tyler joined me outside, lit my cigarette and then her own. 'Having fun?'

'Oh, yes. I'm finding myself perversely aroused by his outrageous sexism. I think it's because I know he doesn't really mean it.'

'Oh, he means it all right. But you can *afford* to be turned on, that's the point.'

'You're not actually going to do this, are you?'

'I've never needed it more.'

Tyler didn't have an upper age limit. I'd once asked her how high she'd go and she just looked at me.

Sixty?

A pouty squint.

Seventy?

Flat palms, Mafioso shrug. *If they were a young seventy. You know all this age talk is bullshit anyway. No one ever feels any fucking different.*

'I just don't get the appeal of younger men,' I said. 'They're so giddy, like spaniels. But then I didn't fancy teenagers when I was a teenager.'

'He's not a teenager!'

'He's not far off.'

'I need distraction. And Nick's getting a bit too close for comfort – I need to stop him thinking we have so much of a thing.'

A flash: had she lied, had Nick hit her, was the whole Marie thing a story . . .'Does he know what happened?'

'Dunno. I've been dropping his calls.'

I eyeballed her. Nothing. 'I don't trust him. That stuff he had was so strong, I didn't like it.'

'Oho, you seemed to like it at the time! What's the matter, puss? Jealous?'

'Fuck you.'

Back inside the inn I let her go on ahead and walked up to the bar and bought myself a Lagavulin.

'Where are you girls from?' the landlord said, dropping my change into my palm as though he didn't want to touch me.

'*Cumbrian Life.*'

'You'll be wanting a receipt, then.'

Two hours and six whiskies later I was wake-drunk. I slurred a word. I fell over in the bathroom. I dropped my drink. Three strikes! That was that. An outdoor piss and then bed. Tyler gave Larry's belt a firm tug for good measure and followed me towards the door of the inn.

'Where are you going?' he shouted after us.

Tyler turned with a flourish. 'Country tradition.'

The landlord dropped a glass and picked it up again. Sam was finishing his pint. I followed Tyler outside and squatted beside her at the edge of the car park. Above us, a mad sprawl of stars. A background chuckle.

'THE EXISTENTIALS!' Tyler said, yanking up her pants. 'They've found us! Quick – back to warmth, light, strong booze and sexual frisson!'

I left her an hour or so later, helping herself to crème de menthe behind the bar. Sam had gone home, Larry was indecipherable. I went up to the room, got undressed, took my phone into bed with me and opened Marty's picture message. And.

Yep.

I woke up alone, the other twin bed still made.

'Tyler?' I looked under the bed and in the wardrobe. I looked at my phone. A message from Jim in reply to one I'd sent him before I fell asleep. I couldn't remember sending it but it contained only two spelling mistakes. The time on my phone told me that I had missed breakfast so I packed, crept downstairs and smoked leaning on the car, my foot up behind me on the wheel arch. The cold air woke my brain as I breathed. *Water, I should probably have some water*, I thought, listening to the waterfalls, now visible as jagged white streaks down the hills, static from a distance, like stars.

A door banged and Tyler came running out from round the side of the inn.

'GET IN!' she yelled, opening the passenger door, throwing her hold-all in the back and haring round to the driver's side. The black eye was back. Her hair was haunted. I clambered into the passenger seat. She started the engine.

'What the – ?'

We were halfway down the track before she said anything.

'Landlord's son. Just turned twenty. His mom just threw me out of his room.' She took a hand away from the steering wheel to wipe the sweat from her brow and then put her hand back and gripped the wheel tighter. A car had to swerve out of the way as we passed in a non-passing place.

'And that's not the worst thing.'

'What's the worst thing?'

'She threw his skateboard after me.'

I saw red in the hair at the back of her head. 'Hang on . . . Tyler, you're bleeding. You're actually bleeding.'

'I'm CONFUCKINGCUSSED!'

I wound down the window. 'Stop, I'm going to be sick.'

'That's what *she* said . . .'

I CAN RESIST EVERYTHING EXCEPT METAFICTION

I smoked a cigarette in the street outside the B&B, bilious with exam-nerves in my old university city. *This is not a test*, I reminded myself. *ENJOY YOURSELF. ENJOY YOURSELF HARD.*

When Tyler was dressed we walked across town to Charlotte Square Gardens. We bought a quarter-bottle of whisky on the way and passed it between us as we walked along the humped footpath that ran round the Castle. According to myth a serpent lay stretched out beneath the city, the path curving over its rounded back. In the gardens we bought two cups of white wine from a stall. Tyler flicked through the programme. Festivals, like cities, were places to lose yourself: pop-up holiday towns with all the attendant lawlessness. Bandit country.

'AHA,' said Tyler, stopping on a page and pouting, 'I wondered whether *he*'d be here.'

'Who?'

'Marty.'

I downed my drink. Pulsed once down low.

'In fact, he's on right now, interviewing someone over there.' Tyler nodded to a marquee. 'It's just started. Here, grab this a sec.' She handed me the programme.

'Is there nothing else on?' I said, leafing through it frantically. 'I mean, it's good to have options, isn't it? The very essence of festivals is options, no?'

She put her hand in her pocket, fumbled around for a minute, pulled her hand out, sucked her finger. 'You want?'

'Where's that from?'

'I siphoned some off and hid it in the Christmas tree. Who says poetry doesn't have its uses.'

Now.

You can judge me for this, but I think I'd reached such a point of disbelief and angst that . . . Yeah. Anyway. Whatever. I had some.

We walked across the gardens. When we got to the marquee, there was a NO ENTRY sign and a chain – an actual chain – across the door.

'Fuck is this?' said Tyler, yanking at the chain. A man in a suit with an earpiece came running over.

'Sorry, ladies, no latecomers admitted,' he said. 'It says so on your tickets.'

We didn't have– well, of *course* we didn't . . .

'She's PREGNANT,' Tyler said, pointing at me. 'She needs to sit down. This is an infringement of human rights.'

'There are seats in the refreshment tents.'

'She has leukemia, too. It's her dying wish to be at this festival and hear some words of comfort and inspiration before the end. With her doomed unborn in her poisoned womb – '

'Tyler, you heard the man,' I said. 'Let's go see something else. Anything else.'

The man glanced at my abdomen and walked away.

'Fuck this shit,' Tyler said. She tore off a piece of her t-shirt, dipped it in the remains of the whisky, set fire to it with her lighter and then lobbed it into a nearby bin. The bin burst into flames. Somebody screamed. The man in the suit ran off shouting FIRE! and returned with a fire extinguisher. As he was extinguishing the flames we dipped under the chain and crawled under the door-flaps.

Inside the marquee there was a sparse audience, intently listening to the writer onstage. We sat on the back row, putting our wine beneath the chairs.

'Would you look at him,' said Tyler. 'The bombastic bastard.'

I would not look at him. I was shaky all over. What if he knew, somehow?

'A question from the audience next!' Marty said.

I looked at Tyler. She was openly dabbing. She swigged her wine and gargled to get it all down. A man in front of us turned and scowled.

'Here,' I said. She passed me the bag and I put it between my knees to needle out a few surreptitious nailfuls. There was a lot in the bag.

'Your novels tend to have happy endings,' said a woman down near the front. 'Don't you think happy endings are unrealistic?'

'All endings are unrealistic,' said the author demurely.

Oof – this woman was good. I looked to my right again. Something was amiss. It took me a moment to work out what. Knowledge crashed in; the proverbial china shop reduced to smithereens. Tyler wasn't in her seat. I scanned the room, panicking. Her wine was still there beneath her chair and so was her jacket, slung across the back. Then I saw her, haring down the side of the marquee towards the stage. Oh holy fuck of fucks I couldn't cope with this, couldn't cope with this at all. When she reached the stage she clambered on and grinned. The writer noticed her and stopped talking. A terrible hush fell over the marquee. Someone stood up on the front row and said something to Marty but he gestured for them to sit back down again.

'Ladies and gentlemen, please welcome Tyler Johnson – my old spar!'

Mortifications. Mounting.

Tyler took a little bow and then took the microphone from the writer's hand. The writer sat there, confused.

'Say, this obsession with realism – or what I think you're pertaining to here is better defined as naturalism,' said Tyler into the mic. 'It drives me up the fuck-ing wall.' I shrank further into my seat, my fingers finding the rim of my wine glass. 'I can honestly say I've never stopped reading a book and thought, *What am I doing here, sitting in this room, reading? I was just on a ship at sea, with one arm in a sling and the mother of storms approaching and sharks circling the hull. Thank fuck! It was just a story* . . . I like a bit of style. Craft. Panache. Self-consciousness. Whatever.'

'Are you a writer?' said the writer.

'Yes,' said Tyler. 'In every other way apart from the actual writing of things. I often think of getting my thoughts down on paper, to process them, to leave something behind. But I won't be put in a box until I'm put in a box, know what I mean?'

I went down for my wine again and stayed low.

Tyler said: 'Does anyone up here have anything to drink?' The writer and Marty shook their heads. 'Right then,' said Tyler, 'that's me. Enjoy the festival, mufux.' She made a peace sign, dropped the mic and jumped off the stage. As she bounded back to her seat the whole marquee – the canvas itself – was watching us.

'Tyler,' I said through gritted teeth, 'that was the most revolting display I've ever seen, which where you're concerned is saying something. We're leaving.'

'What do you mean? They loved me. I'm made for this shit.'

'What, bad manners?'

But then, a sea change: the irrepressible swell of fuckedness. Neurons failing to receive, kicking back, muting their phones and signing off for the day. I felt my eyes peel, my brain warm through, my limbs align. She was right. Everything was cool and fine. They loved her. They loved us both. Which was handy because we loved them, too, everyone in the tent. Everyone loved everyone and we were all made for all of the shit all of the time.

'You should lecture at universities,' I said.

'Yeah, I've often thought about that.'

After the applause we waited outside the tent for Marty. Tyler said *Thank you* to everyone as they left, like it was her wedding. 'Isn't this just like old times?' she said.

The good feelings. The good feelings. Was it just the drugs? Was it not the truth? I didn't care, and not caring was a kind of purity in itself. Anything could feel pure when you were under the influence. Licking a toilet cistern. Talking to a moron. Putting on a purple jumpsuit and doing star jumps to 'All Night Long' by Lionel Richie. The most dickish and dull of activities, ideas and objects were suddenly invested with an intense and intriguing glamour. Who wouldn't want to reside in that place, that world? *Only a fool, my friend, only a fool.*

'Laura! Tyler!'

He grinned. 'How are you?'

Oh, you know, wanking over your cockshot occasionally.

He kissed us both on both cheeks and put an arm around each of us. He smelled of new leather. Aftershave. My stomach boaked.

'What are you two reprobates doing here amongst all the proper people?'

'We came on a whim,' I said.

NOBODY TRAVELS THREE HUNDRED MILES ON A WHIM, DICKHEAD.

'Impressive whim.'

'Yeah.'

'Your wine's run out.'

'Probably for the best.'

'Probably not.'

Stop it, I thought. This is categorically not fair, on anyone.

194

In fact, let's shake hands and bid each other farewell and turn
round and walk off in opp –
  'Fancy another?'
  'Yes.'

Arguably, the joy of the intoxicated world is not reality. (Tyler:
Reality is for people TOO WEAK FOR DRUGS.) Those aren't
your real feelings because we base our concept of reality on how
things are most of the time. The dust settles and the dazzle fades
and you realise you feel nothing for jumpsuits or morons or
Lionel Richie except the embarrassment that the memory of
your involvement with them demands.
  Know what? I *tire* of reality.

We sat round a wooden table outside the marquee. There were
four of us; Liz the author came for a drink, too. She was a good
woman. She lived in Nottingham with her husband and three
sons. She wore a lot of precious stones. Practised Reiki in her
spare time.
  'Laura's a writer,' said Marty.
  'That's great,' said Liz.
  His leg brushed against mine under the table and I moved
away, quickly. My reflexes were catlike. I was enjoying thinking
that sentence. *My reflexes are catlike.* I thought about offering
him some mandy.
  'I wish you wouldn't do that.'
  'What?'
  'Introduce me as a writer.'
  Liz turned to me. 'Have you had anything published?'
  'I'm working on a novel.'
  'What's the title?'
  'Well it was *Bacon* but I'm thinking that's too glib and I had
this like weird epiphany the other night when I was on a plane

on my own and I now think it should be called *Killing the Changes* you know because that's more mysterious and I want the book to be mysterious and complex even though it's about the simplest thing really and that's love.'

'What's your name? I'll look out for you.'

'Laura Joyce.' She looked at me. 'I know. I *know*.'

'In the particular is contained the universal,' said Marty. 'That's Joyce. The other one.'

'In the *sub-atomic* particular now,' I said. Liz looked at me oddly. Was I not making sense? Because I actually thought I was being pretty fucking profound. I thought about offering her some mandy. 'I could always send you . . . if you . . .'

'Good luck with it!' Liz chugged a large mouthful of wine.

'Liz!' Tyler cried, standing up. 'Do some Reiki on me.'

'Oh, I've got to go.'

'Just a little, would you? I'm all tense with driving and being beaten up.' She rolled her shoulders.

Liz stood up. 'So lovely to meet you all,' she said. 'Marty, thanks for a lovely event.'

And she was off.

'So,' said Marty, nodding at Tyler's eye. 'What happened, badass?'

'A drug dealer. Taking everything into account, it was a small price to pay.' I saw Zuzu's face and cast it away. 'I've got some of the drugs I stole on me, too.'

'I'd never have guessed. Share the wealth, then.'

She did. We all did.

When dusk fell we went to a supermarket for cigarettes. The queue for the manned counter was long – just one young man in front of the masked tobacco wall, with eight self-service counters bleeping away to our left as we queued. Unexpected item in bagging area. Approval needed. Everybody and everything was impatient.

'I like those self-service checkouts,' Tyler said. 'You can rant at them and it's not a person. You can take it all out on those fuckers.'

'I once pretended to be blind in a chemist,' I said.

'Oh, this one's great,' said Tyler. 'She – '

' – I was looking for saline solution for Tyler, and I couldn't find the eye section so I found a sales assistant and said, *Can you point me to the eyecare section, please? Sorry – I'm a bit blind* except he took "a bit blind" literally, came and held me by the elbow and made a big show of guiding me across the shop and I didn't know how to correct him, I didn't want him thinking I'd been flippant or worse still made some kind of sick joke, and I was really regretting saying it so I went along with it and pretended I was actually blind. He led me across the shop, moving people out of the way for me, and I let him lead me, thanking him, and then when he deposited me at the eyecare section I said, *I think I can take it from here.* But he wouldn't let it be, he pressed a bottle of saline into my hand and then started guiding me over to the till, and I thought, I'm going to get rumbled here when I have to chip and pin so I said all indignant *I'm not completely incapable, you know!* which saw him off.' I exhaled profusely, which felt good. 'I still feel bad about it.'

'That's because you like feeling bad,' said Tyler, wrenching a pack of ibuprofen off a plastic holster.

'No, I don't.'

'Well, you like a good telling-off at any rate. That's why you like the idea of God. He's the ultimate angry teacher.'

'That's so interesting,' Marty said.

'Know why they keep the toiletries behind the tills?' I said, to be more interesting.

'Because they're more expensive.'

'Nope, there are boxes of chocolate over there worth more than deodorant.'

'Enlighten me, Miss Joyce.'

Miss Joyce. I liked that. No I didn't. Yes I did.

'Because they're what homeless people are most likely to steal.'

'I steal handwash from bars to give to homeless people,' said Tyler. 'I'm like Robin Hood, not in tights.'

I'd seen her help someone out of a supermarket once. The man had bought two bottles of super-strength cider and there were three staff and two security guards around him like he was a dangerous dog. Customers were staring. The man had paid, he had a carrier bag and a receipt in his hand, he was just taking his time to pack up and struggling with the bag handles. Tyler batted the people around him away. *I'll get this gent out, no need for all this.* She escorted the man to the doors. He was grateful. He said *They look at me like I'm shit, you know, but I'm not shit I'm just pissed.* Would she have helped him if she hadn't been pissed herself? Who gave a shit.

Marty said he knew of a place called Deco, a wine bar. We stood outside the front door finishing our fags. Down the street, a busker was singing 'The Boxer'.

'Boom,' said Marty softly as we passed. I liked him better when he was smoking.

'I kicked over a busker's cap once,' I said. 'The money went everywhere. And then I felt so bad I put a fiver in on top of the rest I'd picked up. It's a dear do, middle-class guilt.' This wasn't true but it was a great story.

Deco was dark and busy and everything I wanted. Stained-glass mirrors mystified the walls and a series of birdcages hung still and empty down the middle of the ceiling, between depressed Tiffany lampshades. The bar-top itself was wooden and highly polished like a long flat slide, the sudden flower of a gramophone at the far end.

Tyler went straight to the bathroom and Marty went up to the bar. I found a table in a corner with only one chair so I asked the occupants of a nearby table if they could spare one and they moved some coats and donated what looked like a milking stool. This still meant we only had two seats. I sat down on the stool. It was low, really low, and my chest came up to the table. I pulled the stool back a little way so it wasn't as noticeable how low I was. I looked at Marty's ass, looked away, looked back. Realised he could probably see me looking in the stained-glass mirrors behind the bar.

Marty returned with three squat cocktails. Old Fashioneds, I deduced, seeing the orange peel spiralling in the dark liquor. I took the glass from Marty's hand and as I did so his finger brushed mine. A dopamine rush. I put the cocktail onto the table so that I'd drink it more slowly.

'So you went to university here?' said Marty.

'Yes,' I said. 'You went to Oxford, then?'

'That was for my BA.'

'Impressive.'

He brought his cocktail to his lips and looked at me. 'What made you choose Edinburgh?'

'It's a good university!'

'Of course it is.'

He took off his coat. He was in pretty good shape, his chest and arm muscles slid around under his shirt and his stomach was flat above his belt buckle even though he was sitting down.

DO NOT LOOK AT HIS BELT BUCKLE.

'Did you not want to push yourself?'

HE JUST CAUGHT YOU LOOKING AT HIS BELT BUCKLE.

I looked at him. His face was good and round, his evil Cupid's-bow lips wet from the whisky. Motherfucker.

I said: 'I admire your balls, Marty.'

'Budge up, buster!' Tyler was back from the bathroom. She plonked herself on his knee and helped herself to the remaining cocktail. I sipped mine. Give me credit for that, would you? I sipped.

Tyler leaned forward and then her hand was in my hand under the table and then the bag was there, crackly in my palm, depleted yet still plentiful. I went to the bathroom. When I came back Tyler was sitting down on the stool, whispering in Marty's ear. She stopped whispering when she saw me and stood up. 'Another chair! Another chair is what we need.' She flew off into the depths of the bar. I sat down on the milking stool.

'So,' Marty said. 'This new title. Remind me again?'

'*Killing the Changes*.'

The edge of his shirt-sleeve touched the end of my shirt-sleeve and tickled like a butterfly. Like something delicate, struggling. A rush went up my neck. He pulled at his beard, touched the arm of his glasses. 'It's not right.'

'What do you mean, "not right"?'

'It's too TV drama. I'm seeing Helen Mirren with a difficult home life wrongly accused of sexual harassment in the workplace.'

I belted back my drink and slammed the glass down on the table. 'Tough titty,' I said. 'I was disappointed when *A Room With a View* wasn't about a sniper. It's my fucking wedding.'

'Mm, petulant. Sexy. Not.'

'You know, your age really shows when you say words like "Not".'

He bit his bottom lip, raised his eyebrows, nodded his head, amused. AMUSED. Oh, my bankrupt inner grammar-school debating team! I wanted to massacre them all.

'Okay,' I said, 'I realise that was a little below par.'

'It's fine.' He reset his face. 'So long as it's foreplay.'

A chair landed on one side of us and Tyler landed on top of it. I thought they'd been thrown across the room for a moment, but no she was just . . . bouncy. I moved back in my seat.

'Marty went to Oxford,' she said.

'I'd remembered.'

'You almost went, didn't you, Lo?'

'"Almost" is a bit of an overstatement.'

'Always the bridesmaid?' Marty grinned. I grinned back.

'I went to look round one of the colleges in sixth form,' I said, reaching for my glass, which was empty.

'We're all out,' Tyler said. 'I'm going to the bar.'

'Do you want some money?' I said, looking for my bag.

'No, what I want is for you to enjoy yourself.'

'I am enjoying myself.'

She went to the bar.

'You should use Yeats for your title,' Marty said. 'If he's your favourite.'

'How do you know he's my favourite?'

'I'm a hardline Romantic, too. Surprised you didn't spot me a mile off.'

'Your event publicity was hardly knavish.'

'Hook, line and sinker.'

'You wish.' I pulled my lip-gloss out of my bag and swiped a scoop out, smeared it across my lips. Marty watched me. 'Want some?' He nodded. I applied. He rubbed his lips together. 'You know, that suits you.'

He pouted. 'Thanks. Hey, do you have the . . . erm.'

I shook my head. 'Tyler's got it.'

His aftershave wasn't so bad, close up. It was strong and alien and could under some circumstances even be a turn-on. I imagined.

'So does your fiancé like poetry?'

'Jim? Of course he does.' (I wasn't sure. My mind was a blank where Jim was concerned.)

'But he doesn't write?'

'He plays the piano.'

'He covers other people's songs?'

'He channels. He pulls music through himself and puts it out again. It's very creative. His process.'

'Others because you did not keep that deep-sworn vow have been friends of mine. "Friends". That's a sweet way of putting it, don't you think?'

'I don't want to think about anyone's face right now, thanks.'

A dimple appeared. 'Oh, okay, so we're going to hell. Shall we hold hands on the way down?'

I nodded towards the bar and Tyler. 'Go over there and say "Three Bloody Marys" and everything will be fine. I'm half-Catholic.'

Oh this was really really really bad. He moved closer. Tyler turned to glance at us and quickly turned back again. I looked at Marty and thought, *I could just kiss you, just kiss you, right now.* I tilted my head to show him his mouth might fit on the side of my throat.

He said: 'You spend too much time guilty.'

'I'm a writer. Guilt helps analysis.'

'You need more to analyse. Less conversation, more action.'

'Maybe you're right. I have too much thinking time. Really someone should just put me in a mill or down a mine – '

'How about I just put you over my knee?'

Three cocktails landed on the table, Tyler's fingers in them. I shot back, looked down, told myself I must have misheard him. But I was wet and I was afraid he might know it. Jesus and all the fucks. Marty was taking me apart, layer by layer, piece by tiny piece. An autopsy with cutlery. I felt that feeling of being the focus, of the focus sharpening – even when you know it's to your own (small-scale) destruction (oh fuckit, *especially* when you know that). I thought of the sailor Quint sliding down the deck towards the shark's open mouth and there was something in his eye that wasn't pure horror, there was a part of him contracting, a last kick from being the sole object of the beast's desire. I looked at Marty's hand around his glass, mentally transplanted it to my breast, my arse cheek. I looked at the chunky zip of his trousers, imagined opening his flies, pushing my fingers inside, feeling him stiffen as I pushed him back on his chair and swung my leg over and shoved the fingers of my free hand in his mouth . . .

In the quantum multiverse all eventualities are possible. Which means, paradoxically, that all eventualities are inevitable. They have also quite possibly already happened. Make of that what you will, not that your will has much to do with it. Because here's the thing. *If* you believe that consciousness is an accumulation of memory; *if* you believe that you often know what's going to occur either through some animal instinct or a human subscription to fate, then you are a walking and talking embodiment of everything happening all at once. There is no x and y, no cause and effect. Nothing is inevitable because it doesn't have *time* to be inevitable. You just are, all at once. Living for the moment isn't even a choice.

Another bar. Another round. The street, a path through a graveyard. A shortcut. It's quicker this way. I had hold of Marty's hand. No time to think about the meaning or lack of meaning, just hold the buzz. Another street. Fag-ends. Chip wrappers. A discarded Peperami sheath like an anteater's condom. A small fence to step over. *Is the line this thin, then?* I wondered, lifting my foot and landing on the other side of the fence. My other foot followed. And there it was, I was over, all of me over. The line was elastic. Life and death, unreality and reality, right and wrong. You could step from one to the other with no bother. It was eleven and midnight and morning and –

Marty's hotel. The man behind reception had *Sorry, residents only* in his eyes ready for us. Tyler sashayed up to him and placed her palms on the desk.

Tell me, good sir, do all your rooms have wig stands?

I'm sorry?

Wig stands. For storing one's wig overnight. Do all your rooms have them?

I'm sorry, I –

May I speak with the manager?

He eyed her: *I am the manager.*

She held the desk and rocked up onto her toes. *Prove it. Give us four bottles of wine.*

And he did.

I caught up with myself in Marty's bathroom, admiring the miniature toiletries, resisting the urge to pocket a few. I sat on the toilet and pissed hard, holding the soft ballotine of my stomach as I pushed. Someone had pulled the toilet roll holder off the wall and there was a hole in the tiling where its fixture had ripped out. It reminded me of a hole that was in the wall of my bedroom at university. It was about the size of a macaroon, half an inch deep, jagged round the edges. I grew attached to that hole. The second time I took ecstasy I sat having a conversation with it for about an hour. Know what? I've had worse conversations. Out in the bedroom I could hear Tyler arguing with Marty. *The thing is, you've internalised a norm, that's all. It's not actually your* desire *to wear trousers, even though you think it is . . .* I finished pissing and stood. Zigzagged my pants up and zipped.

KNOCK KNOCK.

You okay in there, darlin'? A girl's voice I didn't recognise.

Fine thanks, just taking a minute.

Do you feel sick?

No.

If you feel sick I could rub your back.

I don't feel sick.

I could paint your nails then.

Okay.

I opened the door and let her in. Hieroglyphs on her arms. Long brown hair tied back and slicked with sweat. A hole in her tights just above the knee that stretched into a screaming mouth as she kneeled.

'Who are you?' I said.

'I'm Alice.'

Alice? Who the fuck was Alice?

Back out in the room there were more people, sitting on the bed.

'You were telling us about your ill-fated trip to Oxford,' Marty said when he saw me.

I couldn't look at him, couldn't meet his eye. 'They gave us salmon en croute and put fish scales on the pastry, that's my most enduring memory – that and the smell of the history. That smell. You don't get it when you grow up in a terrace. Books, leather, dust, whatever it is, we had none of it.'

'An Irish Catholic family,' Tyler said. 'Ten of them, living in just one shoe.'

I looked at her. Black eye or no black eye. My hands were round her neck and she was spluttering. 'GET OFF ME! GET OFF!' She started to wrestle back. I swung for her good eye and missed. She swung for me and didn't. My jaw cracked and I held it even though I couldn't feel it. We both sat back down.

'It's fine,' I heard Marty say to the other people in the room – who were they? I could taste metal in my mouth. Tyler was clutching her throat.

'Fuck you,' I said, looking around for my things, how to get them together. 'No, really. Fuck you.' I was all but ready to leave.

Tyler gasped. 'I'm – '

'No, you're not. And my dad worked until the blood burst into his face, and you know it.'

She looked down. *Yes*, I thought. *You stay there a minute.*

I looked over to the window, the open window. The Night was there, tapping on the glass. *If you should need me* . . . The Universe was microwaving popcorn for the show. God was . . . God was at the bar, if he had any sense. I looked around for a drink. Marty handed me something. I drank it. 'I wasn't immune to the kudos,' I said. Marty nodded. Tyler sipped her drink. Her throat was reddening. My jaw was starting to ache. 'Far from it. I wanted in. Badly. But then . . . well, I convinced myself I wasn't academic enough, I was too creative yadayada, I wouldn't have time to write blahblah, but really I knew why I didn't apply. I'd bottled it. Reached my limit with all the trials and tests. Fear of failure – is there a word for that?'

'Normal,' Tyler said.

Oh, Tyler, see, you can be so nice when you try . . .

I said: 'I bet there's a proper word for it.'

She got out her phone. Tapped on it. Scrolled. Tapped. Scrolled. Squinted.

'Atychiphobia.'

'There you go,' I said. 'Also known as the fuse-box.'

'Also known as the ego,' said Marty.

I looked at him.

He followed me to the bathroom. Locked the door. Got hold of me. I pressed my hands over his kidneys. Our faces were centimetres apart. Eyes to eyes, nose to nose, mouth to mouth, there we were, matching up. A feeling like falling asleep and jerking alert, the rush of the plunge, the clit-to-jaw synapse . . .

'Take your knickers off and bend over.'

'What?'

He started unbuckling his belt. 'You heard.'

He pulled me to him and smacked my arse. Hard. He did it again. I pushed him away and slapped his face. 'Come at me again and I'll knee you into oblivion.'

SHE'D TOLD HIM.

SHE'D FUCKING TOLD HIM.

Oh, she's totally game and besides she needs it, you should think of it as a noble act, we've got to get her away from that douchebag so anything you can do really, she's a bit Othello about the whole infidelity thing so it should do it – or you could get her a book deal? I dunno, whatever's easier. The infidelity? Okay. Sure. Yeah, a bit of garden-variety S&M, nothing too rad, there's a weird childhood spanking thing involving her sister that you could work with, that's probably as deep as her perversions go . . .

He was between me and the door. Fast mathematics, physics, logistics, spatial awareness, was he stronger than me, more fucked? I could draw on a lot cornered and reminded myself but still: orthodox terror, the avian curve of his mouth, arms that could break my arms. Without further assessment I shoved him to one side and unlocked the door, ran.

Tyler was standing on the bed holding court. She looked at me and raised her eyebrows. I retched. She got down off the bed and came and put her arm around my shoulder. 'You need some water.'

'Fuck you.'

'No, listen, Lo, I put a rock in your drink.'

I retched again. 'What?'

'I put a rock in your drink, thought you could use it, so you need to loosen up and have some water or you're gonna flip out.'

I put my thumbs on my temples, pounding, struggling. She was in my ear, her voice loud and hot and horrible.

'Oh, Lo, have you forgotten the intense *joy* of getting fucked with someone when you know that later you're going to fuck them? It's the best feeling. I know you know that.'

Marty came out of the bathroom zipping up his flies.

All I needed was my bag.

As I slammed the hotel room door I heard her shout 'You bailed first, Lo! Remember that! YOU BAILED FIRST.'

INFINITY STRETCHES AWAY EQUALLY IN ALL DIRECTIONS

'They've found it, Laura.'

A voicemail from my dad. I listened to it on the train, squashed into a window seat, hot and thirsty and heavy in the middle. My stomach went when I heard his voice. There was only one 'it' where my dad was concerned. I realised that the cancer coming back, a negative check-up, rogue cells gathering into a shadow on an x-ray, was still what I was expecting to hear whenever he or my mum called.

I called back and he answered before it even rang. 'Laura – did you get my message?'

'Yes. When – ?'

'Can you believe it?'

'Uh – '

'They're being cautious, saying it's just *Higgs-like*, but that's scientists for you – '

I shook my head to clear it. 'Dad, what are you talking about?'

A pause. 'The Higgs boson.'

I burst out laughing. Then I remembered myself and stopped. 'No way.'

'Way, love. Way.'

'Look, Dad, can I call you back in a bit?'

I got up – *Excuse me, sorry, sorry, sorry* – and walked down the carriage and then through the next carriage and the next carriage until I reached the shop. I picked up a paper and bottle of water. My jeans pockets were heavy with coins, pirate's pockets: the result of spending notes and forgetting when you got change. As I stood in the queue I read the front page of the paper. Sure enough, there it was, albeit with a caveat (the restraint of scientists struck me as a more glorious thing than usual that morning): the Large Hadron Collider in Geneva had reported 'a new boson with Higgs-like properties'.

I went back to my seat – *Excuse me again, sorry* – and devoured the story, thankful for the distraction. The text and the thrill of the news evaporated and I was left with guilt again, heightened by the thought of bodies – mine and my dad's, of care and lack of care. I closed my eyes as the train flew through a tunnel. Always, always the fantasy of collision, of points not moved, of screeching, sparks, warped metal and fire-illuminated brick-work.

I hadn't slept back at the B&B. I'd sat in bed listening to the street, waiting for the telltale splutter of a cab engine or the clatter of boot soles hitting stone. She hadn't come back. I had a series of fast-dismissed sordid visions of what she might be up to with Marty in his hotel room. Bottles and furniture featured heavily. I tried to force a dream upon myself, backwards, one I'd had a few weeks ago, the strangest of my life so far. The only way I can describe it is that it felt like travelling through sedimentary rock. In the dream I'd murdered someone; had all the guilty horror of such a nightmare, the kind that normally stays with you all day, like a hangover. I came out of the dream through what felt like layers. First, the relief of innocence, but bodiless, a spirit; then the sensation of a body but not my body, a kind of physical peace; then up and up, through several more layers, each one a little more individually sentient, a fraction more sentiently filled until, finally, me, complete, Laura Joyce, in my bed in my bedroom, innocent (of murder at least). I was in bed with Jim and I'd rolled over and woken him.

You won't believe this dream I've just had.
Shhh.
But I think I've just travelled through my own consciousness.
You take too many drugs, Laur.
I haven't taken drugs for – oh, never mind.

I called Mel from the train.

'Minibus?'

'Train. Listen, has Julian got any flats going? Anywhere. Anywhere at all.'

'Have you won the lottery?'

'No, but I'll work more hours, I'll get another job, I don't care – look, just ask him for me, would you?'

'Have you fallen out with Tyler?'

'No – it's just. Time.'

Train toilets offered little in the way of solace. All that plastic and crèche-style primary colours, plus the pressure of knowing someone's likely to be waiting outside. In the early days of Pendelinos Tyler hadn't realised she had to lock the door and someone had come along and caught her mid-wipe. *Could have been worse*, she reasoned, *I could been inserting a tampon. And anyway, they were so embarrassed they bought me a can of Stella from the buffet. Result.*

Back in my seat I opened my laptop and took the lid off my tea. It was grey in there, weak and watery. It looked like the most unsatisfactory brew in the world. I longed for a whisky. The train was quiet. A woman and a little girl got on at Lockerbie. Age-gapped sisters, I thought at first, and then when I'd seen them interacting a few minutes I thought more likely mother and daughter. They sat on opposite sides of the carriage, the little girl stretching her legs out on the seat next to her, taking care not to put her shoes near the upholstery. She looked tired, like she could sleep if she lay down. They both looked tired.

The woman was holding an open bag of chips. Now and then the little girl reached over and took a chip and then reversed back into the double seat, chewing on the chip thoughtfully for a few minutes in a sort of trance. The woman munched through the chips more quickly, sucking the salt off her fingers and shaking the paper so that more chips were loosed from the sides. When the chips started to run out, the little girl moved over and sat beside her mum. They got off at Carlisle.

My phone rang. An unknown number. Pluses and too many digits. Jim. I picked up. 'Hi.'

'Good night?'

'Oh, you know.' My voice was shaky. Thank god it wasn't a video call. I felt like I was at work, carefully managing a situation.

'Everything okay?'

'Yeah, I'm just on the train, you know what it's like on trains.'

'I thought you went in Tyler's car.'

'She stayed on.'

He tutted.

'Sorry, Jim, bad reception – I'll call you back.'

I hung up and sat there hyperventilating. The train picked up speed. I lowered the phone from my ear and stared at it, hard. I looked up to see a couple sniggering, a little way down the carriage. Had they heard what I'd been saying? Had they seen me gawping at my phone? Agonies! I glanced a few times to get the measure of them – she was a reddish brunette, he was wearing a flat cap, they looked trendy. Trendy. I hated the word and I hated them. I took a breath. They are a new couple and they are bonding and they are using me to do their bonding and that is fine, I am big enough to take this. It could even be their first date. In which case they're welcome to ridicule me. They need all the help they can get. Make the most, young hearts. Run fucking free.

When I got up to get off the train I walked past to see that they were watching YouTube on a phone, sharing a pair of headphones.

At Jim's I washed my hair and put on my pyjamas. Tyler texted. I didn't reply. There were some eggs in Jim's fridge, they would do for my tea. There was a bottle of wine in a gift bag in Jim's dried-food cupboard. *No*, I told myself.

Hey, Laura. Just Say No!

Somewhere in a parallel universe, a Laura Joyce was constantly saying no. This thought was spiritually comforting for two reasons: a) that a version of me with perpetual willpower could exist, and b) I didn't have to be her. (Tyler: *I DID say no, it's just that the drugs wouldn't listen . . .*)

I opened the wine and poured myself a glass. Mel called.

'Ju says there's a flat if you want it. Just don't piss him around, okay?'

'Do I – ? Okay.'

Jim got back a few days later. I was in bed and felt something move in the bed next to me and I woke in a blind panic, limbs flailing. Where was I where was I –

'It's me.'

'You scared me to death.'

He put his arms around me and we lay like that, me on my side with my knees and feet together. I felt vertiginous. I wanted to shrug him off so I could balance.

The next morning over coffee he said: 'There's a party tonight at the town hall. A new signing by a classical publishing house. We don't have to stay long but I thought it might be nice to go, together.'

'I'm not sure I fancy it.'

'Come on, party girl.'

'Look, Jim, there's something I need to tell you. I'm viewing a flat next week. One of Julian's.'

He looked at me. I had to say more.

'A stop-gap, if you like.'

A lie.

Fear – it's an aphrodisiac. His thumb working its way from my knee along the tendon beneath, round to my inner thigh. Crossing my legs and squeezing his hand, rolling my thighs around his fingers, letting my toe nudge the hem of his jeans, up, up. Falling through the bedroom door and kissing him deeply, stretching my tongue, feeling the entirety of his mouth. The smells of him booming like pulses of sound, each stroke and slide a new reveal of sea and timber. In the bedroom he dropped to his knees and pulled down my skirt and pants, held his face down there for a moment and then clamped his mouth, his tongue wide and fat. The cold air made his tongue feel warmer. I ran my fingers through his hair, pressed the bands of muscle on his neck. He got up, kicked off his trousers. Sat down on the bed and reached for me, put one hand behind my head, the other in the small of my back, holding my hands there. *Don't move.* Owning me. In that moment I think I wanted to be owned.

We missed the food but got there in time for the speeches. The Great Room was just that – majestic, candlelit, dotted with linen-draped tables and vases of flowers.

'Classical publishers are like thoroughbred stables,' Jim whispered as we walked in. I could smell myself on his breath. 'New composers are rarely signed. Believe me, this is a big deal.'

A waiter went past with a tray of champagne and water. I took a champagne and downed it, not looking at him as I drank. I stared across the room.

'Oh look!' I said. 'There's Kirsten!'

For there she was, standing by a pillar, talking to a man in a tuxedo. She looked relaxed, her hair loose on her shoulders, her black dress flowing off her thighs and moving as she talked.

'She's talking to someone,' said Jim.

She looked right past me a few times. I was waving for five minutes on and off before she spotted me and made her way over. She had a wicked weave on her, bumping into people, spilling drinks. Was she? Yes, she was. Absolutely fucking goulashed.

'Hello!' I said, gripping and kissing her. She swayed and righted herself. Still classy. Clean fingernails and smooth clothes. If you were truly classy then nothing could tarnish you, not even excessive alcohol. I imagined Kirsten spent weekends at the cinema or theatre when she wasn't practising the cello in bijou hotel rooms around Europe. Her breath revealed her poison: brandy. Boy, was she classy.

'James,' she said.

I looked at Jim. He was looking at his shoes. Clearly classical musicians didn't deserve a night off, even at a party. Perhaps Kirsten and I should just run away to a balcony and have a fag and shit-tons more brandy. I could hold her up. I wondered if she smoked. I bet she would smoke if I offered her one. It could be something we did together, something she always remembered from the beginning of our friendship. *I didn't know how to smoke until I met Laura. Laura brought the joy of nicotine into my life.* No, not Laura. What would her nickname for me be? Something elegant. Lorrie. And I could call her Kirst, or Sten.

'I like your jacket,' she said.

'Thanks,' I said. 'You'd suit a leather jacket.'

Then someone tapped a mic and we all turned.

I suppose I should have known when she took two glasses of champagne from a passing tray and tried to hand one to Jim. I should have known when he refused the champagne in a tone of voice I couldn't remember hearing before, more of a growl. I should have known when she poked him in the ribs with her finger when she thought I wasn't looking. I should have known when she downed the two champagnes, got another two, and downed those. I should have known when she started talking softly but not that softly during the speeches: *You really have stuck to it, haven't you?*

Yeah, said Jim through gritted teeth.

I hoped you wouldn't, you know.

Jim turned and walked off. I didn't follow him. The speeches finished. Applause. Kirsten turned and said to me: 'You know, Jim's such a special guy.'

I looked at her. She had a different look on her, a ruthlessness, her face was all hard angles. Maybe Kirsten and I weren't going to be such good friends after all, especially since I usually preferred people when they were drunk.

'Yeah,' I said.

'He's been so supportive. It's a lonely life this, all the travel, all the solo work. Jim's been there for me so many times.'

Suspicion, now. Dripping and trickling and flowing in, walls bursting, villages submerged. 'Yeah,' I heard myself say.

'I'm not always sure I know what I'm doing and Jim's kept me on track. Guided me. He's a real teacher. A nurturer, I suppose you'd say. I feel as though we've been through so many things together.'

'Mm.' Out of the corner of my eye I saw the shape and gait of Jim striding towards us. Suspicion smelted, emotional alchemy, and there it was: clean blue fury.

'Yes,' said Kirsten, 'we really have been through so many things, together.'

I leaned towards her, closer, spitting distance. 'Have you been through a fucking *window* together?'

I felt Jim's hand on my right arm. He pulled me away. 'Goodbye, Kirsten.'

I skidded in his grip and then shook him off. 'DON'T YOU

DARE FUCKING PULL ME.' People turned and looked. Jim raised his hands, *Hands up, crazy woman in the house!* and followed me towards the double swing-doors.

'Stop walking,' he said. 'Laura.' His voice echoed along the stone corridor.

I turned to look at him. I was sick at our sex, sick at our love. 'I need to find a bathroom.'

'This way.'

I sat on the toilet doing nothing, staring at the door in front of me and listening to my phone vibrate in my bag. The tiles on the floor were huge and white, similar to what you'd find in a torture chamber or morgue. At one point it dawned on me that I was hearing voices and it took a moment for me to recognise that I recognised one of the voices and then another moment to tune in to what the voice was saying.

It was Kirsten. Words became sentences, sentences sense.

'You know how cut-up I've been about this.'

'Oh, Kirsten, babes.'

'I'm sorry – I . . .'

Oh god, I thought. Oh no. Please don't be – Fabric rustled against fabric. I could hear the water in the pipes and now and then a low quiet female cough like someone clearing her throat gently.

'Can you believe what she said to me?' Kirsten's voice cracked as she said the words. 'Do you think she knows? She must.'

I paused, held myself taut. I wondered whether I should get up, flush, make a sound, come out, cough, sneeze, call someone? Or just stay still and –

'Nah, she's always pissed, isn't she?'

A snort, sad not happy. 'The way he's been with me, Sylvia, ever since. So cold. Hard to believe it's the same man. Like he hates me and hates himself – oh, I don't know. I felt like what happened had been building up for so long but to him it was

217

obviously just a mistake. And now it's so hard to avoid him, this world is so fucking small.'

Oh for a sinkhole, I thought. *Or a bomb scare. Even an actual bomb would be a blessing right now.* They fell silent. Liquid horror. Had they worked out I was in there? That would be too much to bear. I'd have to run if they saw me, have to. I couldn't endure making them feel better on top of –

'We should be – '

My cunt burned with held-in piss.

'I know,' said Kirsten.

'I'm so paranoid!'

Footsteps. High heels on tiling. Their voices receding and a door creaking to a close. I sat there. After a few seconds, piss trickled out. I had no water pressure. It took a while and when I was done I wiped myself and stood shakily. Pulled up my jeans. What was I going to do what was I going to do? I didn't know. Could I climb through a window? Was there a window? I opened the cubicle door and peered out. They'd gone. I rinsed my hands and wiped them on my thighs. I'd have to leave it a few minutes but not too long before I emerged into the bar. Could I just run away? Just running away would be preferable. I looked for a window. There was no window. I was having a heart attack. I put a hand on my chest and pressed it there.

What would Tyler do?

Just the thought of Tyler made me feel calmer. I knew what she would do. She would walk out there chin-first, down a drink for the road, and get the fuck out. That's what Tyler would do.

That's what I would do.

I opened the door. The noise of the corridor hit me like a train. Jim was standing there, stone-faced, by a sandy beige pillar. I turned and walked in the other direction. I knew there was an exit round the back of the town hall. Would it be open? Would I be granted that small mercy?

The back exit was open. Hosannas! I flew out and started to run.

'Laura!'

He grabbed my hand and pulled me to a stop. I turned and looked at him. Everything had receded within, sucked back like the tide going out or the thaw after an ice age. Just wet rocks remained. A deserted beach. The moraine after the glacier.

'When?'

'Christmas. The party at the Bridgewater.'

'Did you fuck her?'

He shook his head.

'You kissed her, though.'

He nodded.

'What else?'

'I was drunk. I don't – '

'Did you see her tits?'

A nod.

'How about her nipples? Did you see her nipples?'

What was this, soft-porn rules? Yes. Yes, it was.

Another nod.

'Did you touch them?'

Yes, he had touched her nipples.

'Did she see your cock?'

He looked at me.

'Answer the question, Jim.'

He nodded.

'Did she suck your cock?'

Yep.

'Did you eat her pussy?'

He looked down.

'DID YOU EAT HER PUSSY, JIM?'

My imagination didn't spare me the visuals.

'I was so drunk, Laur . . .'

The hotel room. The bed. The two of them grabbing at each other like zombies at a combination lock, futility beckoning, along with some half-awareness of it. He'd had a dopey hard-on, scrabbled unsuccessfully with a condom – the non-application of which had become a momentum-sapping distraction. They'd done everything they could with the tools to hand.

'I get it. You *would* have fucked her but you couldn't.'

'I'm sorry, Laur. I've tried to make this right.'

'Impossible. There's nothing more to say.'

'This is the insane thing with you,' Jim said, sitting down on a step. 'This is why I couldn't tell you. You're so extreme.'

'That's not true.'

'It is. And you've been fighting this wedding, you and your wreckhead friend.'

'YOU LEAVE MY WRECKHEAD FRIEND OUT OF THIS.'

'Look, I made a mistake because I am a human being. It hasn't happened since and it won't happen again.'

'A "mistake"? You didn't use an apostrophe incorrectly or get on the wrong bus, Jim. You fucked someone else.'

'I didn't fuck her.'

'ONLY BECAUSE YOU CAN'T PLAY SNOOKER WITH A ROPE.'

Someone came down the steps, looked at us and jogged across the street to the newsagents.

'Keep your voice down,' Jim said. 'This is my career.'

IT WAS AN OLD NIGHT

3.46 a.m.

I wandered the streets for many hours. In my head I performed several staircase soliloquies and fantasy action scenes. I burst from the toilet cubicle with a gun and shot Kirsten just to watch her die – shot her friend, too. During the speeches I threw my drink sideways in Jim's face without changing my expression. I left the party in a blaze of *Carrie*-like telekinesis, the town hall roaring with fire behind me as I casually lit a fag on a smouldering gargoyle. None of them helped.

When I got to Tyler's I knocked.

No answer.

I knocked again.

Nada.

I found my key and unlocked the door. Stepped into the hall. 'Tyler? Ty?'

No sound or light but a meteorological sense of something not right. Rather, something terribly wrong. I turned on the hall light and went through to the lounge.

A lamp was on and a CD was playing. The Faint. Hilarious. Funny what you manage to appreciate even when . . .

She was on her back in the middle of the rug and there was sick all over her and all over.

TYLER

TYLER

TYLER

I shook her by the shoulders – nothing, nothing oh god fuck – and then turned her on her side into my best approximation of the recovery position. Why had I never taken a first-aid course? Why had I never had a job in a coffee shop? She would have known what to do. She would have. I banged her on the back once twice three times in case more sick was in there.

'TYLER!'

I scooped sick out of her mouth with my fingers, held the back of her head and put my ear close to her mouth, moved my fingers to the side of her neck where the pulse should be. Oh god oh fuck oh please –

Then I felt and heard them, soft, soft – very faint but very there – there was a pulse and she was breathing. Thank all the gods and all the fucks and all the angels and Jesuses. She coughed and retched a long, horrible retch.

'Tyler, it's me – what the fuck have you taken?'

I scanned the room. Wine glasses on the table with purple liquid inside. The mandy was gone, wasn't it?

'I'm calling an ambulance.'

She shook her head. Coughed again. Retched again. 'Nawp.'

'A taxi, then. You're going to hospital. I'll clean you up a bit first if that's what you're bothered about.'

'No no no no no.' She moved her arm and I saw two pieces of paper in her hand, scrunched in her grip. They fell in a flutter as she got onto her elbows, her bottom. Sat up. Brought her fingers to her nose.

'What did you have?'

She looked down at her chest and grimaced at the sick. 'You don't want to know.'

222

'I really do.'

'I need a bath.'

'I'll get a hot cloth and then we're going to hospital.'

She sniffed hard and rubbed her face. 'Look, I appreciate the offer but I'm not going so you may as well drop it.'

'Tyler, we are going – '

'Listen, they don't even pump your stomach any more. They just put you on a drip because they're fucking pussies. Then I'll have to lie there for hours hydrating until some fucker comes in to lecture me or tries to send me to rehab or some shit when really I'm fine. I just had a bad day.'

I looked at the papers on the floor. 'What happened?'

She flapped one hand then the other, like she was trying to bat away a fly or not cry on TV.

I looked at the wine glasses on the table. 'Take it that's not Vimto?'

'It's GHB. Mixed with Vimto.' She retched as she said it.

Arithmetic assaulted me. Two glasses. One Tyler.

'Who was here?'

She rubbed her face again. She had no mascara left on her lashes but plenty on her cheeks. Her beauty spot was smeared with lipstick. 'Nick.'

'Did he bring the GHB?'

'Naturally.'

I nodded. Motherfucker.

'Do you think you can stand?'

'No promises.'

I helped her. She was very weak, leaning almost all of her weight on me and banging the wall as few times as we walked to the bathroom. I sat her down on the toilet while I ran the bath, took her clothes off and helped her step in. I washed her very slowly and gently.

'He didn't hurt you, did he?'

'You mean did he rape me?'

'I mean did he anything.'

'I'm not sore so I don't think so. It hardly matters, though, does it?'

'What?'

'It'd be more like necrophilia than rape. Look at me. My life hasn't changed in ten years, I work for The Man, I'm covered in fungus, I haven't got the memory of the Sixties to keep me going and the Nineties feel like some sort of bad in-joke.'

'You'll feel better when you've had something to eat.'

A series of grunts and snorts. I could hear the night in her chest.

'Come on, piglet, I'll roast you a pizza.'

I dressed her in my clothes – not that fucking kimono. When the t-shirt, baggy on her, was over her head she pulled it down and held the bottom hem.

'Do you love me, Lo?'

Sometimes.

'Tyler, I'd give you my ass and shit through my ribs.'

I put her to bed and went to the shop for food for myself. When I got back she got up and sat next to me on the sofa as I ate pizza (she couldn't eat). We watched the Olympics. A string of mozzarella dangled from the piece of pizza I was eating. Tyler eyed it warily then looked back at the TV.

'Who was it?' she said, still looking at the TV. I put the piece of pizza down. Saliva deluge pre-empting a bathroom dash. On the screen, teenaged girls bounced around, landing and posing. Tyler nodded at the TV. 'Would you look at the American girls nailing this shit. I want them to flick the bird as they land and yell FUCKYEAH! at the apparatus.'

Sparkling leotards flitted across the screen. A tiny American gymnast started doing a routine on the horse. Halfway through a pike she fell onto the horse and banged herself badly between the legs, falling to the ground in agony.

'Get up!' Tyler shouted.

'She's hurt, by the look of it.'

'Get up, you stupid girl.'

'I think she's trying.'

'Don't you know the rules?' I shook my head. 'She has to be back on that horse in ten seconds or she's disqualified. How whack is that? You've just taken a sledgehammer in the puss and you've got ten seconds before your whole country hates you.' She stood up and motioned wildly. 'GET UP, GIRL, GET UP!' She sat down again quickly. 'I feel very nauseous,' she said. 'Will you get the vomitarium, just in case?' She lay back, closed her eyes.

The wine glasses from the previous night were still on the table (they wouldn't be helping) so I picked them up and as I passed the papers on the floor I picked those up, too. I glanced at them in my hand. There was writing on them. They were letters – one long, one short. I read the short one first, almost walking into the door frame.

T,
They found this when they were clearing your father's house and forwarded it to me with some other paperwork, so I'm sending it on. I haven't opened it. It's up to you whether you open it or not. If you want to talk about it I'm here and I love you.
X Mom

In the kitchen I put the glasses down, almost missing the work surface, and read the longer letter, dated 24th of December 2006.

Dear Tyler,

I don't know what else to do other than write you – you won't take my calls and then last week you threw me out of your apartment (which I have to say has deteriorated considerably in the five years since I bought it) after I had made a special trip to England to see you and your sister (I also thought it was particularly mean of you to refuse to give me Jean's address in London and let her make a decision herself about whether she wanted to see me or not). So all I can do now is get what I want to say down on paper in the hope it might help you see things from my point of view and not be so dismissive when you don't know the whole picture.

I know that I was a terrible father, and a terrible husband for that matter, however as a Christian I believe in second chances and while I know you girls never really took to mine or your mother's religions, and we never forced you, I can't help the values mine gives me now especially at this stage of my life, and what it encourages me to contemplate and pacify. I don't expect much, just a few minutes of your time once a week or once every two weeks, to hear what you are doing with yourself and maybe a small amount of news about what it is like to be living in a different place so far away from home. I really wouldn't expect any more but now I suppose I do expect a small something after the financial support I did not deny even for a second the last time we spoke, which was just after you arrived in England. As I believe the laws of physics clearly state, you can only get out of a thing as much as you put in, and I do believe I have put a little in recently not just with the apartment but also with the extra studies you wanted to do, so I suppose the question you have to ask yourself is: will you give a little back?

If you will, I won't waste your time with griping. I've spent enough years now knowing I kicked the whole thing away and sure there will always be moments when any person in their life looks back and feels challenged to decide whether or not they made the grade and I really never meant it to get so bad but as I say I'm not for dwelling although I will say that I never meant that bottle to hit you and that has been one of the hardest things for me to forgive myself for. There are some things you might be interested in hearing about, for example the population over in Crawford is almost down to 1000 now if you can believe it and a few months back a few boys on a school trip from the city drowned in the river up by Fort Robinson so I suppose that makes it even lower, haha! You shouldn't laugh at these things but you'd cry otherwise – a famous poet said that and I suppose you'd know which one. Also your old horse Marshall is doing well, I take him an apple most Saturdays (they laugh at me in the store shopping for myself and a horse – tell that to your mother if you like) and there's a girl from the Normangill place (the Fletcher place as it is now – June Fletcher is her name) who comes and takes him out during the holidays. I'm thinking of saying she can have him permanent but I suppose I wanted to check with you first that that would be alright.

Your father.

There was a phone number at the bottom of the letter.

I wondered when he'd died. I thought it had to have been around the time Jean went back to rehab. I folded the letters in half and put them away at the back of the cocktail cupboard, behind all the glasses. I rummaged around in there until I found the plastic jug we were always sick in, stained orange

227

from microwaving beans. I carried it through to the living room.

I thought she was asleep but as I put the jug down on the table she said: 'Don't leave me, Lo.'

'I'm not going anywhere.'

CRUEL PARODIES

She stayed in bed for four days. I called her every hour from work and walked back via the indoor market. I got her to eat crushed ice at first to get her system used to the idea of solids, then I peeled and mashed fruit and vegetables and gave her mugfuls of purée, which she hated. I cancelled the viewing with Julian. He sounded relieved.

I sat with her every night as she fell asleep, descending with sweating and ranting – one time about making ratatouille, another time about deadheading sunflowers. Childhood whisked in with the dreams. Memories, fabrications, her brain unpacking. I knew she'd been further than her will, grew up in an instant. Did I envy her still, lying broken in bed: her completion? The Night didn't beckon Tyler – she summoned it, saddled it and rode it down the street. My darkness had been drafted in, was unconceived.

While she slept I stood smoking at the kitchen window, looking out. Drinking water. Popping pills. Small ones, primrose yellow, the same time every night to be sure, whatever happened, whoever – A small decision, absolute. Not for me to pass on my greed and ingratitude. And for what? Redemption? I knew I had an ego, but . . . I couldn't be something I couldn't run from, either. I was a swarm, a murder of birds, a shape-shifter, co-existing with my panics and habits and all the ways they flung me. What was it Kierkegaard said about anxiety = dizziness = an overwhelming sense of possibility? *What wine is so sparkling, what so fragrant, what so intoxicating, as possibility!* Anxiety is a privilege when you live with it like that, akin to the privilege of seeking mayhem. My life was full. It had a rotten apple in its mouth.

Ten minutes from the end of my shift. Two phone calls to go, three if the enquiries were straightforward. I sat big-eyed, repeating phrases, my fingers pressing on and off the same keys. I said exactly the same thing over and over again to customers who knew exactly what I was going to say. No one broke from the script. Work felt like a bad dream on a loop, one I couldn't break from. Once a boy at the centre had asked a girl out at the end of a call (she'd lost her card in a Portaloo at a music festival and they got on so well) but even though she said yes he was being monitored for training purposes and got fired. I hoped they were still together or had managed at least to have a brief, life-affirming love affair that he could eulogise about in his darker hours and tell himself that it (life, unemployment) had all been worth it. I was shutting down but mockeries persisted in the high smell of acetone, carpet tiles below, ceiling tiles above, whiteboards like tiling on all sides, peace lilies on every other desk. An office was a parody of a bathroom.

My mobile began flashing, next to my company-issue coaster. I picked it up, answered.

'So I'm in this new bar on Whitworth Street.'

'You're out?'

'I'm fucking *rocking*, baby.'

'Tyler, I don't think – '

'This city needs me. They have dishcloths for napkins in here. It's abominable. The whole square half-mile would go to the dogs – and by that I mean the hipsters – without me around.'

'I think you still need to rest.'

'They sicken of the calm, who knew the storm.'

Dorothy Parker. Irresistible.

'Ha.'

'This place is heaving with promise, they're all revoltingly young.'

'You must catch one for us to drink from.'

'Come help me, why don't you.'

I told myself I was going to monitor her. I told myself that.

She was waiting with a bottle of wine and a bag from a fancy-dress shop. She'd bought us black eyemasks and capes. We stood together in front of the mirror in the Ladies, the same red lipstick on, our hair in suave ponytails. I wasn't nearly drunk enough.

We sank the bottle of wine, sank another, walked to a karaoke joint in Chinatown. I went up first. 'Is That All There Is?' – Peggy Lee. There were six people in the place including us. A quiet middle-aged couple, possibly celebrating an anniversary, sat drinking tropical-looking cocktails in one corner. A pair of teenaged boys nursed illegal pints in the other. She danced with whoever she could drag up while I sang. There was more wine, and more wine, on and on we went, as the place filled up there was suddenly a DJ somewhere and bigger gaps between the songs and more people singing and the two of us disintegrating, losing all our differences.

We sat down and Tyler sparked up a cigarette and I didn't think anything of this until the barman was standing by the table. 'Put the fag out, Turpin.'

'Make me,' Tyler said, taking another drag.

'I just might.'

'Do it and see what happens.'

'What happens?'

'You find the grave a welcome embrace after the wrath of my ju-jitsu.'

I waited to be ejected. He stood there. When she'd finished her cigarette she tossed the dimp into an empty glass. It fizzled. He picked up the glass with our other empties and walked away.

'Fuck me. He's so beautiful it's *humiliating*.'

'He's all right.'

I felt a hot blip and put my hand down my pants instinctively, pushed a finger inside and pulled it out to see a blob of something on my fingertip. Dark blue in the neon. I held it up to show Tyler. She lifted her mask.

'What?' she said. 'You didn't think – ?'

'No. But it's always a surprise, isn't it? All these years, every month since I was thirteen and still it surprises me, like a season.'

The sudden physicality of myself made me weak. Tyler stood up and pulled me up by my hands. 'Let's dance.'

'No, I don't think I can. I feel all hot and dizzy.'

She pulled me onto the dance floor and started whirling me round. Everything was spinning. I broke free of her grip and went and walked to the edge of the dance floor, pressed my palm on a wall. She followed me, patted my back. 'You okay?'

'I need to lie down somewhere quiet. Can we go back to yours?'

She looked over to the bar. The barman was standing behind it, cleaning glasses, watching us.

'Do you need me to come with you?'

'No.'

'You sure?'

'I said so, didn't I?'

As I turned she grabbed hold of my hand. 'I used that flyer on purpose but I didn't know he'd be in the pub.'

I looked at her.

When the end comes you know it's real because it isn't remotely cinematic. I looked round as I reached the exit. She was dancing in the middle, people closing in around her. She kept her arms in as she danced. That was thing with Tyler. She was her own hero.

Outside the club I took off my mask and cape and threw them

into the gutter. Hailed a cab. Got in. At a red light I saw two teenaged girls sitting in a shop doorway, having one of those conversations, smoking their jaws square. They had long mullety hairstyles dyed platinum and pink, brightest at the ends, glam-rock style, dyed over the same sink. As my cab pulled away I felt the smallness of myself and everyone I knew, even the city. The appalling humanity of it all. These mundane things we do to each other, these miniscule effects we mistake for epic at the time.

From the fridge door, half a bottle of wine winked back at me. I poured a glass and carried the bottle through to my room. I lay on my bed in my jacket and boots. My phone vibrated. Clearly things hadn't gone so well with bar boy. I reached into my jacket pocket, thinking I'd turn the phone off before her pestering reached crescendo point –

It was Jim.

In Manchester. I miss you. x

I stared at the text and all I could think was that he had taken the trouble to make the kiss lower case after the full-stop.

Delete delete delete.

Telling someone you missed them was an imposition, all said and done.

Wherever you are, infinity stretches away equally in every direction. Whether you're under someone's fingernail or straddling Saturn, infinity stretches away from you equally in all directions.

I held on to the bed so I didn't fall. Then I called the one place I had left to go.

BALL BEARINGS

We walked arm in arm along the row of empty chairs and closed curtains to a chair ready-rigged halfway down the ward.

'Usual for me, please, love,' my dad said to the nurse. 'And a bag of pork scratchings.'

The nurse looked at him. *Laugh, you bitch*, I thought. She managed a smile. Heard them all before, no doubt. The padded grey chair released a crisp sigh as he reversed onto it. He was wearing a faintly striped pink shirt that did his skin tone no favours but he'd had the shirt so long – I recognised it from my childhood – I thought it might be a talisman for the day. I wondered whether it had been a present from me and Mel, and I'd forgotten (these things we treasure . . .). The fact he'd put a freshly ironed shirt on, that he looked *smart*, hurt.

My mum pulled the curtain round us. The nurse stood in her solid shoes and hung a pouch with a yellow warning sticker on it, DISPOSE OF PROPERLY (*I should have one of those on me, eh* – this time the nurse forced a laugh), on a hook next to the chair.

'I'll go and get some drinks,' my mum said.

'Pint of Guinness, please, love.'

More forced laughter. They hadn't wanted me to come, and now my belated show of solidarity, my half-arsed support act, felt transparent under the strip-lights. The nurse held my dad's hairy, freckled arm and inserted the needle. Previous treatments had left their marks, a line of red tracks branding his skin from wrist to elbow like the footprints of a tiny devil.

My mum walked away down the line of chairs.

'Still furious with me,' my dad said, nodding after her.

I sat down on a buckety visitor's chair. Nuclear light poured through the blinds at the end of the ward, where another curtain was pulled round the last treatment chair, several metres away; respectfully distanced. It was sunny outside – something close to summer. Sometimes the weather had no idea. In the long thin room, dust hung in sun-shafts, as though the air had been suspended at a molecular level and was waiting, stunned by its own potential, wondering what to do next. The nurse stretched a tube from the pouch and slotted it into the plastic slot on the back of the needle. There was a TV up on a wall bracket, showing the news. The rover 'Curiosity' was about to land on Mars. The nurse stepped back from the chair, adjusted the drip. 'There you go, Bill. Button's there if you need me.'

'Oh, I'm fine thanks now, love. This is my last blast.'

She smiled. 'Let's hope so.' She pulled the curtain round so there was just a small gap for us to talk through.

Down the ward, a girl emerged from behind the other curtain. She was in her late teens, dressed in a fluoro-green t-shirt and grungy jeans. We glanced at each other – I supposed I was still young enough (at a distance) to arouse her competitive streak and we sized each other up (I wished I wasn't sitting down) before politeness stepped in and her scrutiny dissolved into an orthodontic smile. I gave her another once-up-and-down for good measure. She knew I was nobody's mother.

'Looks like we just made it in time,' my dad said. On the TV, the rover was descending in its parachute.

'There's a storm coming in,' I said. The gas-station guy to Sarah Connor, *Terminator*.

He got the reference but not my bitterness. 'How do you mean?'

'Well, you can't put that much hope in something's direction and not expect it, sooner or later, to start to assume some sense of responsibility.'

I'd been staying at my parents' for a week. Tyler had called and I'd ignored her. I felt a monkish need for solitude – for starvation and sleeplessness and clarity. I was writing a little at night and sometimes I came downstairs in the early hours for a glass of water and saw the kitchen tidy in the low light and felt tranquil and private and as though all was well.

'I could socialise with robots,' said my dad. 'Cheap rounds, for a start.'

'It's the old ones I feel sorry for. Haven't they just stopped dead?'

'One's still going, I think. The other one took a fall in 2009 and they haven't heard from it since. Resting under a dune, no doubt.'

'If you have to be buried, I suppose Mars is as good a place as any.'

Buried. The word hurt us both, I think – death being the latest source of constant innuendo. He filled the silence. 'It's only a universe because of the things that don't work. The flops. The mutations. Know what this would all be if it weren't for all the fuck-ups?' He swore to save me. Waved his free arm around. I shook my head. 'A perfect line of ball bearings stretching for ever. Or maybe just nothing at all. Look, love, look – I think it's down.'

On the TV people in blue shirts were hugging each other behind banks of desks. Messages from viewers scrolled across the bottom of the news report. *Godspeed little rover! Don't go crunch!*

I looked across the mote-bright air at the drip, eking out its poison. He saw me looking and jerked his head towards it. 'Want a go?'

'Wouldn't touch the sides with me that shit, Dad.'

He looked at me. I looked at him.

'How are you doing?'

'How am *I* doing?'

'Yeah.'

'Fine.'

'Listen, you take your time with things. There's life in the old dog yet.'

I was staying in my old room. Remnants of me remained despite the redecorating. When I went to bed I stuck my head in the many earthy-smelling jewellery boxes on the dressing table, the velvet insides, the leather outside, like they were extinct things displayed in a private collection. There were pieces of jewellery from my teen years – silver pendants, lace chokers, precious stones and crystals from when I used to get my fortune read at the Corn Exchange. I licked the inside of one of the chokers, trying to taste my old skin smells, my old perfume. I used to wear perfume.

Hours later I awoke cold and turned to the bedside table for my phone. 4 a.m. No messages. I turned onto my back, feeling the dull click of my bones going in and out of place. Balls in sockets. Things wearing away. There was water by the bed but water wasn't enough. I needed something with some taste. Juice or squash or something. I got up and crept downstairs so as not to wake anyone. As I crept into the kitchen I saw something outside – ectoplasmic plumes coming off a dark figure on the driveway. I jumped, thinking it was a ghost (at last! I knew it, *knew it* . . .) but no – as I hid there, staring, I saw that it wasn't a ghost.

It was my dad. Outside. Smoking.

Smoking.

I hid and watched him. The party line was that he'd given up when Mel was born. Still, there he was, kicking against the tide. The big Fuck You to the big Fuck All.

*

I sat at the dining table the next day, planning my next move. The table had been in our family for generations. The surface was more like skin than wood. The grain had gone black in its recesses with grease, sweat, ash and old food. It breathed in the patches where the varnish had worn off. It remembered everything. A hundred thousand homeworks. A hundred thousand dinners. I felt the history coming off it as my parents buzzed around in the background, attending to the kettle and the catalogues and things that may or may not need posting. A bluebottle circled the room, lazy with imminent death, regularly bashing against the windowpane and I wondered whether to put it out of its circular misery. I'd once Googled whether insects feel pain while deciding whether to euthanise a twitching beetle on Tyler's bathroom floor. Apparently they didn't have a central nervous system, so it doesn't translate to an emotion, to pain as such. They just respond to negative stimuli. They reverse. Hide. Play dead. Run like hell. In Edinburgh I lived in a student house that was riddled with cockroaches. When the man from Rentokil came I asked him how the poison worked. *It rots their stomachs.* The next day we came down to the kitchen to find hundreds of them lying along the skirting boards, the odd leg daintily flexing. They took hours to die. I'd sat in the living room, holding my stomach, rocking, hating those fucking cockroaches for what they were putting me through.

The way back to Tyler was laid out in repetitions; an executive desk toy, unplayed with. Jim had starred in nightly nightmares. I was full of forlorn foregone conclusions. Sitting at the dining table, the twilight kindling the street outside, I longed for a drink to numb my metaphysics.

I went outside to call Mel and smoke a fag. Through the kitchen window I could see sections of my parents side by side on armchairs in the lounge, his arm and her arm visible, the backs of their heads bobbing in and out of view as they chatted about something on the TV. When my phone rang in my hand I answered thinking it would be Julian calling me back to arrange a viewing on another flat. I registered the name as my finger pad hit the green bar but it was too late.

'Laura?'

'Jim.'

Exhalation, of a kind. 'What's going on? My parents are beside themselves. All this money and everything's on hold. I know you've every right to ignore me but it's been over a week now . . .'

'I don't know what to say.'

Sighing. 'Well, we need to sort this out.' How *romantic*. I awaited more overtures. 'I'll be in the Circus Tavern at 3 p.m. tomorrow.'

Through the window, deep in the lounge, I saw my mum bat my dad's arm as she laughed despite herself. My dad shot her a sideways look. Their song was Simon and Garfunkel's 'America'.

'Noted.'

I hung up and slid down the wall into a ball.

When I arrived at the smallest pub in the city he was sitting in a back corner, two balloons of white wine in front of him. Would he stand up? He would not. Would we kiss each other? We would not. Shake hands? I sat down next to him, looked at the wine and waited. He reached forward, picked up a glass and took a sip. I picked up the other glass. He looked exhausted. *Probably from shagging string players.*

LAURA.

He took a second sip before lowering his glass. Fuck, it was good to see him have a drink, I can't say it wasn't.

'How's that going down?' I said. It felt like a cavalier thing to say, inaptly breezy. But then – what? Darkest dissonance. This man I'd been making plans with, that I'd spent the past however long in love with, and I had not a single thing to say. I wondered whether it was because *there was so much, it was impossible to articulate . . . etc. etc.* I put my glass down on the hammered copper table and held it for a moment to check it didn't wobble.

'Oh, it's disgusting,' he said, taking another swig. He grinned but his eyes weren't involved. And there it was, opening: the possibility of some kind of renewal. I sipped my wine, welcomed the quickening in my blood as it provided the necessary transfusion. 'So what do you think?'

'Would you apologise to your parents for me? For all the fuss – '

The tail-end of the sentence caught my throat as it flew up and out. I sat swallowing with pity for myself and my own tender heart in the mix – I thought I might have been enjoying his pain until that point, thought I might still just be angry. He picked up his glass. Sipped. Put the glass down again. The Spock look. *It's life, Jim, but not as we know it.* I raised my glass again and a familiar bittersweet feeling washed over me, classic futuristic déjà-vu: reassuring on the surface and, beneath that, profoundly depressing. You've been here before. You've always been here.

'I mean how are you feeling about *us*.'

I drank. Drank. Drank. Then I said: 'I think it was the dream itself enchanted me.'

He wrinkled his nose. 'I don't know what that means.'

'It's Yeats.'

He shook his head. 'What the fuck? Do you love me, Laura?'

I put down my glass. Looked at him.

'Sometimes.'

SIX MONTHS LATER

'I never thought I'd say it, but I missed church today.'

I took a step backwards and blew fagsmoke out too fast. My dad stuck his hands in his best-suit pockets and went on. 'It was all over so quickly. I like a bit of decoration round the edges, a few candles and flowers, and then you need the singing to break things up. That way, you can soak it all in and really savour it.' He leaned in. 'It felt like a bit of a production line in that registry office. Is it symptomatic of atheism, do you think, efficiency? Is this what passes for spiritual evolution: speed?' He pouted and released the pout. 'God might be dead, but I tell you what, he knew how to throw a party.'

I took another drag on my fag. Blew the smoke away from my dad – even though, well, you know. 'So what you're saying, Dad, is you didn't miss God today but you missed his canapés.'

'Yes, smartarse, I missed his canapés.' He shouted to the sky. 'Did you hear me, you old get? I MISSED YOUR VOL-AU-VENTS.'

We laughed like laughter was the thing we were made of, like it was the only thing to do. The roof terrace of a posh hotel in a converted Victorian school. Inside: the squares of a mirrorball dappling restored oak flooring, and a fork buffet being served by over-starched emo kids. Outside: colonial wicker furniture and a hot-tub rich with the scurf and sin of premiership footballers.

February. The lace arms of my maroon dress might as well not have been there at all. I berated myself for putting my hair up instead of leaving it down for extra warmth around my neck. The heater on the roof had such a short timer that it was more irritating to keep turning it on rather than just stand there freezing.

Then.

The door of the roof terrace opened and there she was. I knew she'd been invited but hadn't expected her to show. Another girl followed her out.

'Hello, Tyler,' said my dad.

She kissed him on the cheek. 'Hey, Bill. Great news about the cancer.'

'Thanks, yeah, few more years' grace, eh.'

'Ack, you'll live for ever.'

I drank some of my drink.

'Dunno about that,' he said, 'but I do have a cunning plan.'

'Yeah?'

'Yeah. I'm going to do what every rational person should do when they find out their days on Earth are numbered.'

'What's that?'

'Move to Stoke. It'll seem like longer.' She laughed and then my dad looked awkward, trespassing on my awkwardness. 'In a bit, love,' he said to me, and went inside.

She came and hugged me and the familiar smell of her almost knocked me over. 'This is Valerie,' she said. The girl next to her had the same jacket and the same eyes. I donated a long, kind blink. 'Hello, Valerie.'

We shook hands. Valerie's hand was hot. I wondered when might be acceptable to leave your own sister's wedding. I looked to the windows, through to the room and the party. Mel and Julian were slow-dancing in the middle of the dancefloor. I'd exiled myself to the terrace when the seventh person in a row had asked me where Jim was and I heard myself reply: *No fucking idea these days, and it's a real weight off.*

Tyler knew better than to ask at least. Or maybe she couldn't care less any more, either. Who knew.

I looked across the roof terrace. There was an iron staircase on the other side, leading down to the street.

On Deansgate I hailed a cab and asked for Blackley. We drove northeast, through Ancoats and the old newspaper quarter, sullen with redundancy, past the Green Quarter where *To Let* signs prickled the front lawns of artless tower blocks. I got out of the cab early and as I walked along the main road I felt the old rush coming over me – you know that feeling, you know that feeling, the wind in your ears as you stand at the crossroads, elements stirring, the clouds shifting over the moon (and every time you see that, you are mine). Something waiting for me in a small, unchanged room, in the blank screen of my laptop.

I stopped at the off licence to buy some wine. Pulled the coldest bottle from the back of the over-stocked fridge. At the till I put my hand in my pocket and felt the keys there, two rows of hard little teeth ready to bite. I stroked my nails along them as I waited for my change.

I walked another five minutes and turned into a smaller road. An ice-filled drain like a moat, a privet like a portcullis. The streetlights hitting the lids of a row of wheelie bins and bringing them up gold. I stopped outside a semi-detached Victorian house and looked to the skylight in the roof, open a crack like I'd left it.

I pulled the keys out of my pocket but before I could use them the front door opened and a woman came out, dressed for town. She nodded hello and held the door ajar. I heard the rich tut of a lighter flint before the click of the rimlock.

Two sets of stairs, the motion detectors acknowledging me and flicking each bulb on in turn. Right to the top. A blue door freshly painted with no marks or scratches. I opened the door and they were all there, the edges of safe and simple things in the shadows. I took off my coat and hung it on the back of the door, turned on the light. Went into the bathroom, which I'd done up nice (*nautical, but nice* – this amused me too often) but without real sentimentality. I walked out and over to the bed, took off my boots and dress and tights, loosened my hair, unpacked my bags. Zuzu came out from her box beneath the bed, yawning and blinking. She stretched her supple back-legs in turn.

I'd gone for her as soon as I got my place. Drank three margaritas and caught the bus to Belle Vue with a pair of kitchen scissors in my satchel, my heart in my ears the whole way. But when I arrived at Marie's, a cannonball of nerves and bile, no one answered. I heard the bell sounding inside: 'Für Elise' by Beethoven, blasphemed by burbly electronica, sending Jim spinning in the graveyard of my heart. A boy riding sidesaddle on a mountain bike sauntered past on the road. *No one there since last week, love.* (Love? He was half my age.) I turned around and pushed the door. It opened, revealing disaster. The house was ransacked. Clothes and CDs and broken furniture everywhere, a scene reminiscent of poltergeist activity. I put my hand inside my satchel, fingertips finding scissor-handles. Then I heard a faint cry. I walked towards the sound, stepping through the hall, picking my way around the shit. A strangled Anglepoise lamp. An empty dog bowl, the pink plastic grained with gone biscuits. In the front room, alone on top of a crippled sideboard, was a Granny Smith apple; I started at the sight of it, it looked so precise and unlikely. Another miaow from behind the sideboard. I called her and she came.

Now she kept me company these long nights in. On the drainer by the sink was an upturned tumbler. Just the one. Guests got their wine in mugs and liked it, or soon forgot. No pictures on the wall but books on the bookshelf, a few favourites open mid-flight on the carpet by the desk to keep me going.

The desk was under the window. I sat down and poured some wine. Looked up. Dark outside, the sky a great hole for falling into. I was light-headed. I was contemplating gravity. I was here and here and here, everything in its place, everything something like belonging.

Thanks to

Frank, Lorraine and Lucie Unsworth, Guy Garvey, Katie Popperwell, Nicola Mostyn, Maria Roberts, Sarah Tierney, Jo-anne Hargreaves, Natalie O'Hara, Clare East, Glen Duncan, Zoe Lambert, Clare Conville and all at Conville & Walsh, Jo Dingley, Francis Bickmore, Jamie Byng and all at Canongate, Sherry and Brian Ashworth, John Niven, Sally Cook, Romana Majid, Wayne Clews, Emily Powell, Caitlin Moran, Katie Potter, Rebecca Murray, Jesca Hoop, and the members of the Northern Lines Fiction Workshop.